CUPCAKES,
TRINKETS,
and other
DEADLY MAGIC

D1547860

This is a work of fiction. All names, characters,
places, objects, and incidents herein are the products
of the author's imagination or are used fictitiously. Any
resemblance to actual things, events, locales, or persons
living or dead is entirely coincidental.

Library and Archives Canada
Doidge, Meghan Ciana, 1973 —
Cupcakes, Trinkets, & Other Deadly Magic/Meghan
Ciana Doidge — PAPERBACK

Cover image & design by Elizabeth Mackey

ISBN 978-1-927850-00-8

Dowser Series · Book 1

CUPCAKES, TRINKETS, *and other* DEADLY MAGIC

Meghan Ciana Doidge

Published by Old Man in the CrossWalk Productions
Vancouver, BC, Canada

www.oldmaninthecrosswalk.com

For Michael
without whom there would be no reason
to bake

If you'd asked me a week ago, I would have told you that the best cupcakes were dark chocolate with chocolate cream cheese icing, that dancing in a crowd of magic wielders — the Adept — was better than sex, and that my life was peaceful and uneventful. Just the way I liked it. That's what twenty-three years in the magical backwater of Vancouver will get you — a completely skewed sense of reality. Because when the dead werewolves started showing up, it all unraveled ... except for the cupcake part. That's a universal truth.

Chapter One

The vampire stood at the door to my bakery. My heart skipped a beat. The sun hadn't even fully set — damn daylight saving time — and the vampire wasn't even wearing sunglasses or a hat. He was old, then. Or maybe young? I never could remember whether their skin got more or less sensitive with age. But then, I'd never seen a vampire before, so there'd been no reason to remember my vampire lore lessons.

I was a magical dowser of sorts. I found and attracted magical things, so it wasn't completely weird that a vampire wound up at my door — except the wards protecting my bakery should have safeguarded me from magical detection. If vampires were even capable of detecting magic on that level. Again, I had no idea. I lowered my eyes to nestle a sixth cupcake into the box I was currently packing. Maybe if I ignored him, he'd go away. Because that always worked, right?

The bakery's seating area was standing room only. The line of customers at the counter stretched almost to the door, as it always did in the hours after work and before dinner. Three of us regularly worked the counter for the final two hours of any weekday. I moved along behind the display case, parallel with my very human customer, dodged my employees Bryn and Todd, and added another cupcake to the box. Dark chocolate cake with strawberry butter icing — one of my favorites. I called it *Love in a Cup*. I made up cute names for all my cupcakes, and the occasional cookie I decided to bake. My bakery was aptly, though perhaps unimaginatively, named "Cake in a Cup". I certainly never pretended to be a wordsmith or anything. Not all my customers were fully human, but even the magically lacking seemed to believe there was something extra special about my baking. A magical ingredient. There wasn't.

I glanced up to check on the vampire. He was still on the sidewalk but had moved farther along the window to peer through the paned glass. He seemed to be watching a little blond girl, who was maybe four and dressed in the prettiest pink ballerina outfit. The child had climbed off her stool and was straining her cake-crusted chubby fingers to reach for one of the trinkets hanging in the storefront window.

I placed an eighth cupcake in the box — a peanut butter-iced fudge cake I called *Bliss in a Cup* — without taking my attention off the vampire. He narrowed his ice-blue eyes at the child. With his short-cropped, almost-white hair, broad forehead, and lanky frame, all he needed was an uber chic ski jacket to look even more Scandinavian. He was probably sexy — in that angular, chiseled way — to anyone who didn't know his love bites were deadly. I bristled and reassuringly brushed my fingers over the invisible knife I wore underneath my apron. No one was going to be snacking on any children in my bakery.

"*Sex in a Cup*," the customer across the display counter requested. His voice was laced with as much innuendo as he could muster.

I reached for and automatically boxed this ninth cupcake — more chocolate butter icing with a wallop of cinnamon and cocoa in the batter. I ignored the come-on — with a smile that indicated my delight over his exuberance for my cupcakes, but which thwarted his attempt to start something other than buying them. The customer looked familiar, like maybe he'd been in the bakery a few times before. The vampire, however, was new. What the hell was a full-blood vampire doing in Vancouver anyway?

The vampire wasn't interested in the child, whose mother had lifted her back onto her stool and directed her attention to the remainder of her cupcake. No one else seemed to notice the striking bloodsucker at the window, but then again, most people couldn't see magic as well as I could. That was my little bit of talent. Well, that and the trinkets I made from magical bits I happened upon, but they weren't powerful or useful. Just pretty bits to hang in a window and chime in the breeze.

One *Rapture in a Cup*, a yellow/chocolate swirl cake with cream cheese chocolate icing; a *Buzz in a Cup*, a mocha fudge cake with mocha butter icing; and an *Ecstasy in a Cup*, a double chocolate cake with lemon butter icing, rounded out the customer's order. He liked chocolate almost as much as I did. Or he had a thing for anything provocatively named.

I crossed to the till, weaving for a second time around Bryn and Todd, who were moving a hell of a lot faster than me to fulfill customer orders. But then, being human, they weren't distracted by the vampire examining my trinkets through the window.

I didn't know vampires were attracted by shiny things, or I wouldn't have hung so many in the front window. I really should pay more attention to Gran's lessons. Too bad my grandmother was currently surfing in Tofino — yes, at sixty. The vampire might not be so bold confronted by a full-blood witch. I was only half, through my mother. I also had my mother's eyes, medium blue or indigo, depending on whether a part-time, guitar-playing poet was immortalizing them or not. I didn't know any guitar players. I also didn't inherit the Godfrey petite stature, pert nose, or magical prowess.

My father was some Australian backpacker, whom my mother left — at sixteen — before she even knew she was pregnant. So all I'd inherited from him was my golden locks and sun-kissed skin. It didn't bother me much, not even knowing my father's last name or whereabouts. But then, I had Gran, and Gran was better than any other family in the world.

I took the customer's credit card and rang through the order. Customers could run their own cards, but I thought it was better service to do so myself. He was talking to me again. I pulled my gaze from the vampire, who was moving back to the front door, to acknowledge him.

"Sorry? My mind was elsewhere."

"I said that I own the law firm up the street. We just renovated."

Oh. Nice. He was the reason I'd been woken before eight in the morning for the entire week. I always attempted to nap after I baked in the mornings.

"Great," I replied as I handed him his card. "I hope you enjoy the cupcakes."

His smile faltered. Perhaps I, a lowly baker, was supposed to be more impressed with his lawyer status. Then I felt bad for being uncharitable ... it was just that the vampire currently testing the wards on my front door was starting to freak me out.

"Oh. Okay then," the lawyer guy said. "Till next time." He grinned, and I took a brief moment to notice he was rather cute. It wasn't like the vampire was currently slaughtering my customers. I could pause for a moment to exchange smiles with a cute, potentially rich guy — leases on West Fourth Avenue weren't cheap — who had nice straight teeth and an adorable dimple.

"Till then," I called after him.

The lawyer didn't even notice the vampire as he exited the bakery. But then, he was looking back at me. I was accustomed to men — even some women — staring. This time, I was pleased it meant the lawyer didn't inadvertently make eye contact with the alpha predator in the doorway. The vampire was all but blocking the entrance.

He caught my gaze. I flinched. I couldn't help it. His magic coated his pale skin with an icy aura. He lifted his hand to press against the invisible ward guarding the door, which stood open despite it being early spring. It had been unseasonably warm all day, but the weather could be temperamental in Vancouver. The runes etched in the doorframe glowed in response to the vampire's touch. Runes were how Gran anchored her magic, though not every witch used them. I wondered if the vampire could see such things, or if he simply felt the magic blocking him from entering uninvited. I felt the ward magic shiver in response, but the vampire wasn't trying to break through. He was simply ... tasting.

The idea scared the shit out of me.

I let my eyes drift over him like he wasn't the absolute focus of my attention as I crossed around the baking display case. I murmured greetings to some of my regulars, and, as unhurried as possible, wandered over to the bistro table where my foster sister Sienna sat sipping a latte and nibbling on a mocha butter-iced white cake *Thrill in a Cup*. I hated it when she paired similar flavors like that, but my sister did what my sister wanted. We both did. We were as similar in that attitude as we were dissimilar in looks.

I cleared my throat as I came around from behind to the front of the table. Sienna didn't lift her dark eyes from the book of spells she was reading on her Kindle. I was momentarily distracted that such an ebook existed, and wondered where it could be purchased. Sienna seemed to be reading up on binding spells, which made sense given that was her specialty.

A breeze from the door — the unusual heat the day had provided was fading as the sun set — stirred a few of my trinkets and recalled my attention to the vampire.

"Sienna," I hissed.

"What?" My sister glanced at me over the rim of her coffee. She'd skimmed off all the foam and was left with the creamy espresso underneath; her bored eyes almost matched the color of the liquid. "The coffee beans are burned."

"The coffee is not burned."

"Is too."

"Sienna, there's a vampire at the door."

"What?" Sienna laughed and looked over my shoulder toward the door. "Where?"

"Right there! Tall, blond, and fangy."

"You can't actually see their fangs, you know. Ahead of time, I mean."

"Sienna!"

"There is no vampire at the door, Jade."

I looked over my shoulder. Indeed, the doorway was empty, and closed. The last customer to leave must have politely shut it behind them.

"Imagining things?" Sienna murmured, but her attention had returned to her book of spells. Spells that were above both our magic grades as far as I had seen with a glance. Which was why I rarely bothered to practice magic — it was mostly out of my reach. Sienna always liked to know, however, even if she couldn't do.

"Right," I murmured, tracking my eyes from the door along the French-paned windows. I'd had them especially built for the bakery when I opened last year. The mullions were painted white, as was the paneled wooden front door. I had been going for a French provincial look, but with the addition of the slat wood floor and the hodgepodge of trinkets hanging everywhere, I'd achieved more farmhouse than sleek old country.

The vampire was gone.

I was nowhere stupid enough to step out onto the sidewalk to look for him ... okay, maybe just a quick peek. The sidewalk and street were empty of vampires, though. The sun was fully set, the last vestiges of reddish orange still tinting the sky to the west. It was suddenly chilly enough to see a puff of my breath. I folded my arms over my T-shirt-clad breasts, and a light breeze lifted my blond curls from my neck. At least it wasn't raining.

I dropped my hands and smoothed them over my spotless apron. The sidewalk was teeming with after-work shoppers. Strollers competed with teacup pets, the dogs even pricier than the kids. But then, my customers could afford the price tags of both. I held the door open for one mother fresh from yoga and decided that I needed a class before dinner myself.

What the hell was a vampire doing in Vancouver? And why the hell had he wound up at my door?

I locked up and sent Bryn off with the day-olds for the Kitsilano Neighborhood House. The kids in daycare loved my baking, and they didn't need to know the rather provocative names. That was just marketing.

I didn't worry about the vampire bothering Bryn or Todd on their way home. Vampires had their own code about that sort of thing, at least from what I remembered. I needed to drop by Gran's house and pick up her *Magical Compendium*, which was a witches' encyclopedia of sorts. I wondered if I could get an edition of it for my iPhone. I'd have to ask Sienna.

When did Gran say she'd be back? Tomorrow? Monday? Though I wasn't exactly sure my grandmother could stop a vampire unprepared. I also wasn't sure the wards on the bakery were much of a deterrent, not with the way they'd glowed in response to the vampire's touch.

"Still lost in thought about your sexy vamp?" Sienna's voice yanked me out of my head.

"There was nothing sexy about him," I snapped in response. I hadn't heard Sienna come into the office, and it always threw me to be caught off guard. The more magical the person, the less likely they could sneak up on me. My Gran had a terrible time masking her magic enough to play hide-and-seek or catch me sneaking back into the house after hours when I'd been younger and still living full-time under her roof.

I locked the deposit in the store safe in my small back office. I'd take it to the bank in the morning, after I baked. Most of our daily take was card generated anyway.

Sienna's magic was softer, and almost as familiar as my own. In fact ... I looked closer to see that my sister was wearing three of my trinkets like necklaces.

"What's that? Hobo chic?" I crossed by Sienna to leave the tiny back room. Most of the store's square footage was taken up by the massive kitchen, which was my refuge and my ball and chain. Not that I hadn't chosen to settle down and take on the responsibility to run the bakery. I always strove to be the exact opposite of my mother, who at best guess was currently somewhere in Vegas or San Francisco. Scarlett Godfrey was a free spirit. Not even a child at sixteen could tie her down.

Sienna shrugged at my sarcastic take on her necklace, turning to follow me as I crossed through the kitchen. I ran my hand along one of the two long, steel tables that occupied the middle of the room. Spotless. The ovens filled the south side of the kitchen; the walk-in fridge and dishwasher station took up the opposite wall beside the exit to the alley. Nothing was out of place.

"I thought the extra protection, you know, from the vampire, would be a good idea," Sienna said, referencing her trinket necklace. She almost purred when she was being sarcastic. She never had mastered the dry part of wit.

Ignoring Sienna, I smiled, as I always did as I crossed through the heart of my bakery. It would be waiting for me in the early morning, ready, willing, and swathed in stainless steel. It was heaven.

"The trinkets aren't for protection," I said, turning away from my sanctuary to deal with my sister. "And I wish you'd stop selling them under that guise."

Sienna shrugged again. "A girl needs pocket money, and even the normals know there's something special about your creations."

I sighed and dropped the subject. I was as tired of complaining about Sienna's joblessness as I was of her insistence that the trinkets were some sort of protective magic. I could feel magic. I collected pieces of things — buttons, pins, tie clips, and whatnot that had been in contact with enough magic to retain an imprint. But stringing such things together didn't make them any more useful than they were on their own. It was just something I'd done — almost compulsively — since I was young.

"Are you showering before dinner? Maybe I should just meet up with Rusty first."

Dinner, I groaned in my head. It had been my sister's boyfriend's birthday yesterday, but I'd all but forgotten the promise of dinner and dancing. I'd even baked a cake for Rusty yesterday.

"You're not canceling!" Sienna picked up on my thoughts — or, rather, my body language. She wasn't a reader, capable of actually delving into others' minds.

"I'm not. It's just I'm on the schedule to bake to-morrow morning."

"So bake before you go to bed," Sienna said, and then rewarded me with a crooked smile. "It's never as fun without you. You attract all the right sorts."

"Fine." Yes, not only did I have an affinity for mag-ical things, but things of magic — people specifically — were also drawn to me. It wasn't as fun as it sounded coming from Sienna. If it wasn't for the wards separat-ing me from the vampire earlier, I would have assumed that was why he'd shown up at my door. "I'll shower," I said.

Sienna clapped her hands together like she used to when she was younger, before her mother abandoned her after her father's death. That was when Gran had taken her in full time. It was difficult for the magically lacking — *normals,* as Sienna called them — to raise those with magic, even if only a half-blood like Sienna. I wondered how long it had been since Sienna had heard from her mother, but I didn't bring the sore subject up. No matter how free-spirited she might be, at least my mother always showed up on the important dates.

"The trinkets don't really match the goth look, you know."

"I think they go fine. And it's deconstructed, not goth. Welcome to the second decade of the twenty-first century."

"That's my sweater you deconstructed."

"You weren't wearing it."

"At the time."

"Shower, please. You smell like bakery."

"Some people like it."

"Like who, Jade? Anyone you'd actually consider?"

I turned away from Sienna's almost mocking laugh and mounted the stairs to my suite above the bakery. Gran owned the entire block that included the bakery, which I leased from her through her corporation, Godfrey Properties. A real estate investment that had been passed down from her husband, of whom I had only vague memories. The storefronts also had apartments on the upper floors. The rents were high, but the view and the solid building upkeep made for long-term tenants.

When I renovated the bakery, I had stairs built to connect to one of the two suites that occupied the second floor. The apartment also had an entrance from the outside that I shared with the other, currently unoccupied, suite. However, I pretty much used the back alley exit from the bakery exclusively.

I thought Sienna was currently bunking at Gran's, being in between jobs. Which meant she was probably living full-time with Rusty, who was some sort of a stockbroker — he worked from home, keeping almost the same hours as I did. The stock exchange opened early on the West Coast.

I walked through my sparsely furnished living room toward my second bedroom, which currently operated as a craft room of sorts, and which boasted the most amazing view of the ocean and the North Shore Mountains. Kitsilano spread up from the beach in a slow-sloping hill. Many homes managed peekaboo views from their upper floors; I had a hundred-and-eighty-degree vista. The lights of North and West Vancouver spread out along the base of the snow-peaked mountains. The ski runs of Grouse and Cypress Mountains were clearly lit tracks above the residential area, even though mid-April was late for them to be open except to hikers and, maybe higher up, snowshoers.

I ignored the urge to open the large window and let the breeze in. It had a tiny Juliet balcony on which I'd planted chocolate cosmos and strawberries last summer. No matter the oddly warm weather we'd been having, it was still too early for the strawberries to flower.

The room was lined with shelves. I stood before the desk by the window — I liked to look at the mountains while I worked — and trailed my hand over the trinkets on the nearest shelf. I had thousands of them ... bits of magical things, rocks, ribbons, knickknacks. One set of shelves was completely devoted to jade — jewelry, unpolished rocks, and chipped figurines. Yes, my name is Jade and I collect jade. The stone held magic like a sponge. My fingers strayed down to stroke the jade knife I always wore at my hip, covered by an invisibility spell — courtesy of my grandmother, of course.

It had taken me a year to hone the knife from a large stone I'd found on a remote hike outside Lillooet, and another year struggling with the spells I'd wanted to temper it with. It was practically unbreakable and would cut through pretty much anything now ... well, anything I'd tested it on. Why I needed such a knife, I didn't know. I just wanted it. Gran hadn't questioned it, and had even supplied me with spells from her personal spellbooks on request. Some of the items needed to perform those spells had taken months to secure, and I took classes on how to wield the knife while waiting. It was the length of my forearm, just thicker than my thumb. It was perfect.

The vampire was perched on my Juliet balcony. My jaw dropped and stayed down. He was leaning against the ancient iron railing, which was in no way rated to take his weight. Juliet balconies weren't meant to be stood on. He crossed his arms and looked at me. Coolly assessing, completely unruffled, though he had just climbed — or jumped — two storeys.

"Vampire," I said, naming him before I thought it best to shut my mouth.

He tilted his head and said, "Witch." I could hear him clearly through the glass, and hoped that was because it was single paned and not because he was somehow in my head.

The same wards that protected the bakery protected my apartment. Actually, the wards here were stronger, more focused. They were anchored to the walls and windows, covering the entire inside perimeter of the bakery and apartment. No one could enter the apartment without being invited by someone keyed specifically to the spells, such as myself or Sienna, who had a habit of living with me between boyfriends. Whereas the wards on the bakery had to allow human customers through. Anyone with a bit of magic in them had to request the right to purchase my baking, though once keyed to the ward they could come and go.

My pulse was loud in my ears. I wasn't sure that had ever happened before. I wished I'd gone to that yoga class ... though maybe the vampire would have just followed me there, where I'd be unprotected.

My hand involuntarily strayed to the necklace I wore. I also collected vintage wedding rings, pairs if possible, all magically imbued. I soldered the rings like charms on a bracelet to a long, thick gold chain, also vintage. It wound three times around my neck easily. The magic in the rings was barely discernible, but still I collected them together like a magpie. I wore the necklace constantly, even in the shower.

The vampire's gaze stayed on the knife at my hip. I'd taken off my apron, the sheath worn over my jeans. The supposedly invisible sheath. He could see through my grandmother's magic.

The hair stood up on the back of my neck. He was old, then, and powerful. That was worse, even though it meant his control was probably unshakable — the bloodlust sated by centuries of drinking — because I didn't know that the wards would keep him out.

"What have you been up to, witch?" The vampire spoke so quietly that I barely heard him through the glass. Okay, so he wasn't in my head. The wards were stopping that at least. As I tried to remember my lessons, I was pretty sure that that was one of a vampire's talents. Along with immortality, strength, invulnerability, and the pesky need to drink blood for sustenance.

I wasn't too sure he couldn't also hear the beating of my heart, or cut through witch magic like softened butter.

Belatedly, I remembered to not look him in the eyes, and he laughed as I tore my gaze away from his. He laughed like I was easy prey. Suddenly furious, I clenched my fists and glared at him. He wasn't smiling; could you laugh without smiling? It was odd. If it wasn't for his eyes, which were again locked to mine, he could have been carved out of stone. Dense ice, actually. Expensive jeans, cashmere sweater, and all.

I stepped toward the window and lifted my hand to the latch without even deciding to move.

He smiled then, pleased with himself. He was obviously trying to compel me through the wards. Powerful bastard.

I clenched a fist with the hand I'd lifted toward the latch, then dropped my arm to the side. I smiled back at him. Two could play the smiling-without-mirth game. Not that I'd ever been compelled before — that was more than a little frightening — but still, I covered well.

He frowned and dropped his gaze to my chest with a raised eyebrow. But it wasn't my breasts that impressed him, though I've been told more than once that I was a perfect handful. It was the necklace.

Maybe Sienna was somehow right ...

He pulled something from his pocket, a long string of blackened and crumpled objects. I stared at this item without comprehension for a long moment before my brain figured out what I was seeing.

One of my trinkets, burned and crushed.

I flicked my eyes questioningly to the vampire. He was waiting for my reaction. Well, I was mad.

"Why? Why would you ruin it? What did you do? Run it over and then set fire to it?" I could see a piece of sea glass hanging wired in the middle ... it was one of my new favorite trinkets. And he'd destroyed it.

"Not me, witch. You," the vampire said, and he slipped the trinket back into his pocket. No ... not a pocket. He must be wearing a spelled satchel or something. If I looked closely, I could almost make out a shape. The wards worked both ways, keeping magic out and in, so I couldn't be sure.

"Why would I do that to one of my own pieces? I make them."

"Why do you make them, witch? What purpose?"

I frowned at his question. "No purpose, just because the pieces work together ... like they're meant to be."

The vampire shook his head as if disgusted by me. The condemnation hurt, even though I had no idea where it was coming from or what he meant by it. Or why his opinion should mean anything to me at all.

"Next time, I come in," he said, his voice empty of warning and more terrifying for it.

"Let's see if you can, vampire. I'm game." I wasn't, not even remotely, but I was good with the bravado. I placed my hand on the knife at my hip but didn't draw.

The vampire showed me his teeth. It wasn't a smile. It was the lip curl of a predator. "No. I sent a request. I'll await official confirmation. I won't have the Conclave question my right to your blood truth."

I had absolutely no idea what he was talking about. Request? Conclave? Blood truth ... well, that one was half obvious. He was a vampire, after all.

Then he left. Just like that. He dropped, or climbed, or perhaps disappeared quicker than I could track him.

I didn't wet my pants, but I was glad I hadn't drunk anything all afternoon. Usually I was an eight-glasses-a-day sort of girl.

I was being stalked by an obviously insane vampire. It didn't get much more terrifying than that.

Chapter Two

*D*espite my numb, shocky state, I made it into the shower. Though not before I seriously thought about leaving a message on my Gran's voicemail. The chances of her cell phone picking up in Tofino were slim, but I was loathe to interrupt her yearly vacation. I never had, not even the day Sienna found out her dad was dead and I'd moved her into the guest room at my Gran's house. We'd gathered as many things as we could grab quickly and toss in a backpack. Sienna's mother — drunk out of her mind — screamed obscenities about us and our "kind" the entire time. She also threatened to dump Sienna in the foster system.

Actually, Gran had been upset I hadn't called that day. When she'd returned from her annual trip, she'd dealt with Sienna's mother somehow and made sure there was legal paperwork in place that made us officially sisters.

It was pretty stupid to think I could take on a vampire by myself, but I was twenty-three. Did I really need my grandmother to be constantly overseeing everything and every choice I made? In the end, I decided Tofino was only a few hours away and I didn't yet know if the vampire was a real problem, so I didn't call.

I dried my hair and halfheartedly pinned it up. After I added some eyeliner, blush, and lip gloss to the look, I was pretty much done procrastinating.

The vampire said he needed approval to bite me. Could he get that approval in the next couple of hours? Was it safer to stay behind wards that I wasn't sure could hold him or be out among people? Vampires were careful about exposure — all the magically adept were — but could he grab me without anyone even noticing? Maybe ...

A key turning in the lock announced Sienna's return to the apartment. She'd come through the main door rather than the bakery, for which she didn't have keys.

I pulled a hand-painted silk jacket over my 'Attempted Murder' T-shirt — it has two crows on it; think about it — and a pair of Seven jeans. The jacket was the nicest and most expensive thing I owned. Sienna was out in the living room chatting with Rusty, though I couldn't specifically distinguish his voice. They sounded far, far away, and I thought then I might still be shocky despite the hot shower. I strapped my knife back at my hip and took a deep breath.

It was just dinner and dancing. The vampire wasn't going to kill me in front of witnesses. Plus, my Gran was someone to be reckoned with — at least on the West Coast — and she wouldn't be happy to come back to find me dead. Of course, it wouldn't make much difference to me at that point.

I hustled out to the living room to find Sienna cracking one of my precious bottles of wine — a bakery grand-opening gift from the wine store that occupied the retail space next door. As she turned to pour Rusty a glass, she knocked over one of the barstools at the kitchen island flanking the living room. She wiggled the fingers of her free hand and the barstool froze in mid fall. Yeah, it was a flashy move — like I said, binding spells were Sienna's specialty. I was just happy she hadn't broken the globe wineglass in Rusty's hand. I owned exactly three such glasses, made of actual crystal; the fourth had been smashed by an ex-boyfriend when I broke up with him. It had been an expensive lesson. Don't break up with people when they're in your home and holding onto fragile, expensive stuff.

"Hey, Rusty. Happy birthday," I said as I entered the room. Rusty's hair was brown, not reddish-orange as his name suggested. All witches of the earth persuasion — as in, they had an affinity for or sourced their power from the earth — usually took on a name that was also a color when their powers manifested. Unless they'd been born with that name, as Sienna and I had. Given our parentage, there was no doubt that we'd manifest some sort of witch gift, even if that gift was limited in our cases.

It was an odd, outdated witch tradition. Rusty's mother was a necromancer, while his father was a witch. The necromancy — the ability to communicate with ghosts or in some rare cases revive the dead — tended to only manifest in the female bloodline, so those powers were all but dormant for Rusty, which in my mind was less creepy all around.

Sienna's boyfriend looked paler and more wan than usual as he leaned over to fuss with my jasmine plant. I always forgot to water it, but Rusty's ministrations kept it two steps away from dead. By morning it would look practically as good as new. That was about as much necromancy magic as Rusty could wield, though.

"Up late last night?" I asked him as I snagged the third wineglass and held it out to Sienna. That was a fifty-dollar bottle she'd cracked, and I was damn well going to have a glass of my own wine.

"Yeah, you know," Rusty answered. He slanted his eyes toward Sienna, who giggled.

"It was his birthday, we had to celebrate!" my sister said.

"Yeah, I've never quite celebrated like that before. I didn't get up until two this afternoon."

I could feel the binding spell on the stool weaken and grabbed it before it could finish its crash to the floor. Sienna pouted at me. She liked to leave things hanging in midair, which, now that I thought about it, was a good metaphor for her life in general. Everyone always bumped into those damn stools, but I liked eating breakfast at the kitchen island. And by breakfast, I meant whatever piece of fruit was nearby.

Rusty swirled and sniffed his wine as he crossed by the island into the living room, then sprawled on my beat-up leather couch. I gave Sienna a warning look. Whatever she and Rusty had done last night obviously had an exhausting aftereffect. Rusty's level of fatigue indicated the spell they used was beyond their ability, and therefore potentially dangerous.

Sienna shrugged her shoulders in response to my look. My sister liked boyfriends of a magical persuasion and swore the sex was 'out of this world better' with a little help from a spell or two. Of the two of them, Rusty was the more focused, so he took the brunt of the magical weight — hence his need to sleep. However, to judge by the smile plastered across his face, pale and tired or not, he wasn't complaining.

"Vampires' eyes go red when they're angry, right?" I abruptly changed the subject to the problem occupying my every thought.

Rusty straightened out of his slump. "Your vampire came back?" he asked. Sienna must've filled him in on the bakery sighting.

"I thought you didn't believe me," I said to her.

"Whether you're seeing things or not, it's still good conversation." My sister sipped her red wine.

"Is that black lipstick?" I asked. Yes, I'm easily distracted.

"Really red. Irritated blood red." Sienna smiled.

"Vampires' eyes bleed red when they need or want to feed," Rusty said, bringing us back on topic.

"I want to stop by Gran's to look up vampire lore in the *Compendium*."

"You really think one is stalking you? A full-blood?" Rusty asked.

"He looks it."

"How would you know when you can't even remember the eye thing?" Sienna asked, her regular smirk firmly in place.

"His magic coats him and glistens off his skin. I've never seen anything like it."

"It makes sense," Rusty said thoughtfully. "They'd be classified as magical creatures if they weren't so crazy smart."

"I'm starving, Jade. Get the book tomorrow. Rusty remembers all that stuff anyway." Sienna finished her wine in a single gulp.

I looked down at the glass in my hand. I hadn't even tasted it. As I set it on the kitchen island, it looked a lot like blood.

Rusty scrambled off the couch. "I got you covered, Jade. Ask away. I studied magic and dead things my entire childhood. When, you know, the parents thought I might come into some actual talent. That included a lot about vampires."

"After the restaurant," Sienna said as she spun toward the door. Her short, brown plaid skirt lifted to show a generous portion of upper thigh. Her dark hair was flat-iron straight and shiny.

I was so out of it that I hadn't even noticed yet what she was wearing. I felt bad that I hadn't made more of an effort with my appearance. But then, Rusty wasn't my boyfriend.

Sienna led the way from the apartment. I forced myself to step through the wards, only breathing again after I wasn't instantly attacked and drained.

I locked the door and turned to see that Rusty had waited for me at the top of the stairs, his face in the shadow of the overhead floodlight.

"Just what is a full-blood vampire doing in Vancouver?" he asked. His voice was pitched low as if he didn't want to startle me, but I had no answer.

"The better question is, how do I kill him if it comes to it?"

Rusty shuddered. "You don't, Jade. Killing a vampire is serious business. There aren't many of them in the world. They're super protective of their ... everything."

"According to them."

"Right. Well, that same 'them' have a strict set of rules. A code against randomly draining people. Their very existence would be in jeopardy pretty quickly if the rest of the Adept ever united against them. No one likes vampires. Biting the granddaughter of Pearl Godfrey would be a serious offense."

"I'd prefer to not be bitten at all, rather than just have my death avenged."

"Right. Well, if he was crazy, there'd be bodies everywhere."

Oh, that was comforting. Insane vampires were slaughtering fiends. Since I hadn't noticed anyone dead, I must be first on his list.

"Guys!" Sienna howled up the stairs. She was waiting at street level.

"How do I kill him, Rusty?"

"I doubt you can, not with a spell at least. I don't think even Sienna's binding would slow him for long. They're pretty impervious to magic, crazy strong, and maybe immortal."

"Fire? Sunlight?"

Rusty shook his head. "Maybe with a newborn or the newly risen. No, decapitation and fire, maybe. Think your knife can cut faster than he can heal?"

"I doubt it."

"So do I. Stay out of his way and get your Gran. Her magic will give him pause."

"It's not like I sought him out in the first place."

Rusty laughed. "You attract magic, Jade. You were probably his second stop after he got off the plane. Check into the hotel, follow the pretty magical signature —"

"I was behind the bakery wards."

"Oh?"

Yeah. The vampire shouldn't have been able to feel any magic from me behind those wards.

"I'm just going to lie down and die of starvation now," Sienna yelled up the stairs.

I turned away from Rusty with a sigh that felt far too heavy for my typically simple fun life. I headed down the stairs.

"Jade, you want me to call my mom?"

Vampires didn't like necromancers at all. I'd probably get Rusty's mother killed on sight. I shook my head and Rusty nodded, looking relieved.

Then I tried to forget all about it and get my sister to the restaurant before she threw a temper tantrum on the sidewalk.

We walked to the restaurant — the best Mexican in Vancouver. Hell, the best I'd ever had, and I'd been to LA a couple of times. Then we cabbed it to the dance club.

We were early, and the line still stretched around the block — clubs always liked to appear packed — but Sienna didn't wait in any line in the entire city. The bouncer looked like he might be one-quarter troll, but his smile softened his face as I passed under his arm. Though he held the rope barrier up for us, Rusty, situated between Sienna and me, got a definite scowl from him.

I was accustomed to being smiled at. A bouncy blond with a light permanent tan stood out in Vancouver, no matter the season. The greens and blues of my silk jacket would only make my eyes brighter blue. Problem was, smiles rarely progressed into anything deeper, at least not with anyone magical. Like I was too much to handle, too much to commit to — and then those rare men who did want something long term bored me easily.

I returned the smile anyway with a brief flash of teeth as I followed Sienna into the club. The music, already loud at the street entrance, promised to drown out any thoughts in my head. I welcomed it.

I left Sienna and Rusty at the bar and skirted the half-full dance floor to the bathrooms. I was still feeling uneasy about the vampire and had only agreed to come dancing because I thought there was a chance there'd be more than humans here tonight. Vancouver wasn't exactly a destination of choice for the more powerful of the Adept, but a few low-level spellcasters, small-time sorcerers, and a couple of part witches could usually be found in this club. Not that I had anything against humans — I was half-human myself, of course — but they didn't offer the extra layer of protection I was seeking. I couldn't even hide within the small crowd on the floor; my magical affinity was like a beacon to anyone who could sense that sort of thing. However, I could blend among others of the Adept even if they themselves didn't know they had magical ancestry, which was the case in Vancouver most of the time. The Adept were a dying breed. My Gran thought witches were diminishing because of the ongoing destruction of the environment. The earth was dying and so was witch magic.

Actually and regrettably, I usually had to firmly dissuade any new boy that came into Sienna's life — unbeknownst to my sister, of course. It was purely a magic thing, and had nothing to do with the guys actually wanting to be with me over her. Rusty had kept his distance, and once Sienna started sleeping with him, he seemed to completely relax around me. Anyway, I usually kept my guard up around any of the Adept, with a few specific exceptions. But tonight, I would have put up with a lot of looks and maybe even some handiness to be surrounded by more magic.

The club was playing popular hits tonight, which I preferred over techno or electronic anyway, and I felt more at ease in the low light of the club. Occasional strobes of black light flashed over the dance floor — they were going old school tonight — and some more of the tension eased from my neck. I always got a stiff neck when stressed.

I slipped into the women's bathroom, lamely called *Dames* according to a sign on the door. I wove around a few tipsy ladies to a sink to wash my hands and refresh my lip gloss.

Suddenly, without even feeling myself move, I was standing in a bathroom stall — door closed and latched — held by the neck and pressed against the steel dividing wall by the vampire.

His grip on my throat was light, but I knew that with one wrong move, he would snap my spine just by squeezing his fingers. I exhaled in a brief moment of panic, worrying for a moment that my lungs weren't going to reinflate.

He'd moved so quickly that the other women in the outer bathroom hadn't even reacted. He'd probably only registered as a slight breeze or blur to them, which they were certainly tipsy enough to ignore.

The vampire had his other hand pressed against my right one, effectively pinning it against my knife at my hip. I'd apparently attempted to defend myself by grabbing for it. Good to know that my instincts had kicked in before my brain, which still seemed delayed.

Up close, the vampire's magic danced across his skin. It was almost distracting. His frown and ice-cold eyes kept me focused, though — even as I once again forgot to not make direct eye contact with him. Maybe the women in the bathroom had seen him and assumed this was a planned rendezvous. He was good-looking enough to be titillating to those who didn't know that his idea of a tryst came with pointy teeth and serious blood deprivation.

"I thought you weren't going to bite me tonight," I said, pleased that my voice sounded much calmer than my mind.

He tilted his head and gazed at my neck ... actually, at my carotid artery. My pulse sped up; I was surprised it could get any higher.

"I wasn't," he murmured.

"Well, watching my blood move through my veins isn't going to be helpful, then."

He lifted his eyes to mine, and for a moment seemed almost ... amused. But then, he just stared at me. My back started to ache from holding myself so stiffly against the wall and away from him, but hell if I was going to relax into his neck hold.

"Your hand is cold," I finally said, having no idea what to do when a vampire just stared at you.

"I could warm it." He flicked his eyes to my neck again and showed me the very tips of his teeth — but no fangs and no red eyes. He wasn't going to bite me. And if I wasn't completely crazy, his tone sounded almost ... flirtatious.

"What do you want, vampire?" I asked, putting as much steel as I dared into the question.

His face blanked like a sheet of ice once again, and he moved away where he'd been leaning forward before. "Just to see you outside the wards, witch."

"So you tracked me here?"

"You're not difficult to follow. You move like a human" — this was not a compliment — "and you ... feel ... odd."

Well, that was terribly flattering news. I'd always wanted to feel odd.

He released my neck and took a half-step back. It was all the room the stall would allow him. I was hyperaware of all the other women in the bathroom with me. All the other very human and vulnerable women. I curled my hand around my knife; he'd released that as well.

He raised an eyebrow. "That won't hurt me."

"You might be surprised."

"I never am."

"Never is a sort of long-term word, even for a vampire."

He was touching my necklace before I'd even realized he'd moved. He seemed enamored with it, weaving his fingers through the wedding ring charms until they resembled brass knuckles. His fingers were slim. He'd plucked the chain off my left breast; I tried to not squirm.

"This is remarkable."

"I'll make you one and we'll be twins."

"A fine gift," he said, somewhat surprised as he lifted his eyes to mine. Obviously ignoring my sarcasm.

"I aim to please."

"Do you?" He seemed suddenly thrown, off kilter.

"You know, this isn't normal behavior, accosting me on my balcony and in the bathroom stall at a club. People will think we're having sex in here."

He looked aghast, dropping his fingers from my necklace. "I just wanted to see you out from the wards."

"Well, now you have." I opened my arms in a 'here I am' gesture. I would have done a twirl if there'd been more room and I thought my shaky legs would hold.

"Half-witch, and what's the other half?" he asked.

I dropped my arms. The scary conversation was going to continue ... "Human. Half-witch, half-human."

The vampire shook his head. "Don't lie to me, witch. I'll know all anyway, once I get my blood truth release. Of course, you could save me the trouble of waiting and give me permission yourself. Get all this sorted out quickly."

"Get what sorted out?" His attention was on my neck again. I felt like snapping my fingers to pull his eyes to mine, except I wasn't sure what scared me more — looking into his cold, emotionless gaze or watching him watch my blood flow.

"The murders, of course," he murmured, sounding more mesmerized than was healthy for me.

"What murders?" I snapped. That caught his attention. I decided it was actually way scarier to look him in the eye. "You didn't mention any murders."

"I didn't?"

"No."

"The evidence obviously points to you, but you don't seem right ... you are very ... blond."

"Being blond makes me less capable of murder?" What the hell was I arguing that point for? He mixed me up, scared me, and then attempted an almost normal conversation.

He grinned and suddenly looked good. Human good. Sexy. Available.

"I'm blond," he whispered.

"And more than capable of murder."

His smile widened. It wasn't comforting, and it didn't inspire me to return the gesture as it usually would. He scared me more than I liked to admit, no matter what rules supposedly governed his behavior.

"Jade? What the hell are you doing in here?" The bang of the outer bathroom door and the shrillness of her voice announced Sienna's entrance.

"Jade?" the vampire said, suddenly too close to me again, though he didn't touch me.

"Yes," I replied, as steady as I could be around a predator.

"You're not half-human, Jade. I can tell you that even without tasting you." His whisper breezed across the skin of my neck and ear. My breath caught in my throat ... just for one awkward, oddly arousing moment. "Anyone with an ounce of ability could tell you that."

I shook my head, just once, but I wasn't sure if I was denying his assessment of my parentage or my reaction to his sudden ... allure.

"Jade? What the hell?" Sienna called, the sound of her voice moving closer. "Which stall are you in?"

The vampire almost reverently brushed his fingers along the rings of my necklace. "I grant you safe passage. For tonight. You are intriguing, half-witch, half-not-human."

Then the stall door was hanging open and I was alone. I slumped against the wall, relieved but more riled up than I'd like to be given that I'd just been practically mauled by a vampire.

Sienna poked her head around the door. "Who the hell was that?"

A few women behind her tittered at the vampire's exit. It seemed he could choose to move slowly when he wished to make an impression. Sienna sent them scurrying with a glare.

"The vampire," I sighed, pitching my voice low to not be overheard. I crossed by her to the sink.

"And you were ... what? Giving him a blow job in the bathroom stall?"

"Yes, Sienna. I was giving a vampire a blow job, because that's all vamps really want from a girl."

"You let him bite you?" Sienna hissed, clamping her mouth shut as a couple of tipsy girls exited another stall together.

"I didn't let him bite me!" I thrust my wet hands under the dryer.

"What did he want?" Sienna murmured into my ear. "Besides the obvious. Was he just drawn to your magic?"

"No. I don't think so. I don't know. Someone has been murdered. He thinks ... or thought ... that I did it."

"Thought?"

"Supposedly I'm too blond to murder anyone."

Sienna looked thoughtful, like she might agree with this assessment. I began to bristle. Not that I would murder anyone, but please — it wasn't because I was weak, or sweet, or incapable. I just had morals and a heart.

"Did he tell you anything else?"

"Yeah. He thinks there's no way I'm half-human."

"That is interesting."

"Are we going to dance, or what?" I was tired of conversations about nothing going nowhere I had any control over.

"Oh, yes. I think you'll like the crowd." Sienna smiled and looped an arm through mine. "They're just your type. More magic than mere mortals, more brawn than brain."

Well ... that did sound promising.

Chapter Three

The dance floor had filled out since I'd been in the bathroom. Strobe lights alternated with black light, creating a staccato effect with the dancers. The blown-out whites generated by the black lights left residual streaks across my retinas. I loved it. The tables surrounding the floor were firmly in the shadows as usual, but I had no interest in sitting and watching. The vampire, who might still be lurking, had scared me. I could feel the adrenaline — the high of escaping a predator — flooding my limbs.

I needed to move, to dance. Rusty sidled up out of the shadows around the tables and laced his hand through my arm. Sienna still hung off the other one. He held up some sort of dark martini in front of me; with the lights flashing it was impossible to distinguish its color. I ignored the offering and stepped toward the dance floor. Sienna snatched the drink, downed it, and followed me. Rusty, left with the empty glass, lagged a little behind as he paused to drop it on a nearby table.

I pushed through the crowd. It was still thin around the edges, but it wouldn't be for long. Sienna joined me, Rusty by her side. They began to move to the beat — some Flo Rida song — but I waited. I stood as the crowd shifted around me. I closed my eyes. I breathed, opening my palms to the room and feeling them ... first Sienna and Rusty, their magic familiar and light ... fragrant, with a touch of sweet floral like sugared violets.

I tilted my head back and pushed my senses past the humans currently occupying the floor. Then I found them on the outer edges. Sienna had been correct in her assessment that I would like this magic. They tasted like dark, fruity chocolate — more berry than citrus, with earthy undertones like red wine or truffles. I'd never tasted magic like this before.

I felt a smile spread across my face ... the music stuttered and then a Kesha song thumped through the speakers. I opened my eyes.

Sienna laughed and pulled Rusty closer.

I shifted my hips ... testing the beat. My shoulders followed.

The crowd shifted, stepped back and turned to face me almost in one motion, one moment.

I lifted my arms slightly to the sides, filling the space around me as I let the beat of the music take control of my body. I twisted and pumped and swayed.

And they approached ... drawn to my magic as much as I wanted to taste their own.

First a woman, her hair an unnatural shade of green as best as I could discern it underneath the dance floor lights. Her body was lithe and muscular. She flashed a smile and slipped in as close to me as she could without impeding my own movements. Her magic brushed against me and I immediately peeled off my silk jacket to expose my arms. Rusty took the jacket from me.

I twisted around the woman, sliding across her body ... not touching, never touching, just sipping. Her magic tasted of deep, dark chocolate, almost too bitter, sharp, and smoky with the slightest of berry finishes.

Then there were more of them — a blond boy who towered over the rest of the dancers but looked barely old enough to be in the club, and a petite brunette with her bee-stung lips painted purple. They formed a tight circle around me, pushing Sienna and Rusty to one side. I wasn't sure I'd ever felt this many of the Adept in one place before, especially not here in Vancouver. It was a small community.

I'd run across a few more powerful witches — or even sorcerers who accessed their power through books or objects rather than the earth itself — in larger cities such as LA, but I never engaged with them directly. I didn't even know what kind of magic these three wielded, but it was nowhere near weak, and they were fantastic on the dance floor.

We danced. And danced.

The magic circled around us, spinning and kissing.

I threw my head back and laughed. The dancers closest to me howled in response — the sound thrilling but terrifyingly inhuman — and pressed closer.

Wolves. Werewolves, to be exact.

A chill ran down my spine, cutting through the heat generated by the dance. Magical beings, not just magic users like Sienna, Rusty, and me. No wonder they tasted so strongly.

Suddenly the wolves, all except the girl with the green hair, pulled back a step. A man moved into their circle.

I looked at him. He looked at me.

Then he smiled. An answering grin spread across my own face. He was a few inches taller than me, and dressed as I was in a tight T-shirt and jeans, his clothing a rather snug fit over his well-muscled frame. He was pushing past two hundred pounds, all of it muscle. His dark hair was cropped short, its styling effortless. He hadn't bothered to shave in a couple of days.

I flicked my hands up over my head in time with the beat, rocking my hips in his direction.

He instantly closed the space between us. Brushing against me but not grabbing. His magic — even more potent than the others — slid across my skin. I almost shuddered with the divine feel of it. He tasted of expensive dark chocolate — fine and smooth, citrus middle notes, and a clean nose with no aftertaste.

I opened my mouth just a little, and tilted my head toward his neck. I inhaled his clean scent. He laughed, his hands brushing over my hips, and did the same to me. The light touch of his breath was warm and welcoming, so different than the vampire's icy touch.

Another song had started, but I didn't even notice the music other than keeping time with the beat. The wolves surrounded me, brushed against me, sharing magic. I should have been scared out of my mind. I wasn't. I lost track of Sienna and Rusty. I felt teeth against my arms, which were stretched up, out, and surrounded by wolves.

The dark prince — I guessed his hierarchy based on the deference of the others — ran his fingers through my hair and loosened my hair clip. My curls tumbled around my neck and shoulders. He dipped his head to smell me, as if I were a glass of fine wine. He ran his fingers along my arm, which was currently twisted up over his shoulder. I danced my fingers at the back of his neck — hardly touching — and he shuddered in response.

The magic built between and around us.

I wanted to press myself against him. I wanted to taste him with my actual mouth, not just my magical senses. I wanted a different kind of build and release, but that wasn't how I played this game.

Everyone knew that witches didn't run with wolves. Very few of the Adept intermingled at all. Rusty's parents — a witch married to a necromancer — were definite anomalies and were treated as such. Plus, I had a feeling these wolves were just visiting, because with magic that tasted like this, I would have noticed them before. Visiting werewolves were definitely not relationship material.

The song ended.

The beat just dropped and left me hanging, raised slightly on my toes, hands in the air. Practically wrapped around a stranger.

The club was closing. I hadn't even noticed the hours passing. Wolves could apparently dance all night.

I moved back, just a half step. My breathing was ragged.

The lights came up. It was definitely closing time … where had the evening gone?

I turned my head slightly and caught sight of the perfect jawline of my companion. The other wolves melted into the rapidly thinning crowd. The dark prince brushed the curls away from my ear. His breath was hot as he whispered, "Take me home, little witch. I like the way you dance."

A shiver ran down the side of my neck and into my spine to pool in my nether regions. My limbs were loose and compliant. I could take him home. I could forget I didn't know him at all. I could share magic, and touches, and bodily fluids …

An ache of regret spread through my chest. I wasn't going to … no matter how tempted. My grandmother's warnings about being intimate with the magically inclined, about the vulnerability of such actions, echoed through my mind.

I stepped back and flicked my eyes over his shoulder to see Sienna waiting for me on the edge of the dance floor. My sister didn't look too happy. I'd let it go too far with the wolves for her comfort ... Sienna's arms were folded, which meant she was scared. Just as I should have been, surrounded by werewolves. But their magic, which still swirled in a dying ebb around us — heavy enough that even Sienna could probably feel it — didn't feel frightening to me.

The dark prince groaned lightly as he turned his head to follow my gaze. "Your friend doesn't approve of me?"

"Witches don't run with wolves," I answered.

He laughed. "Don't be so sure."

His laugh was infectious, so I grinned back at him.

"At least give me a name."

"Jade."

"I'm Hudson."

"Of course you are."

"Is that funny?"

I smiled and stepped around him.

"A phone number would also be nice," he said, but I'd caught sight of the man seated at the table behind Hudson — if man was the right word at all. If I thought Hudson to be the perfect male specimen, this guy was epically more manly. More brutal. Hudson was long and lean. This guy was hard and terrifying. This was who had scared Sienna.

And he was currently staring at me — glaring actually — his arms crossed and his lip almost imperceptibly curled in a snarl. Emerald green glinted off his eyes, as if the overhead lights were casting a strange glow.

"Scary ... eyes," I murmured, frozen in place like prey.

"He won't hurt you," Hudson said, but he honestly didn't sound all that sure.

Sienna, her hand low at her side, snapped her fingers — a warning we'd used as children. The sound woke the part of my brain that controlled movement and I ripped my eyes away from Mr. McGrowly — yes, it helped to make fun of him in my head — as if painfully, slowly, peeling a bandage from my brain. I was pretty sure he was going to eat me, but only after he played with me for a while. And not in a satiating, mutual bliss sort of way. This one liked to hunt, and he kept what he killed.

I found Sienna's eyes instead and moved toward her. She stepped back and into the crowd, heading toward the exit. She'd been standing just to one side and behind the peripheral vision of McGrowly. Rusty peeled off from the bar where he'd been waiting, following her into the crowd at the doors.

Hell, they were scared enough that they were distancing themselves from me.

"Ah, Jade, don't be like that," Hudson moaned behind me.

I kept walking. Once I felt buried in the people heading toward the exit, I chanced a look back.

Hudson was standing next to McGrowly, both of them watching me leave. Hudson looked regretful, but he smiled when I turned back. McGrowly barked something at him that made his grin disappear, and he dropped my gaze. The green-haired girl was perched on their table, but at a nod from McGrowly, she slipped off toward the staff exit.

Sienna appeared beside me, wrapped a hand around my arm, and began pulling me through the crowd. We stumbled out the doors hand in hand.

I raised my face to the crisp air, the chill easing the last tinges of intoxicating magic. Rusty slung my jacket over my shoulders and I thrust my rapidly cooling arms into the sleeves. The fine dew of sweat from the dancing suddenly didn't feel so pleasant.

They didn't talk. They just tugged me across the cobblestone street — one of the few left in Vancouver — while dodging slow-moving cars. The sidewalks were thronged with people exiting clubs and bars. No one in the immediate vicinity was over thirty. This area brimmed with nightclubs, all of which closed at 2:00 A.M.

Time to go home.

We turned a corner onto another street, Carrall or Abbott maybe. I get turned around easily. The crowd thinned to a few friend groupings and a couple of homeless people wandering in and out of the side alleys. The pavement here was wet. It must have rained while we were in the club.

"You're freaking me out," I said, needing to break the oppressive silence.

"We can't go home yet," Sienna murmured to Rusty, completely ignoring me.

"Right. After-hours club?" he answered and asked.

"Guys, it was just a dance," I said, wrenching my arms out of their grips. I wasn't going to be yanked across town. I needed at least a couple of hours of sleep before baking.

Sienna rounded on me. "Do you know who that was?" she whispered, her voice soft but harsh.

I shrugged. "Wolves."

"Wolves," Sienna spat. "At least four of them, plus the one who didn't dance ..." She finished with a shudder.

"You're overreacting —"

Sienna turned her head sharply toward the mouth of the alley we'd just walked past. "What's that?" she asked with a hiss.

"It's nothing," I replied. That was, as long as being stalked by wolves was nothing. I could feel the magic of the green-haired girl emanating from the shadows. I was surprised Sienna had noticed.

Sienna's lips pulled back off her teeth. Most of her face was eclipsed by the shadow of the overhead street-light, which darkened her eyes until they seemed like nothing but pupil. "Do you have your knife?" she asked.

"Sienna, it's just the wolves playing. They're not going to hurt us. We don't need knives." Sienna turned back to me into the light, and what I had mistaken for dark anger was fear. "Sienna, it'll be fine. I'm going to grab a cab home. You and Rusty enjoy the rest of his birthday."

Sienna nodded and looked to Rusty.

He wrapped his arm around her. "It's okay, babe. It's not the first time Jade's attracted attention."

"That was a lot of attention," Sienna said. She placed air quotes around the word attention, her voice a snarl of sarcasm.

I sighed. Sienna had issues with taking anger out on the wrong people. Especially when her fear masquer-aded as anger. I turned my head toward the alley. The wolf magic was moving away. "See. No wolves bursting out of dark alleys … I'm sorry I scared you."

Sienna snorted a laugh, but it held none of her usually playful tone. "You didn't scare me, Jade. I can handle myself."

"You bet you can," Rusty said, getting her atten-tion with a leer.

Sienna giggled, sounding a little more like herself.

I raised my hand and flagged down a cab trolling the street just behind us. We'd lucked out — the streets were one way around here, and the cab must have just dropped off a fare before circling back to the crowd seeping out from the row of clubs all along this strip.

I asked the cab to pull over at the north side of Burrard Street Bridge. I felt like walking home to burn off the residual magic still coating my skin, though not in a bad way. The after-hours club Rusty and Sienna were heading to was on the north side of the water anyway. No sense in doubling back.

Sienna protested but was pretty wrapped up — literally — in Rusty. They already had an outlet for their 'residual magic.' I was a bit envious. Sienna didn't worry about sexual dalliances with the magically inclined. But then, Rusty was low in the power department, and the wolves had been much, much higher.

Was I worried the vampire was still lurking somewhere? Maybe. But I knew he couldn't hurt me without breaking his vampire code — Rusty's info had been confirmed by the vampire's mention of 'safe passage' earlier — plus, I wasn't going to let him play me. I wasn't some toy.

So I walked, happy that my Fluevog boots were sexy yet still practical. I tucked my collar up, lowered my head to the wind as it rushed over the bridge, and hoped it didn't rain.

I didn't hear or see the vampire until he was matching me stride for stride.

I fought back the instinctive urge to run, reminding myself I wasn't going to let him scare me. But being on a long cement bridge over a wide inlet pretty much limited my escape options, so that didn't help with the instincts. Plus, he'd be faster than me. Way faster. I knew that much about vampires at least.

"You don't happen to fear water or heights, do you?" I asked without looking at him.

"No. Why?"

"I was thinking about jumping and wondering if you'd just follow."

The vampire threw his head back and laughed. I could clearly see the stretch of his neck and tilt of his head in my peripheral vision. It was a purely human sound, and for some reason, that scared me more. He could pass for one of them … walk among those who couldn't see the magic simmering off him, then rip someone's head off with a flick of his wrist.

"I wasn't attempting to be funny."

"And yet you are."

"So this is your safe passage?"

"You can't get any safer than with me by your side."

"Right. That doesn't sound creepy stalkerish at all."

He didn't respond further. Apparently, he was okay with being a creepy stalker.

"What do vampires care about murders in Vancouver?"

"It's the missing blood that drew our attention."

"So … it looks like a vampire kill?"

"Yes, but not on closer inspection."

"And if it was done by a vampire?"

"Then I would have found and sentenced the killer already."

"Capital punishment?"

"Not unless I had no other choice."

"Because vampires are precious."

"Yes."

"I still don't understand why you care, if it wasn't a vampire."

"Appearances must be maintained."

I had no idea what the hell that meant — maybe bad PR for the vamps? But I didn't want to look more ignorant than I'm sure I already did.

"The shifters seemed enamored of you tonight, especially the wolves. I can see how your magic could be intoxicating."

"What do you mean 'especially the wolves?' What other shifters are there?" I deliberately ignored the intoxicating comment. He didn't need any more reasons to think that drinking my blood might be a treat.

"I'd be careful. They aren't the cute playthings they seem to be, especially when they've lost one of their own."

"What do you mean by 'especially the wolves?' " I repeated. "And 'one of their own?' Did someone kill a werewolf here in Vancouver?"

The vampire didn't answer. We continued to walk across the bridge side by side. I tried to keep my pace steady, though every few moments my steps unconsciously quickened and I had to slow.

We were approaching the crest of the bridge, almost halfway across. A cement outcrop stood there, rising off one of the central concrete pillars thrust up from the water below.

The vampire suddenly dangled the burned trinket he'd showed me earlier in front of my face. I nearly walked right into it, but then the magic hit me straight in the gut. It rolled over me, dark and terrible, like ashes in my mouth. I faltered. I twisted away from the cursed thing in his hand. The vampire followed me. The stink of magic coated my nose and forced its way down my throat. My stomach protested.

I held up my hands, backed away, and hit the concrete side of the bridge, hurting my hip and back. I was getting frantic. I thought the night had already featured a number of terrifying moments, but this ... I wanted to flee and hide.

I twisted away again, retching the contents of my stomach onto the sidewalk. What an awful waste of an expensive meal.

I retched again but my stomach was empty.

The dreadful magic disappeared. The vampire reached for me, perhaps to steady me — I could feel rather than see him — but I fought his hands. I probably would have been less bruised if I hadn't tried to knock him away. It was like hitting granite — and I know, I've taken a header in my kitchen before.

A car slowed on the bridge, honking. It probably looked like the vampire was assaulting me. I looked up — I was still hunched over, waiting to see if I was going to heave some more — and caught the concerned eyes of a carload of twenty-somethings.

"Wave them off," the vampire murmured. Yes, wave off the fragile, blood-filled humans.

I flapped my hands and attempted to straighten. "Thanks, guys," I called. "Just too much to drink, I think."

The driver nodded, though his companions looked a little unconvinced. The car slowly pulled away.

I took a few hesitant steps. A show of independent movement for their rearview mirror. Plus, I wasn't interested in continuing to stare at my own puke.

I wiped my hand across my face, and my stomach spasmed at the remembrance of the sickly magic that had emanated from the burned trinket. "What the hell was that?" I said. I tried to snap, but my protest sounded a lot more like a pitiful moan.

"Black magic," the vampire answered easily enough. He certainly was chatty now that I was practically incapacitated and trapped.

"The trinket was used to kill someone? That can't be … can it?"

The vampire shrugged. "I'm not a black witch."

"Well, neither am I."

"I can see that. Your reaction was rather extreme. Unexpectedly."

"Is that an apology?"

The vampire fixed his icy eyes on me and didn't answer further. It seemed he only stayed in human mode for short periods.

"I'm not some interesting bug!" I spat.

"I'm not the collector here," he answered. He meant the trinkets. It was true that I was a collector — the proverbial magpie — but somehow that smug observation pissed me off further.

As I tried to soothe my rage, I realized how surreal it was to be standing in the middle of a four-lane bridge in the early morning — in the slight breeze, underneath starlight — having just puked up black magic, while being stalked by a vampire who believed that my little trinket could kill someone.

"The trinkets have no power —"

"They are magical."

"No, the items I collect have some glimmer of magic. That is what you feel."

"I'm not a sensitive like you. I would not be able to feel a glimmer."

"Then someone else has somehow harnessed this tiny bit of magic and turned it."

"Yes, but it should not be possible to harness minor glimmers — as you call them — this way. The trinkets must be far more magical than you let on. Why do you make them? For profit? Do you tailor them to certain spells? Who are your customers?"

I just stared at him, mouth wide open and everything. What he was suggesting was ridiculous. That I could make objects of any power ... the trinkets were worthless decorations, wind chimes —

"Answer me," the vampire said, more inflection in his voice than before.

I eased away from him, looking over my shoulders both ways. A few cars were on the bridge, but I wasn't about to get anyone killed. "I really have no idea what you're talking about. If you would just wait until my grandmother —"

"I know who your grandmother is —"

"Well, then you know she'd be better equipped to help you —"

"I have no need of help. I just want answers. Give them to me now or wait until I get the clearance for the blood-truth letting."

"Are you going to kill me, then, for making trinkets?" I sneered.

"What's the fun in that?" He didn't leer, but his tone was just as obvious. He planned on getting pleasure with his blood. One-sided pleasure, I was certain.

I had my knife out and an inch away from his right eye almost before I made the decision to draw.

He looked as surprised by my action as I was. I'd never drawn the knife in self-defense before; I'd never needed to. I knew I had to be prepared to use it once I drew … so I never had.

"You think that blade will cut me?" he asked, cool and collected now, looking at me rather than the knife.

My hand was steady. My stomach settled as if the knife soothed it. "Hand hewn in jade by me. Took me a year to shape it. And another year of strengthening, sharpening, and accuracy spells. It will cut you. It will take out your eye."

"You made this?"

"God, you really need to get your hearing checked, old man." I sneered, then quickly learned that sneering at a vampire was a bad idea. Or maybe it was the age slur.

A sheen of red rolled over the vampire's eyes. He knocked my knife hand away with the side of his arm and stepped into me. I shuffled back a panicked half step and found myself pressed against the concrete wall. I had a brief moment of contemplating the suicidal bridge jump when he brought his hands down on either side of me onto the concrete wall. His eyes were squeezed shut, but whether in rage or in an attempt to control himself, I didn't know.

I moaned in fear as he sucked in a breath through his teeth — I'm not sure he'd even been breathing before — and turned toward the space between my ear and my neck.

"You will not bite me without permission," I spat, and my fight-or-flight instinct kicked in — finally. I thrust the knife I still clenched in my right hand into his stomach.

Chunks of concrete snapped — yes, just snapped — off in his hands as he stumbled away from me. He looked confused by this for a moment, staring down at the concrete in his palms. Red still tinged the edges of his eyes, and he didn't seem remotely bothered that he'd just been stabbed.

And me ... well, I ran.

He let me go.

I wasn't a runner. I baked cupcakes for a living, tried to not eat too many, and took a yoga class once in a while. But, nevertheless, I ran.

I could feel muscles I never used lengthening and stretching as I sprinted the second half of the bridge. Thank God it was downhill. I tried to block everything, every thought between me and the next step. My right foot hit the sidewalk while my left foot flung forward. I was airborne for a moment as the right foot rolled forward and off the concrete, just before the left foot landed. Repeat. And repeat. And repeat.

Ignore the enraged and most likely impossibly fast vampire behind me. Ignore the fact that my heartbeat was pounding in my head — possible oxygen deprivation ... oh, God, I was going to suffocate before the vampire had a chance to rip out my throat ...

If I'd had a moment to think beyond my terror — it had been a hell of a night, who could blame me? — while breathing, or attempting to breathe, I would have noted I was faster, stronger than I would have thought of myself. Maybe dancing for three or four hours every couple of weeks was more cardio building than I thought.

The sound of a bus broke through the terror relentlessly scrambling my brain. I chanced a look back — yep, a bus was coming over the bridge. I looked ahead. The bridge joined the main road, curving right or leftish a few feet ahead. I picked right, heading for the bus stop nestled underneath a streetlamp. I flung my arm up just as the bus passed, desperately hoping that the driver had seen me fleeing for my life and mistaken it for a dash to the stop.

The amber light of the bus's right-hand indicator flashing and the squeal of its brakes were the most beautiful things I'd seen and heard in the past two hours. Well, almost ... Hudson the werewolf really had been something else.

I flung myself at the bus, attempting to not simply collapse on the stairs inside the open door. I worried I wasn't going to manage the couple of stairs to get fully inside. I was becoming uncomfortably aware of the yawning darkness of the vampire-filled night behind me. Okay, so it was just one vampire. He was one too many. I lifted my left foot and it thankfully rose on command. I clutched the railing, practically pulling myself into a seat behind the driver. These spaces were reserved for the disabled, but he didn't seem to care as he closed the door and pulled away from the curb.

I couldn't breathe. The driver didn't find this particularly charming. I tried a smile, though, and got one in return. Though I thought he might have also just noticed my heaving chest. Good. Maybe that would distract him from the fact that I had no fare.

"Hi ..." I managed to speak between gasps. "Thank you for stopping."

"It's my job," the driver answered, but his smile indicated how much he liked his job at this particular moment.

I flashed him another smile, vaguely getting my breathing under control. His smile widened in response. "I don't have fare." I thought it best to be as upfront as possible.

"Public transportation is free after 2:00 A.M. It's a city-wide drinking-driving initiative."

"It's my lucky night."

"Mine too."

I laughed, but I was seriously distracted by my suddenly shaky legs and didn't attempt to continue the conversation. The driver seemed content to simply have me in his rearview mirror.

I pressed my hands on my shaking knees. It was one thing to look drunk, but another thing entirely to look like a junkie coming down off a bad trip ... I didn't need an intervention right now.

I tried to peer out the back of the bus, but the interior lights blacked out the windows so much that I couldn't see beyond the passing cars and streetlights. Most of the other singles on the bus looked as if they were heading home after a long evening of work rather than play; their once freshly ironed, white dress shirts wrinkled and stained. Though a young couple were getting cuddly in the backseat. Her makeup had seen better days, and I imagined so had mine.

I prayed — to whoever might be listening — that I wasn't wrong to involve the bus and the few souls just looking to get home to their beds. The vampire wouldn't lose it so badly that he'd slaughter humans, would he?

I mean, I knew vampires needed blood to live, but the red that had rolled over the vampire's eyes was the scariest thing I had ever witnessed ... scarier than McGrowly at the club. If vampires supposedly policed themselves and had a code of ethics, why were there any rogues at all? Was it a choice on the individual vampire's part to go rogue, or did they just suddenly snap?

I orientated myself. The bus was closer to my grandmother's house than my apartment. I pulled the cord to request a stop, trying to not worry about whether the vampire hunted by scent or sight. I could make it a few blocks, and no magical creature could get past the wards on the Godfrey house. Those wards were over a hundred years old and fortified by each new generation. In fact, despite my lack of spellcasting ability, Gran had me reinforce the wards with her just last spring.

I flashed another smile at the driver — he deserved it, not only for stopping but for not harassing me with small talk afterward — and swung down off the bus. My shaky legs were happier to be moving.

I waited for the bus to drive away before I pulled out my knife. It was back in its sheath, though I couldn't remember replacing it during my mad dash. I held the knife pressed against my right thigh and stepped quickly in the direction of Gran's house. No need to inadvertently upset any neighbors being drowsily walked by the tiny bladders of their high-priced dogs. Plus, I'd grown up in this neighborhood — yes, silver spoon and all. Any bad behavior would be held against me and reported to a higher authority, namely Grandma Pearl.

I couldn't walk down the middle of the street, like I would have preferred to do in order to be out of easy arm's reach from anyone lurking among the ten-foot laurel and cedar hedges. Even after three in the morning, Cypress Street, now technically Point Grey Road, had a fair amount of traffic. It was the main thoroughfare running past the waterfront homes in Kitsilano.

I hurried, but didn't run, the last three blocks to my Gran's beachfront mansion while a Porsche and then a BMW SUV sped by me. I practically dashed through the wrought iron gate that always stood open at the top of Gran's driveway. A security light flicked on, and I felt the welcoming magic of the outer wards slide over my skin.

I waited a couple of heartbeats, but no one was being obvious about following me. No shadows detached from any of the houses across the street, no scents came on the sea-tinged breeze. But I knew ... I knew the vampire was in no way finished with his interrogation.

I turned back to the dark house — Gran recently had its white-painted shutters and siding refreshed — and wished that I could open the door to the smell of chocolate chip cookies or homemade macaroni. But then I shook my head. I wasn't a child. I could handle being alone in the home of my childhood. For one night, at least.

I jogged up the slate-tiled stairs — the slate was new enough that I hadn't laid eyes on it yet — and grabbed the handle on the native-carved double door. I didn't need a key. The house would recognize me.

I entered with a flush of relief and promptly kicked over a can. I scrambled for an overhead light, turning it on to see that I'd managed to dump a bucket of paint-filled brushes soaking in water across my Gran's white marble entranceway. The gray paint water had sloshed everywhere. Delightful.

Gran was obviously having the house painted while she was away on her surfing trip. Could this evening get any worse? I didn't want to jinx it, but probably not. I trudged into the kitchen to grab some rags to clean up the mess.

Chapter Four

My cell phone alarm blared rudely in my left ear. I reached for it — suddenly aware that my neck was killing me — and managed to knock it off the desk. That didn't stop the damn trill.

Desk?

Why was I lying on a desk?

Oh, hell. I'd fallen asleep poring over the *Magical Compendium* in my grandmother's study. My cheek was currently stuck to the page opposite a blurb about verisimilitude, aka reveal, spells. Witches were a wordy and elitist bunch, or at least they wrote like they were ... I hadn't met many, myself. I must have finished reading the vampire entry before I collapsed. Not that I currently remembered any of it. Hopefully it would come back to me.

The alarm was being rather insistent. It was Sunday; why was the alarm even set?

I peeled my cheek off the seven-inch thick book. I couldn't straighten my neck properly. I blinked my blurred eyes in the hope of calling up some moisture. It didn't work. I tried rubbing them while I batted at the phone with my foot, but the screen didn't recognize my toes' right to shut off the alarm.

The sun was rising. Grandma's den faced east. It was far too early ... oh, damn. I was due at the bakery this morning to cover a shift for Bryn, who had just moved up from apprentice to a single — solo — baker shift on the weekends. Unfortunately, she had some sort of wedding to go to today. Not her own ... I remembered that much at least.

I had to bake delicious, sexy cupcakes on less than three hours sleep, and my body felt like it had been rolled over repeatedly by a dump truck. Why the hell did I feel like ...? Right. The vampire.

I curled my fingers around the hilt of my knife. I'd apparently slept with it on the desk underneath my right hand.

I tried to stand up. My weary legs held, though barely. I felt utterly hungover, even though I hadn't drunk a drop all evening ... except for the magic high. It was probably important to count the magic of four werewolves.

I had a magic hangover. I should have just drunk myself silly instead; I'd feel much better than this. In fact, since it was only six in the morning, there was actually a good chance I'd still be drunk and feeling fine. But no, I'd been responsible because I had to bake in the morning. I was a professional businesswoman. If only I'd remembered that before all the wolves with all their magic had shown up. I'd feel a hell of a lot better.

I tucked the *Compendium* to my hip, really wishing I could get it in ebook form — maybe I should ask Sienna about that — but left the family chronicle on the desk. I'd apparently also pulled it out of Gran's library last night, probably to see if any of my ancestors had direct experiences with vampires. Or werewolves for that matter. I wasn't stupid enough to take it through the wards, though; for all I knew, removing it from the house would destroy it. Witches were rather protective with their knowledge.

The *Compendium* was basic and honestly excruciatingly boring, but the handwritten, meticulously kept family 'diary' was where the real information was to be found. I'd have to come back for it tonight. Again, it would be nicer to have it in a searchable PDF.

I thought about borrowing a car from Gran, because I wasn't sure the vampire's 'safe passage' clause was still in effect or if the confrontation on the bridge voided it. But I really wasn't functional enough to drive. The *Compendium* mentioned that vampires hated the early morning, even if they could stand the afternoon sunlight. However, this reasoning was based on some religious hokum about Christ rising on the morning of the third day, so I wasn't sure I should bank on it. Of course, who was I to question the accumulated knowledge of witches passed down through the ages?

The fifteen-minute walk took me twenty. The neighborhood was dead quiet. Even the dogs and their bladders were smart enough to still be inside sleeping. Isn't that what Sunday morning was for? This was exactly why I'd had Bryn take over the Sunday baking shift. Though some customers claimed the cupcakes weren't as tasty, they couldn't tell me specifically what was missing. They tasted the same to me. I'd thought about just closing on Sundays, but it remained a profitable day even if Bryn was baking.

I cut through the alley behind West Fourth Avenue, preferring the back door and the immediate comfort of the wards rather than taking the front stairs.

A wolf — well, a werewolf — was curled up by my back door. The young woman from the dance club, with the green hair.

I thought about leaving. However, I was pretty sure that even though she looked to be sleeping, she'd already heard and possibly scented me a block away. I remembered that much at least from my reading last night. And running from a wolf would be a bad idea. Her predator instincts could kick in.

"Um, hi," I said. I shifted the book to my left hand, freeing my right for the knife in case everything went rapidly wrong. Why I'd been stupid enough to walk with a book in my right hand for twenty minutes, I didn't even want to think about. I'd miscalculated about what predator I was attempting to avoid.

The werewolf cracked her eyes, and the green of her hair rolled across them for a blink. She was triggering her magic somehow; I could feel that with my 'other' senses. Then she smiled without revealing any of her teeth. "You didn't come home last night," she murmured. "And you didn't spend the evening with Hudson, though I know he asked."

A question was hidden in there somewhere, but I ignored it. Perhaps it was just plain disbelief. Perhaps Hudson never got turned down.

"How did you know I lived here?"

The wolf shrugged. "Smells like you."

"It smells like me?" I echoed. Because, when surprised, I tended to sound like an idiot.

"Yes. Your magic is tasty." This time the wolf did show her teeth when she smiled. I thought that might indicate the conversation was moving in the wrong direction ... the woman-eating direction, and not the good kind.

"I have to bake."

"More cupcakes?" the wolf asked hopefully, but how she'd tasted my cupcakes before, I didn't want to ask. She shouldn't have been able to get past the wards and into the bakery.

"Yes."

She stood without pushing off her hands or knees, just simply straightened out of her slump against the concrete foundation. Graceful, strong ... intimidating.

"The vampire left you alone, then."

It wasn't a question, but I nodded in answer anyway. I wanted — desperately — to ask her what she knew of the vampire and the murders and me. But I also really wanted to be behind the safety of my wards and within the peacefulness of my bakery.

She shifted away from the door but stood nearby. I belatedly realized I wasn't supposed to be looking her in the eye, but when I shifted my gaze, she laughed and said, "I won't play dominance games with you, not unless you ask. You're not a wolf, and I'm not ranked high enough to make you an exception."

I nodded and steeled myself to step by her. She leaned in just a little, to smell me as I passed. I turned the door handle in my hand.

"No key. Nice," she said. "I'll be back. I need food. Don't go anywhere without me."

Then she was gone. Just to prove to myself she hadn't vanished into thin air, I leaned back to peer around the dumpster. She was at the mouth of the alley. Fast, but not impossibly so ... if you measured everything in magical scale, as I was apparently having to do now. I was beginning to wonder at my own willful ignorance. Why had I never bothered to learn all the things now bouncing around in my head? The information of the *Compendium* had always been readily available. I knew Gran sheltered me in a way, but I'd always thought it was because of my mother's long periods of absence.

And because I was mostly a magical dud except for the dowsing ability.

I didn't bother showering as I was late enough already. I did text Sienna as soon as I'd gotten my hair tied up and my apron on. My sister wouldn't be at all happy with a six in the morning text if it woke her, but, seeing as how I was being stalked by werewolves and vampires, I needed some familial circling of the wagons. If Gran was out of town, and I didn't want to call my mother — who would think it was all fun and games anyway — then Sienna was third best. Not that I suspected her binding magic worked well enough to even slow down a werewolf or a vamp, I just preferred to have her near.

I didn't get an immediate response from the text, but I didn't expect one.

I checked the stock list, cursed when I noted we were pretty much out of everything from yesterday, and then set up to bake the minimum amounts necessary. While I waited for the eggs and butter to reach room temperature, or at least warm a bit, I melted chocolate and measured flour and buttermilk. I decided that today's customers could do without one of my more complicated cupcakes, *Sin in a Cup* — a spice cake topped with mocha butter icing. But then I found some leftover batter in the fridge and decided to give them a go with that.

I quickly fell into the peaceful rhythm of baking, my hands moving and mixing while my mind and eyes were on the next ingredient. I was a particular fan of icing, sometimes piling it high enough to double the height of the cupcake. My grandmother often dropped in when I was baking — as I still did five out of seven days a week. She said watching me bake was like watching an adept witch work a spell. Flattery will get you treats from me every time.

By the time Todd arrived to prep for opening, I had three-quarters of the list completed and the other quarter in the oven. I was efficient under time pressure. Todd's curly dark hair was flattened on one side and his neck sported at least three shaving cuts. He looked as if he'd had as little sleep as I had — that's college life for you — as he immediately started brewing coffee. Normally I'd caution him against making it too early, but by the shadows underneath his blurry eyes, I figured he'd go through the first pot before opening. I'd been debating investing in one of those single-cup brew machines, maybe a gently-used Clover brewing system, but didn't think I could float it until next month. I sourced the beans from a local roaster.

Seeing as I had extra egg whites sitting at room temperature, I decided to bake my gluten-free chewy chocolate cookies. They were easy to make, though it had taken me weeks to identify and source just the right chocolate — a 75 percent single origin from Tanzania. I had to charge five dollars a cookie just to break even, so they weren't a regular menu item.

The trinkets by the front door tinkled — Todd had left the passthrough to the kitchen open — and I looked up to realize it was already eleven o'clock. By the sounds of Todd's greetings, there was a lineup at the door. I should have been out front myself, but I suddenly felt utterly weary. Thoughts of red eyes and sharp teeth — not that I'd laid my eyes on any actual sharp teeth yet — filtered into the peaceful place I'd cocooned myself in for the last five hours. I felt a curl of fear settle back into my belly.

I glanced at my phone even though I knew Sienna hadn't returned my text yet — she probably wouldn't until after two in the afternoon or later. Then I smoothed my hair to shake off the fear and weariness, and stepped into the bakery to help Todd with the opening rush.

Tima, the perky high school student who only worked Sunday afternoons, showed up for her shift fifteen minutes early. Which, according to her grumbling, was the only way she could score a ride from her big brother. She lived all of ten minutes away and had forgotten her lip gloss. She had to borrow one of mine, but who was I to complain?

I raced up to the apartment, executed a wickedly quick change of clothing, and was heading a block down the street with my yoga mat underneath one arm, five minutes before class. I made it to the studio without vampire intervention. I'd kept an eye out for him all morning. Either the vampire was engaged elsewhere or the *Compendium* had been correct about their dislike of the early morning.

The green-haired werewolf joined me in the change room, tossing flip-flops into the cubby next to mine. I wondered if she'd stolen the new-looking mat she was carrying, though it was practically the color of her hair, which might have required some forethought, so maybe not. She was wearing short, tight Lycra shorts and a tank top. The diameter of her waist matched that of my upper thigh. I wasn't the only one who noticed — the change room was co-ed.

Beyond noticing that she didn't make any noise while walking alongside me, I attempted to ignore her as I crossed to the far side of the large classroom. I rolled my mat out over the one the yoga studio provided, then wandered over to the equipment area to grab a belt and a foam block. The wolf didn't follow, choosing instead to fold her toned, trim frame into a perfect lotus position on the mat next to mine.

I settled down onto my foam block as the teacher entered the classroom. About thirty or so people filled out the class. The green-haired wolf had eyed them all as they filtered in. Unsurprisingly, no one had chosen to sit next to either of us.

I closed my eyes and tried to pull my hyperawareness of everything in the room deep into myself. I was going to stretch, and move, and refresh my body. The werewolf wasn't going to rip my throat open in the middle of a hatha class. A power class might have been touch and go, though ...

The door, which the teacher had closed as she'd joined the class, opened as someone entered. I heard nothing except some odd murmurs that sounded like involuntary appreciation as whoever this was crossed the classroom and settled in beside me.

I didn't open my eyes until I felt his magic hit me. It was softer, tamer than last night, but unmistakable. Hudson.

I twisted my head toward him in disbelief. He flashed me a grin, and as the teacher called us to our feet to begin the first sequence, I caught sight of the reason for all the appreciative murmurs. Hudson, who'd chosen to wear thankfully loose jersey shorts and no shirt to class, was the most perfect male specimen I'd ever seen outside of a magazine. Broad shoulders, tapered waist, well muscled ... you name it, he had it.

We moved forward into a front bend at the teacher's cue, which forced me to tear my eyes from Hudson's impressive chest. Out of the corner of my eye, as I hung my head upside down, I watched him spread his long fingers palm down on the mat by his feet. He reached easily ten inches across — with each hand — and

I desperately tried to block the image of those hands across twenty inches of my body. I tore my eyes away a second time — I shouldn't have been cranking my head at that angle anyway — and carefully studied my prettily pedicured toenails. The polish, Chocolate Moose by OPI, matched that on my fingernails, though they were French manicured.

The teacher cued us to move through and into our downward dog position and "just breathe." I tried ... really ... but doing yoga was already a challenging practice of patience for me. Being stuck between two werewolves was seriously distracting.

They moved smoothly, effortlessly from pose to pose. They didn't slowly move deeper into any one position; they simply articulated the most advanced version of each position perfectly at first try. As I 'walked' to the front of my mat to restart the sequence, they leaped. Their footfalls made no sound. Forward bends for me turned into handstands for them. They executed their side planks on one leg; I had a hard time lifting off my knee.

My shoulders and wrists screamed at me, as they always did by this point. Why did I do this to myself? It was a question I asked every class, but the werewolves' presence made this session intensely worse.

And then, gradually, as I tried to not notice the tiny beads of sweat accumulating in the small of Hudson's back, I relaxed further into the poses. My muscles loosened and my mind eased. By the time we rolled down into our final resting pose, the corpse pose — the wolves on either side in perfect unison with me — I was happy I'd taken the class, and not even remotely worried about the werewolves stalking me. I was quite sure wolves didn't do yoga with someone they were planning to maim.

Ten minutes later, I rolled to my side to find Hudson unabashedly watching me. The teacher's hands fluttered to her chest to bid us, "Namaste." She seemed more revved up by Hudson than she was by having taught the class. I wondered if he'd been staring at me like that for some time.

As I stepped back to roll up my mat, Hudson leaned across to whisper in my ear. "And I thought you were beautiful last night, all done up and underneath the lights. I see I was too quick to judge. I'll take your cheeks naturally pink and your body relaxed after a yoga class any day, all day."

I laughed softly as I straightened to tuck my rolled mat against my hip. I'd placed my blade, still concealed in its invisible sheath, at the top edge of my mat, but I felt no need for it now. Who knew that wolves liked to flirt so? The *Compendium* had indicated they were separatists by nature, preferring the company of their own kind and rarely cooperating with others, especially witches. But then, some books don't age well, and the witches' bias was pretty clear even to someone as ill read as I was.

"So what do we do after yoga class?" Hudson asked, the energy practically sparking off his skin. I figured wolves would probably find more use in a kick-boxing class — or three — than a hatha yoga class.

"I go back to work." I turned and headed out of the classroom, though not quickly or dismissively even though I totally should have. I swayed my hips, rolling heel-toe on my feet — just a little, proud of my straight back and curves.

Hudson padded after me all the way to the change room. Perhaps a little like a wolf moves through a forest, but I didn't feel like prey.

"Kandy," Hudson murmured to the green-haired wolf as I crossed by her to grab my runners.

"Kandy?" I asked in disbelief, belatedly thinking I probably shouldn't make fun of wolves. She just flashed her teeth at me in that non-smile and nodded her head in Hudson's direction.

As Hudson pulled on his shirt, I — along with every other person in the change room — tried to hide my disappointment. By his smile, I was unsuccessful. Like Kandy, he wore flip-flops, but they looked odd on his manly feet somehow. He checked his phone, then seemed to dismiss Kandy with a nod. The green haired woman left and I followed her out.

I paused as I hit the street and looked up the block toward the bakery. It looked busy from this angle. Kandy cut through the crowded sidewalk in that direction, never knocking shoulders with anyone, though she was moving swiftly. I also didn't see the vampire anywhere.

I hesitated. I checked my phone ... no text reply from Sienna yet. I sent another message, though her silence wasn't yet unusual. I needed to go back to the bakery. I needed to nap, actually, but I wouldn't. I would chat with the customers and give broken cupcakes and cookies to the kids ...

"So ... coffee," Hudson said, his voice indicating how close he was behind me. He'd followed me out of the yoga studio but hadn't turned after Kandy. The crowd parted around him — around us, actually — without protest, when normally these sidewalks would eat casual pedestrians alive on a Sunday. Vancouver wasn't a massive city by a long shot, with only two million people give or take. But West Fourth Avenue — at least these few blocks — was a weekend hub. Shopping for just about anything, as well as a Starbucks or two, sushi, Greek, greasy breakfast to high-end bistros filled these five blocks east to west.

"I don't drink coffee," I answered by rote, because I didn't actually drink it and never liked to pretend.

"Juice smoothie, then. I think the place on the corner does them." Yes, Whole Foods made six-dollar smoothies. An extra dollar got you a shot of bee pollen, or agave, or whatever.

I raised my eyes to Hudson's hazel ones and tried to not notice the perfect way they crinkled around the edges. I was pretty sure he hadn't stopped staring at me since the end of class; I could feel the weight of his gaze. "Witches don't run with wolves," I said, though I was slightly pained to do so.

He dropped his grin, suddenly serious and sexier for it. "I'm big on firsts."

I raised my chin. "What about lasts?"

"Those too." He whispered quietly enough that the words were nearly lost in the din of the street. I just had to smile at his utter sincerity.

"One juice," I said, "but only because I don't want to go back to work."

"I would never have you do anything you didn't want to do. One first juice, then. But not our last."

"One juice does not imply commitment to more."

"Ah, but you're the one who already wouldn't agree to firsts without lasts," he said. Ever so lightly, he touched the small of my back to direct me up the street toward Whole Foods. "And by lasts, you meant forever, didn't you? Wolves, you will find, understand all about forevers."

I didn't answer. The conversation had gotten too serious, too quickly for me. My guard was down. I was feeling soft and malleable after the terrifying evening and the yoga class. I was feeling like leaning on Hudson would be a terribly easy thing to do ... right before he broke and probably ate my heart. Though I thought I remembered from my previous night's research that werewolves generally frowned upon man-eaters.

I ordered a mondo berry smoothie. Hudson ordered something with four shots of espresso in it. He paid. I let him.

We sat outside. In the sun with my hoodie zipped up, it was just warm enough to do so. Hudson didn't seem to need anything other than his T-shirt and shorts. Not that I minded. The T-shirt was a snug fit and I enjoyed the view.

My smoothie was too cold. Either that or my mouth was too hot. This was a possibility, as I was getting a bit peeved at all the women falling over themselves to stare at Hudson. He didn't look anywhere but at me, of course. But then, he wasn't an idiot.

The courtyard furniture was built out of some sort of wire. I perched a bit uncomfortably on the chair, but the mesh didn't seem to bother Hudson.

"So you grew up around here?" he asked, rolling his mug of coffee in his large hands. He hadn't gotten a paper cup. I liked that about him ... recognizing that the 'pro-Hudson' list was getting rather long. Not that I suspected it would ever get long enough to off-balance the one 'con.' Werewolf was a rather tall and wide hurdle.

"Born and raised." I smiled and sipped my smoothie slowly through a straw. His gaze snagged on my lips and got caught there. He didn't wear sunglasses. I did. "And you?" I asked politely.

We were playing first-date-questions, even though we'd practically had sex — without actual touching

— on the dance floor twelve hours ago. My dance partners, and there had been many of them, had never hunted me down the next day before. Even the one I invited to my bed hadn't stayed longer than the weekend — but then, I'd pretty much uninvited him by Sunday afternoon.

"Portland now, with the West Coast pack, but I was raised in the Midwest."

My understanding of werewolves and packs and hierarchy was a bit more complete than it had been the night before, but it was still murky. Magical groups, or divisions, really didn't intermingle. I had a sense that the *Compendium* was filled with a lot of conjecture, which was why I'd wanted to look through the family chronicle. Of course, this would all be easier if there was some sort of digital database with keyword searches. Maybe Gran would allow me to transcribe the records, after I played on her being away surfing while I was in the hands of werewolves and vampires.

Speaking of hands ...

"Midwest," I murmured to cover my wandering mind, but Hudson didn't take the bait and elaborate.

"Has the vampire been bothering you?" he asked, and completely ruined the first-date illusion I'd been hoping to cling to just a little bit longer ... secretly hoping that Hudson wouldn't bring up murdered werewolves or vampires. That he was sitting across from me due to an overwhelming attraction rather than ... well, than thinking I was elbow deep in the blood of his pack. Yeah, it took me longer than I liked to piece that together. The tiny population of the Adept in Vancouver had risen by six — that I knew of — overnight. What were the chances Hudson wasn't connected to the vampire somehow?

I shook my head and dropped my eyes to sip my drink. He'd finished his, though I hadn't actually seen him drink it. "So ... you know the vampire. Do you think I'm some sort of murderer as well?" I asked, happy that the courtyard patio was crowded and loud, and that werewolves had excellent hearing.

"No." He laughed, but in disbelief rather than amusement.

"Why are we having coffee, then?"

"You don't drink coffee."

I looked up at him and noted that he seemed indecisive. So he didn't always just project never-ending confidence.

"Was he or she a friend of yours?" I asked quietly. If we were going to talk about this, I needed more context. The vampire hadn't exactly been forthcoming, other than the suggestion that the murder victim had been a werewolf. In fact, now that I thought about it, maybe the vampire was actually socially inept. The *Compendium* was specific and detailed about their insular, xenophobic colonies.

"No," Hudson answered, "but we'd met at his Rite of Passage ceremony last year."

"Last year," I said, latching on to a nugget of *Compendium*-gleaned knowledge. "He was new, then. Young."

"Yes, eighteen. Here for university." Hudson held my gaze steadily, every flirtatious vibe wiped from his demeanor. Greater Vancouver boasted two large universities known for different areas of academia. However, Hudson had inclined his head westward when he'd spoken, consciously or subconsciously identifying the University of British Columbia as the school in question.

"Do you ... who do you think ... The vampire indicated that he was conducting some sort of investigation."

Hudson snorted in derision. "The only jurisdiction the vampire had was when it looked, momentarily, like a vampire kill. Even then they wouldn't have sent a rep if it hadn't been the third body. He needs to back off now."

"There've been three murders?"

"Yeah. Same MO. Werewolf, drained of blood, evidence of some sort of magic on the body —"

"My trinkets?" I asked, even though I really didn't want the answer.

"Yeah, but this is the first body in Vancouver. The two previous were in Washington, so we didn't make the connection with the trinkets until Kandy found you yesterday. She and the vampire have been pretending to ignore each other —" Hudson's phone buzzed. He checked it and replied to a text. "I have to go. The boss summons." This was said with more respect than sarcasm. "Kandy will watch over you while I'm gone. I'd like to take you to dinner."

"You're guarding me?"

"Kandy is guarding you. I'm attempting to date you. Seeing as how you're the common denominator, with the trinkets and all, it's kind of a conflict of interest. But I find I don't even remotely care. The vampire must think so, too. About you being the thing to watch, not the dating thing, I hope." Hudson curled his lip at the mention of the vampire. The *Compendium* had obviously been correct with regards to werewolves not liking vamps. Then he settled his gaze back on me with a sweeter, softer look. "Let me walk you back to the bakery," he murmured, and I very obligingly got up. I wondered if it was some part of his magic that made me want to obey him, but I found I didn't care. I just liked the sound of his voice close to my ear and his breath on my neck.

We walked to stand outside the bakery windows. I could see from here that the cookies I'd baked on impulse had sold out already. I didn't like the blank space in the display case.

"Don't worry, Jade," Hudson said. He was close enough that his breath stirred the curls on the top of my head. "I know the smell of your magic now. I don't think you killed the werewolves."

"But before we danced?"

"Well," he said, his grin predatory around the edges. "It was a good way to test, wasn't it?"

"Without resorting to violence."

"It'll come to violence. I'll just try to keep you as shielded as possible."

"And why would you do that?"

"Like I said, I've smelled your magic. No one in their right mind would snuff that out."

Yesterday, I was a mediocre half-witch. Now, I'd been informed by a vampire and a werewolf that there was something special about my magic. Seeing how I was a dowser — not that there was much use for such a talent in Vancouver — you'd think I'd know if my magic was remotely interesting. So, yeah, I didn't believe either of them, no matter how convincing Hudson was or how terrifying the vampire was. Something was going on, but I had no idea why it involved me.

"Save me a cupcake?" Hudson asked.

I flashed him a flirty grin. "I make no promises. Plus I didn't say yes to dinner."

"You didn't say no. See you at seven." He backpedaled with his hand in the air, forestalling my sure-to-be flippant answer, and then took off east in a light jog. As with Kandy before, the crowd offered no obstruction as he weaved between couples, strollers, and groups of hipster twenty-somethings.

I watched him go, aware I was suddenly weary without him — perhaps his boundless energy had buoyed me somehow — and not ready to return to the confusion that was currently my life.

Chapter Five

I pulled my cell phone from my hoodie pocket and dialed my Gran's number. Yeah, I was only a big girl to a certain point. Three werewolf murders, a near vampire attack, and my trinkets at the heart of it all? I needed my Gran. I got her voicemail and left a 'call me ASAP' message. I wasn't sure how to articulate everything else before the beep.

As I hung up, Sienna texted a flippant, *Busy, will see you later.* Nice. So much for familial warmth and the circling of the wagons.

The cute lawyer from yesterday's bakery shift was walking down the sidewalk toward me. Was I supposed to know his name? If so, I didn't remember it. I smiled when he waved and tried to catch my attention, but I was already dialing Sienna's number as I stepped into the bakery. He didn't follow.

The comforting smells of vanilla, lemon, and strawberries enveloped me. Todd must have samples of *Charm in a Cup* out. The wards, which were only supposed to hinder the passage of magic, seemed to have blocked the scents from me until I crossed the threshold. This was odd, and something I'd never noticed before.

Sienna wasn't answering her phone, even though she'd just texted me. I restrained myself from leaving a nasty message. My sister always gave back worse than she got, and I was feeling too vulnerable to start anything with her. I kept the phone to my ear. Yes, it was a rude buffer between my usually chatty customers and me, but I was unsettled and not up for pleasantries. Whatever peace I'd found in yoga and with Hudson was wearing off with my attempts to contact family. I cut around the display case and moved back toward the kitchen.

I needed a nap.

I retrieved the *Magical Compendium* from the safe in the back office. I'd locked it in there before Todd had come on shift. Leaving witchy things out for humans to stumble across was against the rules of witchery as dictated by Gran. I also noted I still hadn't dropped yesterday's deposit at the bank. The bank wasn't even one block west of here; I'd had to pass it on my way to yoga. I was seriously out of my routine and not the better for it.

I trudged up the back stairs to my apartment, thankful that Todd worked the closing shift on Sundays. I wasn't even going to make it into the shower. I simply collapsed, book and all, into bed, pleased that my curtains were still pulled from the night before. I wondered for a brief moment what Hudson and the werewolves were doing — if they were tracking down the murderer with my trinkets — and whether or not the vampire preferred to sleep through the day. I tried to not dwell on the trinket connection; there was nothing I could do about it. Fortunately for me, I was successful as I succumbed to blessed sleep.

I woke to Sienna opening and closing the drawer to the dresser right next to my head. Okay, the dresser was across the room, but it felt that loud.

"What are you doing?" I asked without opening my eyes.

"We're going to do a spell," Sienna answered.

"We are not doing a spell, nor are there any spell supplies in my underwear drawer."

"That's cool. I was looking for this."

I cracked one of my eyes, noted that the room was dark but not fully so, and watched Sienna pull a silk tunic on over her head. She then loosed her straight, silky brown hair from the back of the neckline, along with what had to be five trinkets looped into necklaces from the front.

"Why are you stealing my clothes?"

"You never wear this."

"I wore it last week. And the trinkets?"

"I sell them better this way. I sold all three from yesterday already. Hobo chic is a real thing!"

"Oh, God," I groaned. "Go away."

"Nope. We're doing a spell. Rusty is just picking up the last couple of items."

"No spells. I have a date. And you shouldn't be randomly selling the trinkets."

"Excuse me? Did you say a date? With whom?"

"Hudson." Ah, even saying his name came with that comforting feeling ... like snuggling under a wool blanket on a chill —

"Why are you grinning like an idiot? You haven't even opened your eyes yet. Who's Hudson?"

I attempted to stand up and managed a sitting position on the edge of the bed. I wasn't feeling bad at all; just enjoying the waking. "You know, the wolf from the club."

"You have a date with a wolf."

"I do."

"You have a date with a wolf."

"Same answer."

"That's ... that's ... you don't ... ever even, and a wolf?"

I waited for Sienna to sort out her mind. Normally, she would encourage any and all dating — or better yet, one-night stands. I reached for my phone — no missed calls. I was starting to fret about Gran.

"Does this have something to do with the vampire?" Sienna finally asked, in a completely different direction than I thought she'd go with the conversation.

"Partly, I guess. Have you heard from Gran?"

"Partly how? Partly like having to do with the murder he mentioned or ..."

"Murders. Gran?"

"Haven't heard from her."

"That's odd, isn't it?" I asked. Sienna was twisting her fingers through the trinkets she'd laced around her neck and staring off into space. Or she was especially enamored with my framed Marilyn Monroe picture ... I'd loved that movie last year. "Sienna. It's odd for Gran to not return phone calls right away."

"What? Yeah, but she's on vacation in a fairly remote area. Just let her be, Jade. She can't be with you every minute of every day."

Ouch. That little jab was uncalled for. I gained my feet and padded toward the bathroom. "Listen, I'm sorry about the spell, but maybe tomorrow? It's six thirty already. He's picking me up at seven."

Sienna nodded absentmindedly as she flipped through the *Compendium* she'd rescued from my tangled bed sheets. "Go, go. If he shows up before you're out of the shower, I'll let him in."

"Thanks, sis." I shut the bathroom door behind me and promptly pushed all thoughts of Sienna's prickly behavior out of mind. She'd always been that way. I'd be detached too if my family had abandoned me to be raised by Gran at thirteen. Even Scarlett, my carefree mother, had never been Sienna's biggest fan. Though that probably had something to do with the fact that the two of us got in more scrapes together than apart. Sienna always seemed pretty okay with the arrangement at Gran's. She had a roof over her head, good food on the table, and me always by her side.

I quickly shucked my yoga clothes and dove into the shower. I'd have to wash and dry my hair, which would take most of the half hour I had to get ready. I was surprised I'd slept so long. I was usually good on a couple of hours in the afternoon.

I was just rinsing out my conditioner when I thought I heard the doorbell. I assumed it was just Rusty when Sienna didn't come to get me. A glance at my phone on the counter informed me I still had thirteen minutes. I wrung out and towel dried my hair while attempting to cobble together an outfit in my mind. I was having a difficult time figuring out what to wear on a second date with a werewolf. I was pretty sure a skirt and high heels were out. Though I really did hope that running ... or being chased ... or even jumping on a bus weren't on tonight's agenda.

Just as I was diffusing my curls — a regular blow dryer just frizzes my hair — I thought I heard something bang to the floor in the living room. I shut off the dryer but didn't hear anything further. I opened the bathroom door. Still nothing.

"Sienna?" I called.

"Sorry, Jade," my sister answered from what sounded like the hall. Her voice was a bit strained. "Just knocked over that damn stool again, and dropped your big ceramic bowl. It's cracked. I've told you multiple times to move those stupid stools."

Damn it! I liked that bowl. It matched my plates, and wasn't cheap. I'd been slowly collecting a set from a local potter.

"You okay?" I lamely asked, because it was polite. I wondered if there was a spell to fix the bowl. Gran would have a conniption if I asked though ... magic wasn't meant to be used lightly.

"Yep," Sienna replied, and I went back to drying my hair. I was now three minutes late.

I wandered out into the living room, fully ready but not rushing since Hudson hadn't arrived yet. The wards didn't include the front stairs — technically they were communal property with the empty apartment next door — so the werewolf should have no trouble finding his way to my door. I found Sienna and Rusty poring over some sort of spellbook on the kitchen island. It seemed Sienna liked 'those stupid stools' while sitting on them.

"Hey," I said to Rusty.

"Hey," he answered without looking up from the book. He looked like death warmed over, but saying so would probably be tacky seeing as how his mom was a necromancer.

"No Hudson?" I asked Sienna, even though it was rather obvious that neither the living room nor the kitchen contained a Hudson. "He might not know I actually live — not just bake — here, now that I think about it. I should check the bakery. I promised him a cupcake."

"In the fridge," Sienna said. "I scored a dozen on my way through the kitchen after closing. I knocked the stool over with the fridge door. Like I've mentioned too many times now." I thought about mentioning that juggling a dozen cupcakes and my ceramic bowl, which was sitting — more than just cracked — on the counter by the fridge, was just asking for trouble. I didn't, though. Gee, maybe I was maturing, learning to keep my mouth shut and all.

"Sweet," Rusty crowed. "Why didn't you say so?" He leaped off his stool to cross to the fridge. The traitorous stool fell backward to the floor with a bang. Sienna raised a smug eyebrow at me, but I avoided eye contact.

"Rusty, go see if Hudson is waiting downstairs for Jade. It'll look better if you go. Less desperate." Ah, that's my sweet sister, always looking out for me. "Also keep an eye out for the vampire. If we are waiting on a werewolf, we might as well meet a vampire."

Rusty made an abrupt turn away from the fridge and a beeline for the front door.

"Wow, on command," I said with just a little snark.

Sienna took it as a compliment. "Yes, it's been arduous, but he is training up very well."

I opted to ignore her and plate the cupcakes instead.

Ten minutes later, I had moved the cupcakes to a smaller green jadeite plate after we'd all eaten two each of the dozen. Yes, my name is Jade and I collect jadeite. I was that stereotypical. The six remaining cupcakes looked terribly pretty on the smaller plate. Hudson still hadn't shown.

I checked my phone, even though I was pretty sure there was no way he had the number.

I sent Rusty to look for Hudson a second time.

Fifteen minutes later.

"You don't have his number?" Sienna asked tentatively. Yes, my normally outgoing, brash sister squeaked at me like I was going to rip her head off. I had a super slow simmer but a wicked eruption.

"Like I would call," I snapped, continuing to pace the tile floor of the kitchen. I would have moved to the living room to achieve a longer, huffier stride, but I didn't want to wear the wooden flooring.

"You don't know he's standing you up ... yet."

I glared at her.

"It's a bitch to be stood up," Rusty said, earning himself a withering stare.

"I wouldn't know." I stuffed a cupcake into my mouth. If Hudson did show, he certainly didn't deserve a treat.

Ten more minutes, and I had Rusty go down to look for any werewolf. He complained that he didn't know them on sight like I did, and I told him to look for green hair.

He came back empty-handed.

At eight, Rusty and Sienna went out to pick up Chinese food. They could have ordered in, but I gathered they wanted to get some space from me. I swapped out my silk top for an old T-shirt and ate two more cupcakes. I would have thrown the rest out just to spite him, except I was utterly aware that would just be spiting myself at this point, seeing as he didn't give a shit about cupcakes or me. I guess I wasn't quite as special as he'd led me to believe.

By 9:30 P.M., we were in the basement below the bakery, prepping Sienna's spell.

I would never accept a date from a werewolf ever again. For all I knew, they were gathered together over pizza and beer, and laughing about the gullibility of witches. For all I knew, like their wild brethren, it was just all about the chase. I guess I was too easy a hunt.

Damn him and his sexy, sexy, beautiful body and charming grin.

Sienna was buzzing about some reveal spell she'd found after the vampire had accosted me in the club bathroom and claimed I wasn't half-witch, half-human. While I was napping, she and Rusty had spent the afternoon researching and gathering supplies, which was how I found myself made up for a date and instead squatting on a dirt floor.

The building that housed the bakery and my apartment had been built in the sixties, renovated in the eighties, and then recently face-lifted when I took over the lease from Gran. However, my grandmother had always insisted, renovation after renovation, that the basement and foundations could be upgraded if seismically necessary, but not rebuilt.

I didn't even store things down here — it was that creepy, though at least it had full-height ceilings in this fifteen-by-twenty section. The foundations were brick, not concrete, in places as though they'd been built and patched way before the sixties.

I'd protested the change of location, but Sienna had insisted my living room wasn't the right spot for an earth-based spell. Countering my suggestion of a park, she laughed and murmured something about needing the protection of the wards.

I hated it when Sienna murmured about magic. A murmur had led to many a close call in our youth. I'd lost my bangs at sixteen because of one of her murmured caveats. It took two months for the skin to regrow on the back of my left hand when I was twenty, also due to a casual warning murmured by Sienna that I didn't quite catch.

Why I kept following her into these situations was pure stupidity on my part, but it seemed she always caught me at just the right time. This time, I was angry and needing to prove I wasn't just worthless garbage to be left on the side of the road.

Hence, the grime now coating the ass and legs of my second-favorite pair of jeans. The floor was hard packed, but the dirt still rubbed off.

Sienna had known the location of the door — currently accessed through the bakery's pantry — which mildly surprised me until I saw the witches' circle already inscribed on the floor, about five feet from the eastern wall. It was obvious this wasn't Sienna's first spell conducted in the basement. I bit my tongue regarding her practicing magic on her own. Sienna really wasn't powerful enough to do much damage, so it would be a little petty of me to deny her fun.

A few older boxes that predated my occupancy were piled on wooden pallets against the north wall, but I didn't know what they contained. I hadn't bothered to look very closely. I sat beneath the glare of the single bare bulb that hung from scary-looking wires. I was at the east side of the circle facing west, fuming about Hudson while Rusty and Sienna set out the candles and other supplies.

"Sienna, where did you get this spell?"

Sienna pulled an ancient-looking spellbook from the satchel she wore strung across her body. I could feel magic sparking off the tome in little pings.

"That's Gran's," I whispered.

Sienna shrugged as she spread the book open on her lap. She sat cross-legged on the opposite side of the circle from me, facing east, by choice.

"Shrugging isn't an acceptable answer." Yes, I was channeling Gran a bit, but I was shocked that Sienna had removed a book of power from Gran's study. I was also surprised that the wards on Gran's house hadn't prevented this removal.

"You didn't ask a question." Sienna met my gaze across the circle.

Rusty slumped to the south side of the circle, between and beside us. He was exhausted; in fact, he seemed tired all the time now.

I scanned the items placed before me. Unlit candles were set at north, south, east, and west. Each candle represented water, fire, earth, and air respectively, even though this was an earth-based spell. All witch magic was earth-based, except the kind of magic that had ruined the trinket the vampire had shown me on the bridge. That was black magic, and as the *Compendium* preached, black or blood magic was the ultimate of evils. Within the circle sat what looked suspiciously like the wing of a crow, a broken china cup, and a metal bowl filled with water. Between these items sat a small teepee of incense sticks, which were to be lit to start the spell.

"What's with the crow wing, Sienna? That isn't cool," I said.

"It's long dead, Jade. From Rusty's collection." I looked at Rusty for confirmation.

"My mom's," he said. Right, some necromancers liked to collect parts of dead animals. That wasn't deeply creepy at all.

"I didn't rip it off some bird. You're so squeamish for a witch," Sienna said, the derision in her tone as obvious as it was typical.

I shook my head but didn't bother to argue further. We had no hope in hell of casting a spell from this powerful a book. None of us, even combined, had access to that kind of focused power. I might as well let Sienna play witch and then go to bed in peace.

"We light the incense, then light our candles. I'll cover west and north. Then, Jade, you drop a bit of blood into the bowl of water —"

"Excuse me?"

Sienna huffed out a sigh like I'd impolitely interrupted her, and not at all as if she'd just casually suggested I add a drop of blood to an unknown, untested spell.

"Please, Jade. It's a single drop. You want to be specifically included in the spell parameters, don't you? It's not like I'm suggesting you step into the circle with the other items, am I?"

"But blood —"

"Oh, please. We aren't sacrificing anything. Plus, it's Gran's own spell. There's nothing dark about Gran, is there? You've used your blood to fortify your knife, haven't you? This is a lot less than that."

I hadn't actually fortified my knife with my own blood, though it would have been an extra layer of protection for the weapon and myself. I could then spell the knife to never draw my blood again, or just strengthen its physical properties with the magic bound to my blood. If done correctly, I could stop anyone else from wielding the knife altogether. I had done none of these things, though, because blood magic was dangerous and temperamental. Especially if you were still learning the extent of your own power, as I obviously was. I wasn't completely oblivious to the vampire's observations about the trinkets or my necklace.

"Let's wait. Wait for Gran —"

"Fuck, Jade. You are always like this!" Sienna snarled. "Afraid of your own fucking shadow. I can't believe you actually made a date with a werewolf. Maybe you were mistaken. Are you sure he wasn't just some nobody who likes yoga? You sure he likes girls at all?"

I clenched my teeth, feeling the anger that had been settling into a heartache I couldn't rationally justify refocus on Sienna. A ripple of pain ran up my jawline. "You aren't going to bully me into anything, Sienna."

"No? I guess I'm the wrong gender ... and race. Maybe if I had fangs —"

"Not even remotely relevant, sister," I sneered.

Sienna lost a little of her fierce indignation. "I can't do it without you, Jade. I'm not powerful enough, and I'm ... I just thought you'd want to know what everybody has obviously been hiding from you."

I hadn't thought about it like that. If the vampire was correct and my father wasn't human, then for sure my mother would know that. Even at sixteen, she had to have known if she was having sex with a normal or not. And Gran — with how powerful she was, how could she not know?

"We can wait," Sienna continued. "We can ask Gran, but why would she tell you now? She'll use the presence of the vampire as an excuse to coddle you further, protect you from the big bad magical world. Praise your cupcakes and trinkets, and cash your rent checks."

Sienna was right. If Gran had been in town, the vampire wouldn't have gotten near me the second time.

Hell, if he'd tried, I probably would have been gifted with a ticket to Las Vegas or wherever my mother was. An impromptu vacation, probably with a companion ticket for Sienna. And I would have gone — blissfully ignorant and utterly stupid. Duped ... again.

I reached up and removed my necklace. As Sienna smiled, I tried to ignore the smug edge to it. I pooled the necklace by my right knee, easily within reach if I needed the protection I felt it provided. Before the vampire had admired it, I would have thought it just a useless hodgepodge of magically imbued wedding rings and mixed metals. Now, I wondered if it had blocked or somehow dampened other spells I'd attempted unsuccessfully. Even though I thought it useless, maybe it held just enough magic to interfere.

Sienna didn't remove the trinkets she wore around her neck. She snapped her fingers and Rusty, who must have been dozing, sat up with a start. He leaned into the circle and lit the incense.

Sienna, her eyes locked to mine, leaned forward and blew lightly into the smoke trailing up from the incense sticks. Then I did the same.

Many witches had opening sermons or blessings they invoked to begin, but Sienna and I always chose to start our spells with a bit of breath as Gran had taught us. No power words or evocations that we had no hope in hell of controlling. Just a little bit of our magic carried on our breath and offered to the circle.

Rusty lit the candle at the edge of his side of the circle. He passed the long taper he'd used to Sienna, who lit her candle and the northern one. Taking the taper, I lit the candle in front of me. I felt the magic stirring, contained within the circle. It was familiar and comforting. I could control this ... I owned this, no one could take it from me except by killing me. It tempered my wounded pride and bruised ego.

Sienna bowed her head to the spellbook held open in her lap. She muttered words that spoke to the magic drifting lazily in the incense smoke. I didn't bother listening to the exact syllables Sienna used. Words only conveyed belief or intention, and this was Sienna's spell, not mine. Gran could cast a spell without a circle or written words. She called up her magic, focused it, and it did her bidding.

I pressed my hands into the earth on either side of the candle I'd just lit. Gran claimed that our witch magic was earth based and bound, which is why I always sat east where the earth candle was traditionally situated. I'd never felt magic rise and fall from the earth like Gran described, though. I'd never been able to tap into the spirit of the earth, as Gran called it, her voice hushed and reverent. My eyes never shone blue when I exercised my magic like other witches, though I understood that not everyone could see a person's magic in his or her eyes the way I did. My eyes didn't shine any color at all. Neither did Sienna's or Rusty's.

Sienna turned her palms toward the broken teacup handle that sat before her, just inside the circle. The handle vibrated in the dirt. This I could feel. This I could see, though I knew the same wasn't true for Sienna and Rusty. They could see the effects of the magic, as the teacup appeared to grow out of the broken handle and resolve itself into a fully-formed yellow-rose china cup. Gran collected this Royal Albert china pattern. I hoped Sienna hadn't snapped off a handle of one of Gran's teacups just for this spell.

Rusty laughed. Then he reached toward the crow wing placed in front of him. The magic shimmered and shifted. The teacup reverted to a broken handle

— Sienna pouted a little, but allowed the magic to flow toward Rusty — and the feathers on the wing started to ruffle as if touched by a light breeze.

Rusty's brow furrowed with the effort but nothing else happened. Sienna reached out and wrapped her hand around his left wrist. He grinned at her, but then quickly returned his attention to the bird wing. It flopped in the dirt as if it might be trying to flap. I was surprised that Sienna and Rusty had enough of a connection to share magic. That was something she and I might be able to do, having known each other our entire lives, but I didn't know she was close enough to him to offer him some of her power.

The magic resolved around the wing and a ghostly image of the crow appeared, but I knew this reveal was too much to ask of our magic abilities. It was one thing to manifest a teacup, or some other inanimate object, but Rusty was trying to reveal an entire crow — a complete being — from its wing. Actual life force of some sort was involved in this manipulation. He did have the touch with dead things, such as my ever-suffering plants, that he'd inherited from his mom, but —

"Jade," Sienna prompted with a snap.

I sighed, very sure her unarticulated request was useless, but I reached out to wrap my hand around Rusty's right wrist anyway.

The magic in the circle bloomed, and the image of the crow resolved into a solid figure. I gasped. The crow turned its head toward me.

"Oh my God," Rusty said.

The crow opened its beak and cried at me. A full-throated scream of a caw. I flinched and dropped Rusty's wrist. The image — it had to just be an image, right? — flickered and the crow disappeared.

"Did you see that?" Rusty cried. "It looked so damn real!"

I looked down at the bowl of water before me, shaken but emboldened. I drew my knife.

"Jade," Rusty said, some cautionary but unspoken warning in his tone.

When I looked up at Sienna, she just nodded for me to continue. I pierced the tip of my left forefinger with my knife. The blade was so sharp it didn't even hurt. I reached into the circle, feeling the magic moving around my arm, inviting but not aggressive.

I squeezed a drop of my blood into the bowl of water. It barely broke the surface tension, instead shimmering across the liquid in a blurred ripple. I leaned forward in anticipation, expecting — hoping, really — that an image would resolve itself out of the drop of diluted blood. It would tell me who I was, somehow negating — or perhaps supporting — the vampire's claims of my magic and birth.

I waited, forgetting to breathe, as the magic swirled around and around the blood in the water. Then the shimmer brightened into a glow. A small pinpoint of light rose out of the water, hovering about an inch above and then slowly growing until it was the size of a golf ball and hovering at chest height. I peered at the glowing sphere, not knowing if it was made of water, or blood, or magic ... I guessed that it must be a combination of all three. It hovered as if patient, pulsing lightly ... in time with my heartbeat, I realized with a flicker of fear. This was not what I had expected. A bowl of water was usually used to scry. Not by me, of course — that magic was beyond my ability, but —

"Command it, Jade," Sienna said, her whisper breaking my focus on the glowing magic ball.

I hesitated, knowing it was important to convey exact intention with my wording.

"It's in the circle, Jade. We're warded. Command it," Sienna repeated.

Something wasn't quite right with her assessment of the situation, but I was too enamored with the idea of knowing my true self, and I ignored the nagging worry.

"Show me," I said. "Show me who I am."

The glow brightened and grew to the size of a tennis ball. It wavered as if observing me. I waited for it to resolve into an image. I waited for the spell to reveal some secret hidden in my blood. The secret the vampire suggested he could discern with a single taste.

Suddenly, the glowing sphere streaked toward me. Fueled by my blood, it slipped through the barrier of the circle without impediment — I'd never known something like this was even possible, but I realized instantly what had happened. I had stood outside the circle, reaching through and offering my blood to the spell.

I shouted as the light hit my chest, though I saw rather than felt this contact. I screamed and instinctively grabbed my necklace, which was still curled on the ground by my right knee. Without thinking much about it, just reacting in fear, I reached my left hand to my chest as if I could actually grab the magic that sat there, glowing on my sternum and pulsing with my heartbeat. Perhaps it was waiting for further instruction. Perhaps it was attempting to answer my command on a level I didn't understand.

I grasped the magic and pulled it from my chest. It had grown to the size of a baseball. I didn't stop to wonder at my sudden ability to hold this kind of power in the palm of my hand — not that I had ever tested such a thing. No, scared out of my mind, I simply flung the magic back away from me ... behind me.

I was shaking, but the reveal spell hadn't hurt or harmed me. My heart was beating wildly. I looked up at Sienna and stuttered, "It ... it... breached the circle. Could you see it? Sienna?"

Sienna didn't answer. She wasn't looking at me at all. She was staring behind me, her eyes wide and her mouth forming a small O. Then she smiled. A smile full of satisfaction, and something else I couldn't quite figure out through my own adrenaline rush and fading panic.

I turned and looked back. I must have thrown the spell hard enough that it hit the eastern wall of concrete and brick behind me. But instead of dissipating as it should have, though I hadn't given it specific direction, my 'get thee behind me' intention must have been clear. It had spread its glow — a glow that was now slowly fading into an outline that looked to be the height and width of a large door or doorway. A doorway revealed by the spell I had commanded and then haphazardly flung away. I had never manipulated magic in this fashion before.

"Now what do you think is hidden behind that door?" Sienna asked, her voice husky with anticipation as she rolled to her feet.

"If it's a door," Rusty answered. He quickly leaned over to snuff out his candle.

"Don't," Sienna said, but Rusty had doused the candle and scuffed his edge of the circle before she spoke. The magic within evaporated.

Rusty shrugged apologetically but didn't actually seem contrite. Sienna narrowed her eyes at him, but then returned to gazing at the outline. Its glow, slightly fainter than before, still held its rectangular shape on the wall.

Sienna skirted the dormant circle and crossed by me toward the outline. Still cross-legged on the dirt floor, I grabbed her hand as she passed. She looked down at me with just the tips of her teeth showing in a smile. The light was behind her head and I couldn't see her eyes, just two deep shadows carved out of her face.

" 'Show me who I am,' you said, Jade. And look what it has shown you." Sienna's voice was heavy with implication.

"No, Sienna. The two things aren't related."

"How do you know?"

"I don't see a handle or anything," Rusty murmured, making me start badly. I hadn't realized he'd moved from the edge of the circle.

"It's a door," Sienna said as she brushed off my handhold. "And I can't wait to see what's behind it."

Oh, God. That sounded like the opposite of a good idea. Hidden doorways, if that was what it was, were always hidden for a reason ... 'abandon all hope, ye who enter here' reasons.

"Do you think Gran knows it's here?" I asked.

"Of course she knows, dummy," Sienna answered. Then she reached out to touch the brick wall in the very middle of the outlined rectangle.

I waited for something to happen but nothing did. Rusty and Sienna continued to run their hands around the door outline. The glow continued to fade.

They turned to me in unison.

"No," I answered before they asked. Sienna opened her mouth to cajole me and I said, "That's enough!"

The glow around the door abruptly disappeared.

"Jade!" Sienna cried as she turned to run her hands over the now blank wall.

I stood and brushed off my jeans. I had no idea if I had shut down the spell or if it just blinked out on its own, but I wasn't sticking around to be bullied further.

"You know your way out," I said as I crossed back to the basement stairs.

"Jade!" Sienna cried again, but I didn't look back.

"If I don't get in touch with Gran tomorrow, I'm sending the hotel staff, or the police, or someone to look for her. Clean this up. I'm going to bed."

I left them there, even though I was pretty sure Sienna was about to throw a fit. I was certain they couldn't replicate the spell without me, and I had no intention of ever going into that basement again. I wasn't remotely interested in secret doors that led to hell knows where, and was actually pretty freaked that I had one of them two floors below my living room. I'd seen enough horror films to know when to leave such things alone, or to come back with bigger guns. Guns of the type my Gran wielded.

Chapter Six

I couldn't sleep. I was hyperaware of everything magical around me. Sienna and Rusty downstairs, the collected bits that I made into trinkets in the studio, and even the *Magical Compendium* on top of my bureau seemed to beckon. I'd never had to deal with residual magic from a casting like this before. It was as if the spell had hypercharged my dowser abilities to the point where I saw magic everywhere I looked. If I closed my eyes, I could feel it like the lightest of breezes all around me, following me from room to room and into my bed.

The residual eased a bit once Rusty and Sienna left, though they lingered long enough in the bakery kitchen that I was sure my chocolate supplies had taken a serious hit. But still, even then, lying in bed was getting me nowhere near sleep.

I pulled out the blanket my Gran had knit for me when I'd moved out of the house and into the dormitories at the University of British Columbia. The dorm had only been a fifteen-minute drive from Gran's house and the university hadn't stuck with me longer than two years, but I cherished the blanket. I spread it on the floor between my double bed and dresser, then sat down on it cross-legged. Yes, I was planning on actually meditating. And yes, I was doubtful of my ability to do so.

I removed my necklace and twined it around my wrists and through my fingers. Its supposedly fascinating magic — according to the vampire — didn't bother me at all. I rested my hands on my knees, palms facing down to not invite more energy, and closed my eyes. I inhaled slowly and deeply, and when I exhaled, I imagined all the magic I felt coating me like good quality body cream — thick and luxurious — moving through my limbs, through my hands, and into the necklace.

Yeah, I had no idea what the hell I was doing. I didn't channel magic. Hell, I didn't hold magic in the palm of my hand and fling it away from me. Magic didn't obey me ... at least it never had before. I was just a detector, somewhat useful if another witch was wondering if they had a magical dud on their hands, or when collecting stones — such as jade — from the rivers in Squamish Valley. I could find things easier; that was all. At least that's what I'd always thought the limit of my abilities had been. Then the vampire had showed up spouting off about the trinkets, and my necklace ... and then ... Hudson.

I threw up a blank wall between my thoughts of Hudson and my concentration on moving the magic out of my body and into the necklace. I'd been stupid. It was over now. It's just ... the bed behind me was a big reminder that I'd wanted to invite him here. I'd wanted to see if we danced as well horizontally as we had vertically.

I quashed those thoughts — for the second time. I'd never been good at focusing unless I was baking or making trinkets. I hadn't had sex in six months, and my last romp had been spectacularly disappointing, then had hung around way past his welcome. I wasn't hard up, but I was getting there. That's all Hudson was ... a distraction, a playmate.

I squeezed the necklace until the metal cut into my fingers. This was seriously uncomfortable, but it helped me refocus on my breathing.

I must have fallen asleep like that, upright and cross-legged in the middle of my bedroom floor.

I wasn't sure what had woken me. My legs were going to scream bloody murder when I tried to move, but they were currently nicely numb. I looked down at the necklace draped between my hands and across my calves. It glowed lightly, which even my sleepy brain understood might actually mean I'd been capable of channeling magic into it. The glow also drew my attention to the general lighting of the room. It was nearing dawn.

Something scratched at the window, and there were no trees in the alley. The scratching noise repeated. I wound the necklace three times around my neck, very surprised that my arms obeyed. When shortened this way, it slung just over my collarbone.

The scratching was probably just one of my trinkets moving in the wind ... though it sounded too regular and persistent for the randomness of wind.

It almost sounded like a dog scratching at a door to be let in ... but it had been a long time since I'd owned a dog, and I was pretty sure a canine couldn't climb onto a second-storey balcony.

I moved toward the window, again surprised that my legs had no issue with unfolding and holding my weight. As in my craft room, a small Juliet balcony hung off this window. This one held a few pots of lavender, not that it was nearly hot enough to grow lavender on a north-facing balcony in Vancouver. The plants seemed healthy enough, though, even if slow growing.

I pulled back the gauzy outer curtain and the thick blackout curtain behind it at the same time.

Kandy, her short green hair rain-slicked to her pale face, stood perched on the balcony, as the vampire had done outside the craft room. She'd jumped or climbed two storeys to stand on a wrought-iron balcony that was meant for show, not sunbathing. Wet, her hair looked almost black, but her eyes were the same vibrant green I'd seen them flash before. She stared at me. I stared back at her, wide-eyed.

It had obviously started raining in the night.

"Are you okay?" I rather mildly asked.

Kandy shook her head; she could obviously hear me through the glass. "You've been summoned."

The green-haired werewolf's voice was low and scratchy with dark emotion. Her eyes glowed greener, and I imagined that if I wasn't behind the wards, I would feel her magic gathering around her.

The hackles on the back of my neck rose as my adrenaline kicked in. A werewolf very close to transforming stood on my balcony. The wards should hold her, but my neighbors had no such protection. If she turned, would she understand the idea of innocent bystanders? I hadn't gleaned enough accurate information from the *Compendium* to know one way or the other. It declared all werewolves to be beasts in either form, but I knew now from personal contact they were no such thing — in their human form at least.

"Summoned?" I repeated.

Kandy nodded.

"Who has the right to summon me from my bed before dawn?"

Kandy showed me her teeth. I was sure they were pointier than they had been before. "Desmond Charles Llewelyn, Lord and Alpha of the West Coast North American Pack, son of Charles Abraham Llewelyn, a lord of the North American Assembly, requests your presence. Now."

I didn't like the sound of all those titles, but seeing as how I wasn't a werewolf and was currently dry and warm in the safety of my own home, I kept up the brave front. "You expect me to follow you out into the predawn to meet some guy who has absolutely no authority over me? Ever heard of email or the phone? Hell, or knocking on the front door, for that matter?" And where the hell was Hudson? I didn't ask that last part out loud, but I sure as hell wondered why he wasn't at my door instead of Kandy on my balcony.

"I expect you to resist. I expect to test your wards. I expect to either die tearing through them, or to wrap my hand around your far-too-human neck and drag you from your bed."

Well, that was exceptionally clear. My mind clicked madly through all the information I had gleaned from the *Compendium* about werewolves. Could she compromise my wards? Would they kill her? I didn't like the idea of snuffing out the life of this vibrant, fiercely beautiful woman.

"And if I come willingly?"

"Your safety is guaranteed, from me at least. I'm simply the courier." And I was obviously the package.

I looked beyond Kandy's shoulder to where the mountains should be. The day was dawning gray and with lots of low cloud. The mountains were completely obscured. I knew I was going to go before I made my decision. I felt like my life had taken this odd turn and

I wanted to veer back. If that meant talking to this lord guy, then that was just what it took.

Honestly though, part of me was intrigued and excited. Things such as vampires and werewolves just didn't happen in Vancouver, to me at least.

"Five minutes," I said, and I backed away into the bedroom. Kandy snorted in disbelief, crossed her arms, and kept her glowing green eyes on me through the window. Those eyes had dimmed a bit, actually. I took that as a good sign.

I pulled on jeans, a light sweater, and my Hunter rain boots. You didn't live in Vancouver without wet wear. My boots were Original Tall Glosses in cornflower — a birthday gift from Gran. I pulled them on with an odd tinge of anger as I wondered if I was going through a late rebellion. The thought made me laugh, but only in my head. Kandy's glower was too intimidating to feel lighthearted enough to laugh out loud. "Bakery, alley door," I called to Kandy. I left the bedroom as she dropped from sight. I seriously hoped all the neighbors across the alley were deep asleep and not witnessing that agility display.

I grabbed the last three cupcakes from the fridge as I passed through the kitchen, managing to knock a stool over as I crossed around the island with them in my hands. I left it rolling around on the ground, cursing the fact that Sienna was right and I should probably get rid of them.

I passed the cupcakes and a pink paisley umbrella to Kandy as I stepped from the back-alley door. She sneered at the umbrella but took the cupcakes without comment.

By the time we'd turned on to West Third Avenue, I trailed about a half step behind the werewolf and still had no idea where we were going. Kandy had inhaled all three cupcakes and not said a word to me. I figured the best way to make friends with a dog was to feed it. I hoped that held true for werewolves. Otherwise, I was pretty sure I was about to get the same treatment as the cupcakes.

"We're walking?" I asked as we dodged through the cars parked along Vine Street to cross the road. Even with my Hunter boots and umbrella, I was going to get soaked.

Kandy didn't answer. She walked fast enough that I always dragged a bit behind her. I assumed this was purposeful after I tried to close the gap a couple of times, so I just let it be.

We turned onto West First Avenue at the bottom of the hill, heading west. I could hear a few cars on Cornwall Avenue two streets north, but other than that, the very wet neighborhood was still asleep. We were heading vaguely in the direction of my Gran's house. Feeling guilty about defying Gran's rules of staying away from others of the Adept by traipsing through the early morning dawn behind a werewolf — wow, really not a rebel, was I? — I pulled my cell phone out of my sweater pocket, thinking Gran might be awake, only to have it snatched away.

I hadn't even seen Kandy turn around. But in a blink, she had my phone in her hand. She started to tuck it into the back pocket of her jeans, which were soaked through to the skin.

"Wait! Please, that costs six hundred to replace. I just got it, on contract. You're —"

"What?" Kandy snapped, interrupting. "What am I, witch?"

"Wet," I answered, completely confused at the aggression. "I promise I won't use it. I'll turn it off."

Kandy grudgingly handed the phone back to me, watching me as I shut it down. I tucked it into the front left pocket of my low-slung jeans. It felt awkward, sticking out there, but I thought it better if Kandy could keep an eye on it easily. The werewolf turned west again and I brushed my hand over the invisible knife I wore on my right hip. It was good to know that werewolves couldn't see through magic — or not my grandmother's magic, at least.

Fifteen more minutes trudging through the spring downpour, and we turned off into Tatlow Park. Kandy led me toward the First Avenue entrance. The park ran between Cornwall and West Third Avenue with multiple entrances. A kids' play area, along with a parkboard house, was just off the Third Avenue entrance.

A short run of lawn quickly gave way to old, sparsely spaced fir trees. A little farther along, a walking bridge arched over a creek that usually ran dry. The park also continued across Cornwall to the north, but it was mostly lawn and ocean cliff there. I'd done a yoga class on the grass at sunset in that part of the park in July and August last year.

"We're meeting in the park?" I couldn't keep the dismay out of my voice. The thighs of my jeans were soaked through and getting uncomfortable.

Kandy didn't answer, but she did stop. I closed the last two steps between us and waited. This close, I could see the sheen of magic on her skin. The rain seemed to sharpen it, or perhaps the reveal spell's effect on my dowsing ability hadn't fully worn off yet.

Kandy stilled — stiffened, actually — her gaze drawn beyond the walking bridge. I turned my head to see what she was looking at. I saw him, the brutal man McGrowly from the club, by a stand of trees. Behind him the cedar and fir trees thickened into a grove along the west edge of the park.

He was watching us. I had no idea how long he'd been there, and I couldn't sense any magic from him at all. Though now that I was focused in that direction, I could feel something behind him. A collection of people and something else … something not right …

McGrowly gestured to Kandy and she stepped forward.

I didn't want to follow. I didn't want to step any closer to what I was now feeling behind him, but I did. I told myself I was simply hyperaware because of the reveal spell's residual magic, and that there was nothing to fear in the small wood.

McGrowly didn't take his eyes off me as we approached. It wasn't an admiring gaze. Even calling him McGrowly in my head wasn't helping with the intimidation factor. When we were in front of him, Kandy stepped off to the side, then slid around McGrowly to disappear into the thickening trees.

I waited.

He took my measure and came up unimpressed. My pink paisley umbrella seemed to amuse him, not that he smiled. I doubt his face was capable of such things.

He lifted his nose and scented the air. I'd never seen a human do so before. It looked funny. I smirked. I probably shouldn't have.

"What are you?" he asked, his voice deep and demanding.

"What are you?" I snarked back. I knew without question that my tone was a problem for him, because the next thing I knew, I was pinned against a fir tree, my feet scrambling to find solid footing and my umbrella tossed to one side.

He wasn't hurting me. His thick hand was spread across my upper chest, his fingers splayed across my collarbone. I was pinned, like a cat pins a kitten. I didn't struggle and I didn't meet his gaze, but I only remembered that last part because he wasn't looking at my face. He was staring at my necklace, still wound three times around my neck. He'd been careful not to touch it. He must have been able to feel my heart thrumming against his palm, because I could. He seemed distrustful of the necklace.

I didn't move. Hell, I tried not to breathe. The strength in that one hand scared the shit out of me, and was worse for the fact that he held me so lightly.

He flicked his eyes to mine. They were golden-brown and shot with flecks of iridescent green — emerald, like Kandy's had glowed. However, he seemed completely in control, so I guessed that the kaleidoscope effect was normal for him.

I averted my eyes, and he huffed what was probably a snarky laugh — self-satisfied prick. He was completely aware that I was scared out of my mind, and he enjoyed it.

He leaned into me, his mouth slightly open, breathing in as if he was tasting my neck just an inch or so away from my carotid artery.

"What are you?" he murmured, but it wasn't a question for me. He was just thinking out loud.

I answered anyway. I was stupid that way. Foolhardy, my Gran called me. "Half-witch. Half-human," I snapped.

"Half-witch, yes. But the other half is something I've never smelled before. Something spicy, like Chinese food from Shanghai."

"I do not smell like Chinese food!"

He laughed. It was a short burst of amusement at my expense.

"My back is digging into the damn tree," I said.

"Does it hurt?" Oddly, it didn't. Not exactly.

"It's uncomfortable."

"You deserve it," McGrowly said, but it was a statement not an accusation.

"I told you, Desmond." A cool voice spoke from behind me to the left. "The witch isn't complicit, but she might be able to point us in the correct direction." So McGrowly was Lord Desmond what's-his-name. I should have known, what with all the high-handed pinning to trees going on.

"You didn't tell me she smells like Chinese food, vampire." The curl of Desmond's lip was full of condemnation for the vampire, who had just stepped into my peripheral vision.

"It was not relevant," the vampire said.

"I do not smell like Chinese food!" I repeated, not sure why I was making a big deal of it except it was just ... insulting.

"The shifter is simply articulating, within his limited means, that you are not wholly witch."

Desmond growled and released me. I ignored the urge to collapse against the tree and commanded my legs to hold me upright. They did. I didn't miss the 'limited means' part of the vampire's comment. He didn't think highly of werewolves — or at least of Desmond.

"We haven't been formally introduced." The vampire held his right hand out to me. "I'm Kettil, Grand Conclave investigator —"

" 'Executioner' would be more accurate," Desmond interrupted.

I stared blankly at the vampire's offered hand. I was doing a lot of that lately.

"I apologize for the incident on the bridge. I've discovered that I need to be ... satiated to be around you for extended periods." Well-fed, he meant. I made him lust for blood. Delightful.

"Playing nice now?" I asked as he inclined his head. "I'm still not going to touch you."

Desmond laughed. No love was lost between these two predators, and maybe that was the problem. Vancouver was an awfully small territory for both of them to occupy. And here I was stuck in the middle — right now, literally. A cold wash of fear ran down my spine, but I covered by stepping toward and reaching for my umbrella. I didn't fool either of them. When I turned back, I had two sets of too-bright eyes watching me. Perhaps the predawn gloom didn't help, but I had the distinct impression I was a mouse being tracked by a cat or bat. The bat thought amused me, at least internally, and McGrowly smirked as if he could read my thoughts. He couldn't, of course; that wasn't within his werewolf abilities, according to the *Compendium*. He could smell my fear abate, though, and for some reason, that amused him.

"Come then," he said as he turned toward the thick of the trees, where Kandy had headed.

"I don't want to go in there, do I?" I asked no one in particular, but the vampire — Kettle-whatever — answered.

"The necklace and the knife should shield you, if you access their magic."

"What knife?" Desmond asked. He kept moving forward, but glanced back at Kettil.

"The magic-imbued one she keeps, obviously invisibly, strapped at her hip. I guess your enforcer missed it." Kettil spoke all distantly cool and without a lick of sneer.

Desmond's face turned into a reasonable facsimile of stone as he huffed off into the trees. I felt bad for Kandy. I was pretty sure she was the enforcer Kettil had mentioned, and that her lord and alpha was now probably pissed with her.

The feeling of wrongness increased with each step I took. *Access their magic*, the vampire had said, but I had no idea what the hell he was talking about. Still, I curled one hand around my necklace and one hand around the hilt of my knife. I hadn't even thought to pull it on the damn werewolf, McGrowly, when he was pawing at me. My instincts obviously needed a reboot.

"I thought vampires didn't like the dawn," I muttered. I knew the vamp was somewhere behind me because I could still feel his magic, though I couldn't hear his footfalls.

"Myth," he answered, proving he was hidden within the shadows of the gloom and the trees just to the left of my shoulder.

Desmond snorted, but didn't turn around. I wasn't sure whether he was laughing at my question or undercutting the veracity of the vampire's claim. I guessed I'd know one way or the other soon enough.

I rounded another fir tree. The sun was rising somewhere behind the cloud cover, and I unfortunately had no problem following Desmond's too-broad shoulders in the lightening gloom.

I knew nothing good could be at the dark center I could clearly feel ahead. This darkness was encircled by other magical signatures ... I knew Kandy well enough to pick her magic out from the others.

I was right, of course. My newly honed instincts for horror and misery hadn't deserted me.

Though the gray sky was attempting to lighten with the dawn, the stand of trees was swathed in darkness. The boughs were so thick overhead that only an occasional drop of rain made it through.

I kept my eyes on the center of Desmond's back; he was wide enough to block most of my forward view. I tried to not interpret the magic I was walking into. I tried to concentrate on the warm, earthy power emanating off the werewolf, or even the cold sharpness of the magic of the vampire behind me, whom I could still feel rather than hear. Actually, everyone but me was moving as if equipped with silence spells.

More magic surged up a few feet ahead. More werewolves. I wondered again at my heightened sensitivity, and whether the previous night's reveal spell was more active than I thought. I wondered if this was going to be permanent, and wasn't sure I'd be so enamored with that idea.

Desmond stopped and looked back at me. His eyes glowed green in the gray light. I couldn't interpret his expression. He was too inscrutable for me.

He stepped to the side. The tall blond and the petite brunette werewolves from the club stood with Kandy in a small clearing beyond Desmond. They were all looking down at something on the ground, but shifted their glowing eyes up to me. It seemed everyone had enhanced vision here but me, and I was the only one hesitating to look down at the dark, oily patch of magic I could feel on the ground before me.

I looked down.

I'd already known what I was going to see. Why else would they have hauled me here? Why would all the wolves I'd met — except one — be gathered here?

Still, I expelled a painful moan before my throat closed up with emotion.

Hudson lay, obviously dead, beneath the fir trees. His body was sprawled across their roots, his beautiful, lean, sexy body flung like a teenager's empty beer can — slightly crushed and utterly empty.

My chest hurt. I might not have been breathing.

Hudson's eyes — now a dull, lifeless hazel — were open. His head was canted to one side.

"He was with you last night," Kandy spat, but I barely registered her anger.

I was two steps away from his hand. It was palm up, fingers slightly curled. I wanted ... oh, God, I had wanted to feel those hands on me ... I had wanted ...

"What the fuck is wrong with her?" Kandy asked.

"She's not breathing," the vampire — Kett — murmured.

The gray of the day was starting to blacken at the edges. The necklace, which I was still clutching, was cutting into the soft skin of my hand.

Desmond whacked me between the shoulder blades. The trapped air in my lungs and throat expelled in a sob. I stumbled forward as if only my held breath had been keeping me upright. My body demanded I inhale, and with the painful intake of air, the sickening stench of dark magic filled my senses.

I choked. I fell forward and then twisted to one side as Kett caught my right arm just above my elbow. I angled right, going down on that knee as my stomach heaved.

I couldn't take my eyes off Hudson's dead gaze.

"She's going to throw up," Kett said.

"She can't do that here," Desmond replied.

"What the hell is going on?" Kandy asked with a snarl.

"The magic makes her sick," Kett murmured as I wrenched my arm from his grasp and tore my eyes from Hudson.

I stumbled away but didn't make it far. I fell to my hands and knees, my empty stomach heaving as my body tried to expel the oily, dark magic I'd inhaled.

"Here," Kandy said as she pushed a wet wad of paper towel into my hands. I'd given it to her with the cupcakes.

I had nothing to throw up but bile. Large hands, almost too hot but soothing because of that, brushed my hair away from my cheeks.

"She couldn't have done it, then?" Kandy asked in a whisper to whoever was holding my curls from my face, suddenly sticky with sweat. I brought up another wave of bile into the paper towels cupped in my hands.

"No," Desmond answered. "But she has a scent for the magic now. She's a tracker."

"I'm not a tracker ..." I twisted my head, hair, and body away from him to lean against the tree I'd fallen by. Kandy tried to take the paper towel from me. I fought her for it. It was just gross.

"Let her have it, witch," Desmond snapped. "You don't want it anywhere near here when the human authorities get their hands on the site."

Kandy folded the used paper towel and then took off through the trees. Feeling insanely weak, I peered through my tangle of curls at Desmond, who still hovered over me. I really, really wanted to close my eyes, but was wary of doing so with him in the vicinity.

The next thing I knew, the petite brunette with the bee-stung lips was leaning over me with a bottle of water. Her eyes were rimmed red from unshed tears. I grabbed the water and knocked it back, only to have Desmond snatch it out of my hands after just one sip. Water dribbled down my chin and he wiped it off with a swipe of his thumb.

"Slowly," he cautioned. Could I get any weaker or more inept in front of this man? Probably not. I squeezed my eyes shut, forgetting my earlier caution.

"Thank you, Lara," Desmond said.

By her quick retreat, he was obviously dismissing the girl. Okay, I peeked. He settled down on his haunches to glower at me from a more even level. I refused to look at him, but did accept another sip of water.

"You were with him, then? Last night?" he finally asked, kinder than I had any hope of him being in this moment.

"No," I answered, and then had to pause to work around the sobs that started to choke my throat again. Desmond surrendered the water bottle to me completely, then looked away.

I struggled with the well of emotion a bit longer, then finally gave into the tears, allowing them to stream silently down my cheeks. I banged my head lightly back against the tree trunk and gritted my teeth. "I hardly knew him," I finally cried. My voice was far too loud in the stillness of the trees.

"He had that effect on people," Desmond murmured, but he still didn't look at me. He didn't seem uncomfortable; more respectful than judgmental.

I tried another sip of water as I brushed the tears from my cheeks. "We were supposed to go out for dinner."

"Supposed to?"

"He stood me up."

Desmond fixed his green-flecked eyes on me and raised one eyebrow in a smirk. It was darker than the tawny, untamed hair on his head. "I doubt that."

"Is there ... is there a trinket on him?" I asked, dreading the answer.

Desmond nodded. "Three."

I clamped my hand across my mouth to stop the moan of pain this confirmation triggered. "I'll destroy them all," I said.

"That would be a shame," Kett said. He had appeared out of nowhere to loom over my right shoulder.

"They ... they're obviously evil!"

"No. Someone is using them to anchor their spells. Whoever it is must feel they need the extra magic, because whatever they're doing is destroying all the magic contained in the trinket, as far as I can tell. You might be able to pick up some residual magic. I cannot."

"Who is strong enough in this town to take down Hudson?" Desmond asked.

"Me, I suppose," the vampire answered. "Not many others, unless I have a rogue on my hands. But rogues don't usually dabble in black magic."

"Vampires don't do spells?" I asked, my curiosity momentarily distracting me.

"No, they just are black magic," Desmond answered with a growl.

Kett ignored McGrowly to turn his cool blue eyes on me. For a moment, I thought the vampire wasn't going to answer. Then he said, "Rogues rarely take the time to develop such skills."

"Yes, they're usually too busy running from the executioner," Desmond said.

"The same could be said of the shapeshifters," Kett answered coolly.

"Shifters don't choose to be loners," Desmond snapped, his energy visibly bristling around him. Well, at least I could see it.

"There are exceptions to every rule," Kett said. He turned his attention back to me. The vampire and the shifter assessed me for a moment, and I gathered the subject matter had shifted back to include me. "A group of magic users might be strong enough to take down a werewolf of Hudson's status. Perhaps more easily if he was surprised. A coven, perhaps." The vampire held out a hand to me.

I guessed he wanted to help me to my feet, but I wasn't particularly interested in touching him. He raised a rather mocking eyebrow at me. It was an oddly human expression on his ice-carved face. "Your resistance to the magic will grow," he said. "We need you to take a closer look at the body, to tell us what sort of magic we are dealing with, and hopefully how many casters."

The body ... *You mean Hudson*, I wanted to scream, but didn't.

Desmond stood with the fluid move that freaked me out every time I saw it. I was starting to figure out that the more powerful of the Adept spent a lot of time trying to pass for human when in mixed company. It must be exhausting to do so.

I rolled to my feet, using my knee and then hands to get up. I was unsteady, but I wasn't interested in leaning on anyone. "I have no idea how I can help," I said.

"I'll show you where to look," Kett said. "None of us has your gifts, nor your connection to —"

Kandy appeared suddenly from the trees, once again moving far too quickly to be wholly human. "Too late," she said. "We're almost busted."

Kett and Desmond both turned their heads as if listening, but I didn't hear anything.

"Yes," Kett said, though what he was agreeing with, I didn't know.

"Take her home, Kandy," Desmond said. He stepped back toward Hudson.

"What?" But then I heard the sirens, far off but approaching. "You'll let the cops take him and see this?"

"If we'd found him sooner, perhaps we could have tried to clean up. But it is better to go through official channels now," Kett answered. "Our agendas are not one and the same, the shapeshifters and I." The vampire turned to follow Desmond. I didn't get the warning his last sentence implied.

"Come," Kandy prodded. "We need to go now to not be seen. You move so boringly slow when you're walking, not like when you dance at all."

I ignored the green-haired wolf as Kett turned back. "I'll pick you up as soon as I can arrange a viewing. Though it might not be until this afternoon."

A viewing ... he meant the morgue. They wanted me to see Hudson in a morgue. I wasn't sure I was up for that, and yet I felt utterly responsible and outraged at his death.

"I'll be ready," I said. Kandy nodded her approval as I added, "Don't ... try to limit the number of people who touch him, please. Normals don't really matter, I don't think, except you might not know if they are magical or not."

"That won't be easy. Intimidation doesn't work well with the police, and Desmond and I are not especially —"

"Diplomatic? Relatable? Charming?"

"Yes," Kett said. He walked away.

"That was Hudson's job," Kandy whispered mournfully. She began to drag me through the trees in the opposite direction from which we'd arrived.

"Diplomacy?" I asked.

"Yeah."

"I could see that," I said and didn't bother stopping the renewed leakage at the corners of my eyes.

A side glance at Kandy showed that she too wasn't as tough as she pretended … or maybe Hudson had just been worth the tears.

Chapter Seven

My brain felt bruised — overwhelmed or overloaded, maybe — but I didn't actually have any answers to all the questions bouncing around inside it.

Kandy was no longer dragging me. She walked at my side, unlike before, as we headed back to my apartment. We'd gone a couple of blocks before I became aware of my surroundings again. I was pretty sure that wasn't a good sign in regard to my mental state.

"You thought I killed him," I blurted suddenly.

"He called me off, said he'd take the evening watch. His scent is all over your place."

"Outside, you mean."

"Yeah, by the bakery, stairs, front door of the north-facing apartment, in the alley."

On the stairs? By the front door of my apartment? But I'd sent Rusty out to look for Hudson. Maybe the werewolf had come by earlier when I was still napping, then left.

"Can you tell the age of scents, like how old they are?"

"Not like by a clock or anything. But yeah, fresh, old, that sort of thing."

"And how long does a scent linger?"

Kandy shrugged. "Depends on how long someone was in a certain place, or if they touched anything or held something. I just know ... knew Hudson, so I'm ... was ... attuned to him."

"So he might have just walked by?"

"More than that. But yeah, it wasn't concentrated if that's what you're asking."

So Hudson could have just been checking up on me or checking out my place earlier in the evening. Silence fell between us. Kandy had looped back and up a few blocks from the park, so we were walking east on West Sixth Avenue. The rain had ceased for the moment, and a few early risers were taking the opportunity to walk their dogs.

"Could you really break through my wards?"

"Probably not, but Desmond could ... most likely."

"He's your pack leader."

"Yep. You just putting that together?"

"Yeah, I'm slow like that."

Kandy barked out a humorless laugh.

"And Hudson?" I asked.

"Beta ... or was. I guess the position is open now."

I sighed. Hudson had been high-ranked and probably powerful. I could see why Desmond couldn't believe someone local took him out. The Adept, except maybe my Gran, weren't exactly a powerful bunch in Vancouver, not in the same league as a werewolf. The *Compendium* had suggested that there was a werewolf pack in the North, a larger one in Ontario, and, as Desmond had confirmed, wolves didn't choose to be loners. Vancouver was populated by a lot of half-somethings, like Sienna, Rusty, and me. Some of whom didn't even know their magical heritage. But no werewolves that I knew of. Though, based on the *Compendium's* suggestion of their solitary nature, we could have a resident vampire and not even know it. It was no wonder, as I put all this together in my head, that my mother rarely stayed in Vancouver long. She had to be bored out of her mind here.

Kandy cut left a block before the bakery. "You got any more cupcakes?" She shivered as she spoke. Apparently, werewolves did eventually get cold.

"You should eat more than cake."

"I can eat anything I want. It's all just energy."

"Yeah, but some are better for you. I'll make you break —" I cut myself off midthought.

"You're not going to let me in, are you?" Kandy asked.

"You're ... you are ... a pack." I thought through the magical implications of opening my wards to one werewolf and inadvertently inviting them all.

"We are one," Kandy said, though her tone was snarky.

"You're magically bonded, aren't you?"

Kandy thought before answering, but it couldn't be that much of a secret if I was figuring it out. I wasn't completely dim, though I wasn't a genius by any stretch.

"Yeah." Kandy spoke slowly. "If you invited me, Desmond might be able to get in using our connection. But I don't think the same would work in reverse, or for anyone but an alpha. No matter. You won't leave the bakery without calling me anyway."

"I won't?"

"Nah. You're not that stupid, are you?"

"You never know," I answered with a sigh. "I don't have your number."

"We'll fix that."

We passed through the red light at Fourth and Vine but kept to the crosswalk. The street was practically empty. We turned into the alley behind Whole Foods. They sold cupcakes as well, but they weren't half as good as mine. I never thought of them as competition.

"Will you bake, then?" Kandy asked as we neared my back door.

"Yeah. Not my shift, but I'm up, and Bryn won't mind an extra couple of hours of sleep." I reached for the handle of the back door and paused to look back at Kandy as she stuffed her hands in the very wet pockets of her jeans. She resembled a drowned rat. I hadn't realized her eye makeup was so heavy until I saw it running down her cheeks. "They think I can help somehow," I asked more than stated.

"Yeah. You're a dowser, aren't you?"

"I can sense magic, not track it."

"Same thing, isn't it?"

I wasn't sure, but I didn't want to argue myself out of an opportunity to help find Hudson's murderer … plus, the use of my trinkets by the killer made me literally ill.

"Don't worry about it," Kandy said. "I'll be around till the vampire shows."

"After you eat and shower. I'll stay put."

"You have a deal. Give me your phone. I'll program my number."

I handed my phone over to Kandy and tried to not feel like a complete asshole for not inviting her in and feeding her.

Not only had I never seen a dead body before, I'd never really known anyone who died. Besides Sienna's dad and my grandfather, but they were remote male figures in my mind — our connection intangible. Even Sienna didn't talk about her dad anymore, not like she had at first. I gathered she didn't have many fond memories of either of her parents.

Once we'd found the skull of a cat in the forest that surrounded the Cleveland Dam. We'd been there for a group summer picnic before Sienna's dad had died and her mom took off. We were nine or so. Sienna had cried and cried, and the other kids had made fun of her. She'd snatched the skull away from the idiots kicking it around, and got a black eye for her trouble. The picnic had broken up quickly after that — Sienna's mother threw some sort of fit that ended up being about the evils of magic, as always. After she'd confirmed it was a cat, Gran had coaxed the skull from Sienna by suggesting we perform a burial ceremony.

There hadn't been any such observance for Sienna's dad when he died four years later. I thought it had to do with the lack of a body. Though that conjecture was based on much unsuccessful eavesdropping by my thirteen-year-old self. Whatever Gran had told Sienna in regard to her dad's death, she seemed to accept it without argument. I never pushed my sister with questions about her father's death, because I didn't want to be the one who triggered the grief she displayed that one time over the cat skull. As far as I knew, she'd never cried like that again.

But then, neither had I. Not ever. Not until today.

I moved through the kitchen on automatic. I was numb, displaced from even my own thoughts.

I pulled eggs and butter out of the fridge, but when I went for the chocolate, I realized the bakery was closed Mondays.

I stood there in the pantry, my hand resting on a pound of single-origin Madagascar chocolate and just stopped. Stopped moving, stopped trying to think.

Then I began to shake — the adrenaline wearing off, I suppose — but this wasn't some light tremor. I wasn't in control of my body. I couldn't even collapse to the floor. My breathing became short and labored.

A panic attack.

I was having some sort of panic attack in my pantry. This made no sense. Why now? Why not in the park over Hudson's body, or while walking home with Kandy?

I managed to fill my lungs with air. The bones of my face ached. I raised my hands to my cheeks and realized my jaw was locked, and I had tears streaming down my face.

I made it out of the pantry to the industrial sink. I gulped at the cold water streaming from the tap and allowed it to splash over my face.

My breathing calmed and my limbs obeyed me once again, though I still had sporadic nerve spasms pulsing down my legs.

I remembered to put the eggs and butter back in the fridge.

I made it upstairs and into the shower and sat underneath the hot water for as long as the heat lasted.

I climbed into bed with a wet head. I was seriously going to regret that when I woke — my curls didn't do bed-head well — but I couldn't force myself to stand in front of the mirror drying my hair.

I huddled beneath the covers, realizing I hadn't bothered to call anyone ... realizing that I felt in that moment like I had no one to call. No one who could make any of this better. I felt like I was on a precipice, and that a step in any direction would send me crashing down a rocky cliff.

This wasn't my carefully constructed life. I had no well-honed recipe to follow. I was going to have to take each step forward in ignorance. But then, perhaps I always had. Perhaps any sense of control had been false, or based on a false understanding. Or maybe it was the teaching that had been flawed.

I closed my eyes, afraid my teeming brain wouldn't allow me to sleep, but I did. I was blissfully unaware of murder, dark magic, and my ignorance for a few hours.

Then Sienna showed up and ripped me right out of the sleep cocoon I'd wrapped around my beleaguered brain. And she was loud about it. Insistent. At least she'd brought fries. So she didn't totally suck as a sister.

"You look like hell," she said as she followed me out of my bedroom and into the kitchen. "And what's up with your hair?"

I ignored her. She picked up and perched on one of the stools by the kitchen island. I'd forgotten knocking it over. That had technically been A.H. — After Hudson — but before I'd known he was dead. B.H. — Before Hudson — all had been right in my world, at least to my knowledge. What any of that had to do with kitchen stools, I didn't know. It was just something my brain was obsessing over ... something about the stools falling over, always falling over and crashing to the ground ...

I attempted to focus solely on making coffee. I'd found beans in the freezer where I knew I'd stored them, but for the life of me, I couldn't figure out where to put them in the coffee machine.

"How is it you don't know how to make coffee in your own machine?" Sienna asked.

"It was a gift."

"Ah. And how long did he last after he showed up with that?"

"The weekend."

Sienna made a completely judgmental and unhelpful noise. I'd tried to force the guy to take the machine when he left, but that gesture hadn't made the break-up any easier. I thought the fact that he saw it as breaking up and I saw it as 'had-a-nice-time-see-you-later' was probably the very root of the issue.

Sienna had returned her attention to her spellbook, which she'd spread open on the island counter. I quickly identified this book as unsuitable by the glaringly obvious title, *The Riddles of Death*. Plus, it felt off … yes, a bloody spellbook felt off to me, like a tiny poisonous mushroom sitting in the middle of my kitchen counter.

"Sienna!"

"What?"

"Do you know how to use this or what?" I gestured toward the coffee machine. I knew it made actual coffee; the guy had used it a couple of times.

Sienna sighed, marking her spot in the book with a pressed-flower bookmark. I tried to push the coffee beans into her hands as she stepped by me, but she waved me off. "It's one of those cartridge ones."

She started to open and close my kitchen drawers, amazingly coming up with some sort of cartridge that she then inserted into the machine. I took an opportunity to steal a handful of her unprotected fries.

"You sure can pick them," Sienna muttered. "You have an espresso machine in the bakery."

"I don't make the coffee. I don't drink coffee."

"But you want some now."

"Yup."

"And this all has to do with the terrible hair you've got going on?"

I really wasn't interested in discussing my hair. "Whose spellbook is that?"

"Rusty's mom's."

"And she gave it to you?"

Sienna shrugged. Miraculously, something resembling coffee poured into the mug she'd placed in the machine. I dove for it but it was too hot to drink, which brought my attention back to Sienna.

"The book is off, Sienna. Off enough that you shouldn't be reading it."

"Reading something can't hurt me, Jade. And you know I can't feel it like you can."

"I'm telling you —"

"I hear you." Sienna skirted by me to climb back up on her stool perch, but she didn't immediately return to reading. Instead, she rested her elbow on the counter with her chin in her hand to look at me expectantly.

I tried sipping the coffee. It smelled amazing and tasted like shit. It singed my tongue, but as if proving something to Sienna, I took another sip.

"Why do you date guys who have no hope of understanding you?" Sienna asked. It wasn't the question I thought she'd lead with, but it still wasn't pleasant conversation territory.

"It isn't a goal," I answered.

"Take the coffee-machine guy. He probably loved coffee. That machine isn't cheap. And when he buys you a present, making it glaringly obvious he's not remotely paying attention because you don't drink coffee — except for today — you dump him. Instead of working on it, instead of refining it."

I didn't have any response to Sienna's observations about my love life. But seeing as how she hadn't actually formulated a question, I kept quiet and took another punishing sip.

"You ignore your magic the same way. And you have a problem when I don't."

"I don't do spells —"

"What about last night? You worked that spell, and I've been thinking about that door —"

"No."

"Jade ..."

"No, Sienna. Hidden doors are hidden for a reason. If that's even what it is."

"What else could it be?"

I shook my head and declined to continue the conversation.

"Fine," Sienna said, changing tactics. "Are we going to talk about the fact you're suddenly drinking coffee? Late night?"

"Early morning."

"Did your werewolf finally show up?" A grin spread across her face. "Or your vampire? Is he still here? Hiding from the daylight in the closet, perhaps?"

"No. He doesn't seem to have a problem with light. And he's not my vampire."

Sienna didn't even remotely believe me as she slid off the stool to pad back into my bedroom. I sighed and gave up on the coffee. I dumped the remainder of the mug down the drain and liberated some cookies from the freezer.

"The bedroom is vampire free." Sienna sashayed back into the kitchen and snagged a cookie. "I checked the closet, the shower, and under the bed."

"You think I'd invite a vampire into my bed?"

"You had a date with a werewolf." Sienna crossed to and flipped open her spellbook. I turned away, stuffed a frozen cookie — chocolate chunk coconut oatmeal — into my mouth, and fought off the threatening tears. Damn it! I'd hardly known him, and I was still crying about it.

"What time is it?" I never kept the clock on the oven set properly.

"Three o'clock. Why? You have another date?"

"Yeah. To visit the morgue with my vampire, as you call him."

"What?" Sienna screeched when surprised. It wasn't an endearing trait.

I sighed, crammed another cookie into my mouth, and fled to my bedroom because how the hell was I going to explain anything at all to my sister? How much was I supposed to tell or not tell anyone? I couldn't remember anyone saying to keep my mouth shut, but I was more than a little worried about getting her involved.

Sienna was ... well, she liked to dabble. Rusty was only one of a rather long list of magically touched boyfriends, who normally only lasted as long as their magic kept Sienna's attention. Unlike me, she'd known both her parents and there was no question she was half-human. Though her binding ability was impressive, her casting magic was ... insubstantial, like mine was. Well, like I'd always thought mine was — not that anyone had ever outright told me I was magically challenged. I just assumed that, based on the magic I saw swirling around my mother and grandmother. I had no such swirl, and neither did Sienna.

Lately, all I felt around my sister was a reflection of my own magic from the trinkets she wore constantly as her new fashion statement. Which made me realize that the vampire was correct in stating that I altered the

magic of the bits and pieces I used to make the trinkets
—

"What. The. Hell?" Sienna entered the bedroom seconds after me. I'd heard the stool she knocked over to chase after me hit the ground seconds before her second shriek, of course. Damn stools.

I swapped my tank top for a cleaner one, then stepped into the bathroom to scrub on a defensive layer of deodorant.

Sienna paced the bedroom. I could see her in the bathroom mirror as she passed by the door. She was actually excitedly wringing her hands. "The morgue? Has there been another murder? Or is that just some sort of vampire date thing? No, wait, vampires actually don't like being around dead things. Ironic, no? Jade! Are you going to answer me at all?"

I pulled my unruly hair back into a clip and didn't bother with makeup other than light pink lip gloss. I got weird when I didn't have access to my gloss, but getting glammed up further to visit Hudson's dead body seemed very inappropriate. "Yes, there's been another murder. No, it's not a date. The vampire ... they ... want me to ... they think I can help them trace the magic."

Sienna came to a standstill in the middle of the bedroom. I had to dodge around her to pull on a fresh pair of jeans and a silk peasant blouse. I had no freaking idea how one dressed to go to a morgue, but I figured a T-shirt was probably too informal.

"They? Who are they exactly? And do you think you can dowse the killer?"

"I don't know. I don't think so, but ..." I trailed off. The image of Hudson's body and my blackened trinket in the vampire's pale fingers flashed into my mind and took all thought and breath with it.

"But what?" Sienna prodded.

But ... I didn't want Sienna any more involved than she already was. "But I have to try to help."

"Why? Why you?"

I shrugged and dug a pair of Fluevog Joni sandals out of my closet. They were purple with green laces. "Is it still raining?"

"No," Sienna answered, and immediately followed up with another question. "Have you called Pearl? Have you told her all of this?" Pearl, not grandma. Sienna never called Gran anything else. But for a moment, just now, it rubbed me the wrong way, like it was disrespectful to the woman who had sheltered Sienna since she was thirteen. But then, what else would Sienna call her?

"No, actually ..." I dug around for my cell phone, which must have fallen off the bed while I'd been sleeping. I knelt to try to find it.

The doorbell rang. Sienna dashed out of the room before I even gained my feet.

I quickly grabbed the satchel slung across the back of a chair I'd rescued many years ago from one of Gran's renovations, tucking the cellular into an inside pocket. As I crossed into the hall, I could hear as Sienna turned the bolt and unchained the front door.

"Oh!" my sister exclaimed as she laid eyes on my visitor. Then, her sly smile firmly entrenched, she turned to look at me around the door she held open. "Jade," she singsonged. "Your vampire is here."

And indeed, there was a vampire in my doorway. Well, a few feet from my actual door, as he was most likely avoiding contact with the wards. Good to know he could still ring the doorbell, or maybe that was a bad sign. Maybe a vampire knowing where you lived was sort of like seeing the signature on your own death certificate. Wow, I was in a delightful frame of mind. The visit to the morgue was going to be a wild party. Right.

Chapter Eight

"Was that your sister?" Kett asked as the taxi pulled into midafternoon traffic on West Fourth Avenue.

"Foster, technically."

"Ah. A witch?"

"Half, yes. You couldn't tell?"

"Not through the wards. They are ... impressive."

"My grandmother's."

"Hmm, not entirely."

I didn't argue with him. I had, of course, contributed private spells and reinforcements to the defensive wards on my apartment under my Gran's instruction. However, the impressive part was her alone.

"Southwest corner of Vancouver General Hospital, please. Laurel and West Tenth Avenue, I believe." Kett leaned back from speaking to the taxi driver, who took a quick right onto Vine Street to loop back east toward the hospital. The morgue, specifically. I imagined all hospitals had morgues, but this was the first time I'd thought about it. Actually, I'd never even been to the emergency room at Vancouver General, not once in twenty-three years.

I realized I was subconsciously leaning as far away from the vampire as I could, and therefore cramming my left shoulder into the car door. Though he'd shown up at my apartment looking almost human, I was still riding in the backseat of a taxi with a vampire who was stronger, faster, and far more deadly than me. The fact that his skin looked almost pink-tinged didn't thrill me either. I imagined that meant he'd recently fed.

"So ... the morgue," I said. "We breaking in?"

The vampire — Kett, I had to keep reminding myself — turned his icy eyes from the road and looked at me. I didn't meet his gaze. Everything he did had this deliberate quality to it, as if he thought about moving and then moved. Which was just fine, as I really didn't want to see any more provoked movements on his part. My memory of the chunks of bridge cement in his hands was still fresh, and it was a little freaky if I watched him too closely.

"No," he answered. Well, that was informative. He was in a chatty mood.

"Sienna tells me that vamp ... your people don't like being around the truly dead." I slanted my eyes toward him. It looked like he was staring at my chest, but it was my necklace that had his attention — again. A girl could develop a complex around him. I'd only wound it around my neck twice this afternoon, and currently had the fingers of my left hand twined through a few of the rings — an unconscious mimicry of the vampire's grasp in the club bathroom. I had my other hand resting on the invisible knife sheath at my hip. When had I become this wary, cautious person? Overnight, it seemed.

"Myth," the vampire finally answered. I'd almost forgotten my question. He turned his gaze out the side window and I tried to not shudder my relief.

I'm not sure I could ever get used to this. I fought off the urge to call or text someone, anyone, as I turned to look out my window.

It was raining again. Big surprise.

The taxi ride took twelve minutes that felt like hours. We didn't speak again. I let him pay for the cab.

Though we were parked in front of the emergency entrance at Vancouver General Hospital, the vampire stepped out of the cab and crossed to a nondescript door toward the middle of the sprawling building. Buildings, actually. The hospital grounds were large enough to take up an area of three blocks on the side. It was currently quiet, even in emergency. No speeding ambulances or intense, dramatic doctors. So TV didn't get it right every time.

I guessed I was to follow Kett, though he gave no indication whether he cared one way or the other.

The unlabeled steel door opened to an elevator. The vampire hit the down button.

Great. I totally wanted to be in the tight confines of an elevator with a vampire as we travelled beneath the earth ... to a morgue. Damn — internal sarcasm usually settled me ... but not this time.

The ride was quick and painless. The elevator opened to a tiled hallway. Then the smell hit me — that of heavy-duty cleaning agents attempting to cover ... darkness. Yes, now darkness had a smell. It was faint and gritty. Kett strode forward and paused at an office to speak to a nurse or attendant of some sort. She seemed immediately enamored with him, so I assumed they knew each other. Obviously, he didn't look or move inhumanly to her human eyes. She didn't notice me at all.

She led us down the hall and through double swinging doors into the morgue. And this the TV shows got totally bang on — creepy lighting and everything. Well, maybe I was the only one who thought it creepy.

One wall was lined with steel, cubby-like cooler racks with numbered doors. Everything else was either tile or green-painted walls, if that's what passed for green in a morgue. Washed out, dirty green. Dull, dead green ... all right, I was aware I was obsessing about the wall color.

The nurse wandered over to the cubby labeled number six, pausing oddly with her hand on the levered handle. She turned to look back expectantly at Kett, and he turned to look at me.

It was only then I realized I wasn't hearing properly. He moved his lips again. I inhaled and raised my hands partway to my ears before I understood. Magic. The vampire had been using some sort of magic, and I'd been caught in the wake of it.

In fact, I now suddenly seemed to be in the middle of a mild panic attack, like my body had recognized the magic and immediately fought its effects before my brain kicked in. I inhaled again, attempting to filter the almost toxic smells that coated the air here to find the oxygen my brain needed.

Sound came back, though the room was still deadly quiet. The vampire was watching me like I was some sort of mildly interesting science experiment.

"Are you ready then, Jade?" My name sounded foreign, as if he had to think to pronounce it.

I nodded.

He turned back to the nurse, who had just been standing and staring at him. She smiled and then opened cooler door number six. He'd spelled her — maybe speaking to her telepathically, perhaps compelling her movements. It seemed effortless for him to do so.

My stomach rolled with fear.

The nurse pulled out a long, telescoping tray from the cooler. A body, barely covered in a white sheet, occupied every inch of this tray.

Hudson. All six-foot-something of him. I'd thought he'd be in a body bag ... or ... I don't know. I wrapped my hand around the hilt of my knife, and it helped steady me.

The nurse abruptly turned and left the room without a single glance around. Kett's attention was on the body and some sort of chart I hadn't noticed before. He'd probably gotten it from the nurse.

"You're controlling her, aren't you?"

"We aren't exactly authorized to be here."

"And the ends justify the means," I muttered. Kett looked up at me as if puzzled. I had to stop drawing his attention. Though, now that I had it ...

"Could you spell me like that?"

"It doesn't seem so, though I haven't tried very hard to ensnare you." He returned his attention to the chart.

I thought about fleeing the room but took a firm step forward instead, just to dampen the flight instinct. So ... mind control, just another reason to stay far away from vampires. Not that I needed more reasons.

Yes, I recognized that I was avoiding dealing with the body on the tray table before me.

I stepped up to the head. The sheet masked but didn't completely obscure the outline of Hudson's strong facial features ... high brow, long nose, square jaw. The vampire stood on the other side, a few feet away from the body. He looked up from the chart — at me, not the body — but didn't speak. Then again, he didn't need to; I knew why I was here.

I shifted the sheet off Hudson's face with a suppressed moan. If he wasn't so pale and not breathing, I could have pretended he was sleeping.

I slipped the sheet farther down his chest and shuddered in relief when I didn't see the autopsy cuts I'd prepared myself for. His chest was almost as perfect as it had looked in yoga. Except for the not-breathing thing. That really was the exception to everything, wasn't it?

"How does this work? How do you stop the medical community from discovering he's a ... was a werewolf?"

"Religious beliefs, usually. But if it appears to be a murder or when we're too late, memory spells and misplaced reports, of course. How do you not know that?"

"It's never come up before. I'm a witch, born and raised by witches. We read as human."

"Not if someone looked at your blood closely enough. If they knew what they were looking for. And you — you wouldn't read human at all. How many times have you been to the hospital? Or the doctor?"

"Many times. Countless."

"How many times were you the patient?" The vampire's voice was low, nonconfrontational. It raised my hackles immediately.

"I just answered you! Many, many ... times ..." Wait. I hadn't actually ever broken any bones or needed any stitches. There had been those spell accidents with Sienna, but I guess we hadn't gone to a doctor then. Surely, I'd had my blood drawn for some sort of test? When had I suffered anything more than a cold?

I'd had a terrible fever when I was little. I remember Scarlett — I'd called my mother that even then — icing over wet hand towels with a whispered spell and placing them all over my body. Had she taken me to the doctor? I could distinctly recall the strain that the use of so much magic had placed on her as the evening wore on. She'd also mixed poultices and cast other healing spells. Funny, I couldn't remember where my Gran had been that day. Scarlett had curled up next to me at dawn, just after the fever had broken. She hadn't been much bigger than me, even then. She'd fit on one side of the twin bed no problem. The early morning sun had glinted off her strawberry hair, the glow of her magic the dimmest I'd ever seen it ...

The vampire was smirking. What did he think he was implying?

"How quickly do you heal, witch?"

"None of your business," I snapped. "As quickly as any human."

He tilted his head. It could have been mistaken for some sort of concession, but it wasn't. I tore my attention from him and looked down at Hudson.

On closer inspection, Hudson's lips looked pale, bloodless. And a faint reddened outline of the trinket marred his neck and collarbone. I hovered my fingers over this burn but couldn't bring myself to touch it. "Werewolves heal fast, don't they?"

"In optimal health, yes."

"So, the burn? It would have occurred near or after death?"

"You tell me."

"I'm not a doctor!"

"You're a dowser. Use all your senses, witch. I prefer to linger no longer than necessary."

I thought about ripping his head off, but then dismissed the idea. Where was a good cupcake when I needed one? Right — at the bakery, where I should be.

I touched the burn mark that crossed Hudson's right collarbone, the one closest to me. I ignored the inert feel of his skin and tried to concentrate on the magic.

"His magic is almost gone," I whispered.

The vampire sighed at my apparent stupidity. "That's a side effect of death for most." Except him, of course, being a vampire and all. I didn't point that out. Undeath was supposedly a prickly topic for vamps.

"But before he died, then ... there's a greater residual concentration in the burn marks and ... has he ... has he been drained? Of blood, I mean?"

The vampire moved with that creepy deliberate swiftness, flicking Hudson's left wrist over the sheet. His lower arm was slashed vertically, though it looked like it had had a few days to heal. I slowly turned over his right wrist. Same slash marks.

"On the femoral artery near the groin as well, if you care to look further."

I ignored this upsetting suggestion. "Drained of life blood and magic."

"Yes."

"While he was alive, because the wounds have tried to heal."

"Yes."

"... because our blood holds our magic?"

"Basically, yes."

"Except she wanted all of it. Any magic she couldn't collect in the blood ... so she siphoned off the rest into the trinket?"

"Interesting. Possible, except the trinkets are left behind."

"Through the trinket then, into another vessel or ... her."

"Her? The magic has a female tinge?"

"No ... sorry, him or her."

"Look closer, witch. A witch or sorcerer couldn't do any of this without leaving a trace of their own magic."

"There's none. Just the trace of the trinket —"

"Your magic."

"Not really. I mean the trace magic of the trinket. Yes, I've noticed a residual layer of my signature on the actual trinkets, but I have no capacity to infuse my magic into an object." I was aware I was stumbling around the subject, stumbling around my knowledge and understanding. "Yes, if you work with an object long enough you can get residual, but no one has the power —"

The vampire laughed. God, he sounded human. He'd actually thrown back his head — his long, pale-skinned neck like carved marble — so that a deep, full-throated laugh emanated from within. I, or rather my ignorance apparently, amused the hell out of him. Or was that heaven in the vampire's case? Where did religion place vampires in the heaven/hell spectrum?

"This is not funny, vampire!" I shouted, my fists clenched at my sides. I was suddenly furious. Furious that I was here at all, that I'd been dragged into a situation that was so beyond me ... every fucking step, every fucking guess. "I'm trying! I'm here. I've never even seen a dead body. I've never even dowsed for magic like this, and you're laughing at me. Laughing at my ignorance as you rip my life apart!"

The vampire stopped laughing as swiftly as he'd started. I was surprised he heard me over his own din. I was surprised he cared enough to stop.

"It is not I who's ripping your life apart, Jade. Look beyond the magic of the trinket, as you call it. Please, we should not dally. The shapeshifters will become impatient, and they do not have my talent for subtlety."

I dropped it. I already knew that wringing information out of him was next to impossible, so why bother asking any more questions? Plus, I had an inkling I was mixing a bunch of different feelings and confusions into one pot and that always brewed trouble for me.

I could have loved Hudson, had I managed to get beyond my own shit. I could have loved him.

I touched the half-healed slashes on his right wrist. I imagined the knife that had made the cut. I imagined the position of the wielder. I touched the burn at the edge of Hudson's neck. I imagined the killer placing the trinket over his head. Had he been conscious? Had he fought? I remembered the taste of Hudson's magic in the club, in the yoga studio. The perfect flow and depth of it ... except ...

Except that instead, I caught the taste of ... a trace of something reminiscent of the scent of the morgue ... something dark but not evil, of the earth, of ...

Oh, God. I thought ... I thought I knew this magic.

I ripped my hands away from Hudson and met the eager eyes of the vampire. I opened my mouth. No, I was wrong. I couldn't vocalize. This magic wasn't capable of killing a werewolf at the height of his power. This magic was —

"What is it, witch?" Kett demanded.

I snapped my mouth shut. I took a step away from the table, from the body, but really from the vampire.

My eyes were still locked to his icy gaze. I knew this was wrong, that I should look away. I felt the wall of his mind magic hit me full force. I actually staggered back and put up a hand as if to block the assault.

"Stop it!" I managed to say through gritted teeth. "Stop it!"

Another layer of magic twined through the vampire's — a magic that couldn't be here, in this room, this strong. A magic that felt wrong, felt different than it ever had before, stronger, darker ...

"Stop it!" I screamed at the vampire, who was still trying to crack into my mind. "Something is wrong. Something is happening!"

The pressure of Kett's magic dropped away from me and I stumbled forward. I'd never felt someone use magic against me in such force before.

The wrong feeling grew. It wasn't coming from him.

"Articulate your thoughts, witch." Kett sounded pissed. He sounded human again. I was starting to hate that he could do that, that he could play with my fear centers like that. Human or not human. Blood sucking monster or accessible, even sexy, guy.

"It's ... it's ..."

The body on the tray table moaned as if releasing its dying breath. Then it sat up.

I didn't scream. No, I did something even worse. I threw myself forward and wrapped my arms around Hudson's neck while joyful tears coated my cheeks. "Hudson," I cried. "Oh, Hudson! ... I thought you were ... dead ..."

Hudson, or what remained of Hudson, slowly and ponderously turned his face to me. I gazed up into his clouded eyes. He couldn't see. He couldn't see me. He didn't see any more at all. He was dead. Someone else was looking through his eyes. Not that I knew that for sure, but I was damn sure someone was piloting Hudson's body and that I currently had my arms wrapped around the neck of a zombie.

"Step away, witch!" Kett yelled.

The zombie's head swiveled toward the vampire. Then the creature lurched forward.

And I, for some utterly unknown and stupid reason, hung on. So I'm a slow learner, sue me.

The zombie didn't like me decorating its neck, so it threw me across the room. Literally. As in, I hit the far wall, smacked the back of my head on the tiled surface, and then dropped in a crumpled heap. I'm guessing that last part, because I pretty much lost consciousness when I hit the wall.

I thought there was a chance I'd broken my neck. But I wasn't dead, so I guessed not. The room was dim, patchy through my blurred vision, which certainly didn't bode well for brain damage. I thought my nose was bleeding and I was definitely confused, because the sound of pained grunting drew my woozy attention to the zombie — who had the all-powerful vampire pinned against a wall.

The room was torn apart. Literally. As in, chunks of wall and floor tile were strewn about the room, the ceiling lights ripped down and hanging from their wires. The zombie was missing an arm, or at least I was pretty sure that was what I could see a few feet away from my head. It seemed to be trying to claw its way back to the zombie.

Oh, God. I took a moment to roll over and throw up.

Kett didn't look right. His clothing was torn and bloody, though he wasn't bleeding. He seemed to be missing ... chunks of himself. Like the chunks torn out of the walls and floor.

The zombie had trapped the vampire against the wall perpendicular to the one I was crumpled against. Neck-pinning one's prey seemed popular among the undead. First Kett, and now the zombie. The zombie darted its head toward Kett's neck, but the vampire managed to deflect the bite away to his shoulder. The zombie latched onto Kett's flesh and then ripped a large piece ... off ... a large chunk of vampire shoulder flesh. I had to be seeing things.

Kett growled in pain. I was pretty sure I could see the actual bone of his collarbone.

The flesh in the zombie's mouth dissolved into ash.

The zombie could hurt the unhurtable.

I thought about throwing up again as I watched Kett's flesh seal over the shoulder wound, leaving a dent behind. I made it to my knees instead.

Kett saw me over the zombie's shoulder and shook his head emphatically. His eyes were blood red. He lost a chunk of his neck for his distraction.

I gained my feet and swayed in place. Zombie, zombie, zombie ... what the hell did I know about zombies that was actual truth?

Well, I certainly didn't know that zombies trumped vampires.

I drew my knife.

"Get out, Jade. Get the fuck out. Find the shifter —" This time Kett lost a hunk of his lower arm. He'd been trying to pry the zombie away from his neck.

I needed leverage. My knife wasn't long enough to cut off the zombie's head in one slice. Nor was I tall enough, but I was banking on full decapitation being unnecessary.

The room had settled into a strange permanent tilt, but I was fairly certain that the entire room couldn't be listing to one side. I rolled my neck and felt something snap back into place with a spasm of pain. That felt better, even though the pounding in my head was worse, like I'd just undammed the blood flow.

With my knife in my hand, the next two steps were easier than I anticipated. I jumped up on the now empty — and, oddly, still upright and intact — tray table.

I took one more wide stride forward to the very end of the table. Then, holding my knife in both hands over my head, I leaped upward and toward the zombie.

As my upward momentum became a downward fall, I thrust my knife, tip down, through the top of the zombie's skull. The blade slid in easy and clean, right up to the hilt. A shock of magic — not my own — reverberated through the knife and into my arms, forcing me to let go of the weapon.

I hit the floor feet first, but couldn't catch my balance. As I sprawled against the zombie's back, it tipped sideways, taking me with it.

I scrambled a few feet backward on my ass. The zombie's supine body lay between me and Kett, who had sunk down hunched against the wall.

The zombie — my knife still sticking out of his head — didn't move.

I was aware I was sobbing, and that I had been doing so throughout my leap and stab, but I couldn't stop. I'd just killed something ... something already dead, but still something I'd once thought, however briefly, that I could love.

"You ... stopped it," Kett said. His voice was little more than a moan.

"Yeah, though it was probably a good thing it was distracted."

Kett raised his eyes to mine. He didn't look good. The floor around him was coated in the ash that his magic turned to when it died. That scared the hell out of me, but being scared was getting to be a pretty permanent state of being.

"You need to go. Stand. Move slowly," Kett whispered, never taking his blood-red eyes off me. "Don't look back. Go now." He shuddered and pressed his hands to his stomach. A few of his fingers were sticking out at odd angles. He wasn't healing anymore. "Go!" He also had fangs. I hadn't seen those before.

Red eyes, fangs … injured vampire. I was a walking, breathing blood bag.

His magic hit me as it had before, trying to pin me in place.

I straightened despite it. He copied my movement, though he had to lean against and slide up the wall to do so.

I flicked my eyes to my knife in the zombie's head. It was closer to the vampire than me.

Kett grinned. "I shall enjoy draining you, witch. It's been a hundred years since I've hunted so freely. And I've never tasted magic like yours."

Mr. Nice Vampire was gone. I was really wishing he'd stuck around a bit longer.

I ran.

I didn't have a hope in hell.

His fingers brushed my hair.

I hadn't even taken a second step. I had a feeling he was playing with me, despite his obvious need. He was toying with me just a bit before the big finale.

I was going to die and I'd just saved his freaking life. No good deed goes unpunished.

The double swinging doors from the hallway blew open, and fury burst through in the body of a nightmare. This monster grabbed the enraged, starving vampire and tossed him — yes, tossed, with one massive, clawed hand — through the far wall, all without even sideswiping me. The thing had to be seven feet tall but was partly humanoid in form. It turned to look over its shoulder.

"Get her out of here." It spoke perfectly through a face that was malformed, caught in some cross between human and beast — though what beast, I wasn't sure. Its teeth jutted out of an oversized jaw and were fanged top and bottom. Like a cat's; not like the vampire's.

The vampire was laughing from beyond the far wall, and there was nothing human about the sound. I totally would have peed myself except I was actually frozen in place.

Suddenly, Kandy was trying to pull me from the room, more roughly than was necessary. But then, I was resisting more than was healthy for me. In my morbid fear, I just wanted to watch —

The vampire was on the monster before I knew he'd reentered the room.

The beast raised a clawed hand wider than a medicine ball, and smacked the vampire to the floor. The creature was gurgling some choking sort of laugh, like it was playing rather than in a battle for its life.

Kandy finally managed to yank me fully through the half-unhinged and dented swinging doors and out of the room. Two other werewolves — Lara and the tall blond, who were calm but glowing green around the eyes — waited in the hall. I clicked two and two together and figured out the identity of the monster. I'd blame the delay on whatever head injury I was currently suffering, but ... well, I wasn't known for being quick on my feet uninjured either.

"He's not a wolf," I said as Kandy pulled me past the two werewolves and continued dragging me toward an emergency exit, which opened to reveal stairs, not the elevator. I'd figured out the half-beast was Desmond Llewelyn, the Lord and Alpha of the West Coast North American Pack.

"No, a cat." Kandy shoved me up the stairs in front of her.

"He didn't look like any cat I've ever seen."

"Half-form. Some of us can partly change, and meld the strength of our animal forms into the mobility of our human. Opposable clawed thumbs and all that."

Oh. That was clear. Not. I wondered if he liked cream and catnip as much as my childhood cat, Lester, had. Kandy's stifled giggle informed me I'd wondered that last bit out loud.

"But you're a wolf?" I asked.

"Most of us are."

How had I not known that not all shapeshifters were wolves? The *Compendium* had totally let me down in that respect. Shouldn't the werewolf section have referenced a shapeshifter entry? I'd noticed the vampire calling the werewolves 'shapeshifters,' of course, but I'd thought he was just being all correct and elitist, as usual.

Kandy slammed her palms on the bar of the emergency exit door at the top of the stairs, and we were suddenly in the fresh air. Well, the fresh air of an alley between two four-storey hospital buildings — but still, I breathed deeply, over and over again, to get the smell of morgue and undead out of my nostrils, out of my brain.

Kandy propped me up against a cement wall and began to pace the short strip of pavement twenty or so feet in front of me. Like she was securing her territory, or perhaps securing her prisoner. I was happy to be out of her bruising grasp. My upper left arm was tingling as if she'd actually hindered the blood flow.

"He's going to kill him," I said.

"Nah, they're sort of friendly, as much as a shifter and a vampire can be. He'll just subdue him. He looked pretty beaten up already."

"I meant Kett would kill Desmond."

Kandy barked out a laugh. I was pretty tired of being the butt of everyone's jokes, so I chose to ignore her and rest my aching head against the concrete wall.

My neck really was killing me. And whether vampire trumped were ... cat? Well, that was way out of my hands and league.

Ah, damn it. I'd left my knife in the zombie's skull.

Chapter Nine

I was proven completely wrong about Kett killing Desmond when, before I'd even caught my breath, Mc-Growly sauntered out of the emergency exit. Of course, I had no idea if it was Desmond's strength and skill or Kett maintaining enough control to hold back that kept the werecat whole but bloody.

He was back in his full human form, clothed in a rather ratty, bloody T-shirt and jeans. He was just a couple of inches taller than me, though I was sure he'd been closer to seven feet and covered in nothing but fur in the morgue.

I was going to need to start running an abilities-that-scare-the-shit-out-of-me list on the shapeshifters now, not just for the vampire. It was one thing to read about such abilities in a book and completely another to see it with my own eyes. Especially since the *Compendium* was obviously missing chunks of pertinent information. Or I hadn't looked in the correct section. I could never rule out my own inability to focus on things that didn't interest me.

Anyway, each hour with this group of Adepts was a whole new terrifying experience. Lucky me. Shapeshifters, who came in forms other than wolf, could transform into a half-human/half-beast over seven feet tall. Delightfully scary. Then they could throw a vampire through a cement wall. Though maybe that was a far more chilling fact about the vampire than the shifter. Also, they too, like the vampire, could casually pin a helpless half-witch against a concrete wall and stare at her intimidatingly until she wanted to pee her pants.

Um, yeah ... speaking of which ... Desmond turned on me the instant the door had closed behind him. Kandy took two big steps away and turned her back on us. Traitor.

Desmond didn't actually have to touch me to pin me against the wall; one green-glowing-eyed look was enough. Plus, he was so wide that he pretty much created a wall himself. He practically occupied all my peripheral vision just by standing a foot-and-a-half away.

He narrowed his eyes at me, assessing, I supposed. Then he held his hand out, palm up. He'd rescued my knife from the zombie's skull. It was wiped clean and I was grateful for this. Overly grateful, in fact, because I felt like Kett and Desmond were to blame for the fact that I had to stab Hudson's reanimated body through the head in the first place. Therefore, they deserved very little of my gratitude.

"Is Kett ... dead?"

"Not any more than he was before," Desmond said without smiling. It was a joke nonetheless; lame shifter humor, I supposed. I didn't laugh either but Kandy snorted, even with her back turned.

"Nice knife work down there," Desmond said. "Brave. The vampire is in your debt. He won't like that, so use it well." Then he reached up with two fingers to touch my chin. He added a bit of pressure to slowly rotate my head. I thought about resisting, but my neck was really killing me and I didn't want to strain it further.

Desmond let out a low whistle. Kandy turned as he lifted the hair off the side and back of my neck. My curls had fallen out of their clip and I hadn't even noticed.

"That is an impressive bruise," Desmond said, referencing my neck. Even Kandy looked momentarily impressed. "I haven't ever seen a bruise like that on a human. Not one alive, anyway."

I kept quiet. The headache was now pounding at the back of my skull, and I just wasn't up to bantering.

Kandy's eyes fell on Desmond's shoulder and she uttered a short, blunt curse. I looked myself — Desmond had freed my head — and ogled the half-healed chew mark on the bridge between Desmond's neck and his meaty shoulder. His neck had been savaged, T-shirt and all, so his shirt must have stretched and ripped in places to accommodate his half-beast form. It was a similar enough color to the deep beige of his fur that I missed seeing it.

Kandy reached over and extracted a long, broken canine tooth from this bloody wound.

Desmond took the tooth from her and started to laugh. The green-haired wolf growled impatiently and started her pacing game again, only now her track encircled Desmond and me.

The wound on Desmond's neck sealed as he laughed. He was practically clutching his belly with mirth. I was surprised he was capable of such emotion.

"He found me a difficult meal," Desmond managed to wheeze. "He just hung on chewing, waiting for me to drop from his damn venom shit. It takes more than that to get me on my back." The shifter flashed me a grin, and I deliberately ignored the sexual allusion.

Scary venom shit — that was one more check mark in the vampires-are-walking-talking-nightmares box.

"It'll take him time to grow that back," Kandy said. Satisfaction laced her growl.

Desmond, who was now wiping tears from his eyes, pocketed the tooth. "Blackmail," he whispered as he winked at me.

I wasn't impressed. I just wanted to go home and find solace in a fresh batch of double fudge brownies. Desmond dropped his smile and stepped closer to me again. This time he leaned in and actually smelled me. He took a great big sniff just underneath my left ear, then clasped and raised both my hands to his face. He inhaled at my wrists, then pinned me with his gaze again. A green glow rolled over his green-flecked, golden brown eyes. Again, I assumed the glow must have something to do with the shapeshifters accessing their power. Maybe scent this time?

"What are you?"

"We've done this dance before. It's boring," I answered. I guess I did have some lip left in me.

"You haven't danced properly with me," Desmond said, his voice growling low in his chest.

I couldn't figure out if he thought he was being sexy or flirty or whether he was threatening me. I just sighed and turned my head to fix my gaze over his shoulder. This pissed him off, and I could actually feel his anger rise. But then, that had been my intention.

"You owe me a life debt, half-witch, and I'm about to collect."

I shuddered as the power laced through those words rolled over me. I shuddered at the thought of owing anything to this man-beast who could command such magic in mere words.

He'd saved my life.

I couldn't even pretend to dispute it. He could have let the vampire kill me, but he obviously wanted something more from me.

I looked back at him. He was waiting for my acknowledgement. I nodded and felt the magic settle between us. It was a light connection, but it felt heavy to me; I'd never accepted a life debt before. I understood it was a serious binding, fueled and enforced by the magic of the caster — Desmond, in this case — and reinforced with my own magic. He didn't own me or anything, but it felt like I'd signed some sort of lease agreement nonetheless.

I knew then that even if he owed it to me, I wouldn't be collecting such an acknowledgement from the vampire. I didn't want to play with magic that felt so tangible and terrifying.

My grandmother was going to freak unless I could cancel out the debt before she laid eyes on me.

"What do you want in return?" I asked. I was back to looking over Desmond's shoulder and attempting to ignore the tug of the bond.

"What? No thank you for saving your life?"

"You felt the bond seal as surely as I did. That's thanks enough." I'd seen that much in the satisfaction that had flitted over his face, before it settled back into its usual grim lines.

"Hudson was my second. He was invaluable. Irreplaceable."

My eyes flicked to Kandy, who was currently on her guard rounds. If she could hear the conversation, it didn't seem to interest her.

"Kandy is a warrior. One of my best. And while Hudson could be fearsome, you have to be more than just fearsome to reach and hold the second position. He was a diplomat. Charming, agreeable —"

"Everything you're not." I couldn't help saying it. Desmond scared me.

"Exactly." He wasn't insulted easily, it seemed. "I hold you responsible for Hudson's death. Somehow, being around you called him to the attention of the killer."

"That's not fair," I said as calmly as possible, even as guilty tears threatened the corners of my eyes. "You were already investigating murdered werewolves when I met Hudson."

"Why do you think he danced with you?" Desmond said with a sneer. "You think a half-witch held any thrill for such as him? Yes, your magic is appealing. Intoxicating in the right circumstances, I suppose. But shifters don't mate with weak humans."

"Well, you all keep telling me I'm not human at all, so I guess that wasn't an issue. Perhaps you didn't know your precious Hudson as well as you think."

Anger momentarily edged Desmond's chiseled features, but was gone as soon as I'd glimpsed it. Which was good, as I'd momentarily forgotten I didn't want to provoke the beast.

"I can see why the vampire likes you," Desmond said. "The same won't apply to me."

"You prefer your followers with their noses shoved up your ass."

"You have me completely figured out."

Desmond bared his teeth at me. I returned the non-smile as he took an aggressive step forward. I didn't step back. Of course, I was already practically plastered to the concrete wall, so that didn't mean much. But I didn't back down.

The metal emergency exit door slammed open. Kett, with a werewolf supported under each arm, wandered out into the alley. The vampire looked completely human for the first time since I'd met him. His skin was practically pink with health, and he was grinning like he'd just had the most amazing orgasm. I instantly wanted to slap the smile from his face — or maybe throw myself at his mercy, I wasn't sure. The werewolves, Lara and the tall blond whose name I still didn't know, looked drunk out of their minds, buzz and all.

"Kandy, get them to the car," Desmond ordered.

She relieved Kett of the burden of the young wolves by coaxing them up the alley. They stayed on their feet, barely.

Kett ran his hand through his hair — another terribly human gesture — and turned a high-wattage smile on me. "I'm glad I didn't kill you, witch."

"Half-witch," Desmond said — for some reason he was stuck on that point — as he pinned me back against the wall. His touch was light but it cleared my head. I'd been listing toward the vampire as if he was exuding some sort of magnetism.

"Oh? Yes, indeed," Kett graciously acknowledged. "And thank you, alpha, for the gift of your werewolves. They are young and strong. I haven't fed on such for many a year."

"We needed you focused on the correct hunt," Desmond answered, his sneer turning sour around the edges.

"Yes," Kett agreed good-naturedly. This sexy, languid vibe of his was seriously freaking me out. I avoided eye contact, though he hadn't taken his gaze off me.

"I've claimed a life debt from the half-witch," Desmond announced.

Kett's smile fell abruptly away, along with whatever magnetism he'd been exuding. His thoughts were once again hidden behind his icy mask in an immediate and complete transformation. The hair stood up on the back of my neck.

"Difficult magic," the vampire said. "Not for the light of heart." Me, he meant. Not for me.

"We sealed the bond without concern. The half-witch will deliver me to the killer. Once Hudson is avenged, the debt will lift."

"If the terms were clear, and I hope for both of your sakes that they were, then all will be well."

"And if the terms weren't clear?" I squeaked just a little, but at least I'd found my voice. Nothing had been clear to me for days now.

Kett eyed me coolly. I was once again just an interesting bug to him. "I'm sure the Lord and Alpha of the West Coast North American Pack knows what he's doing, one way or the other."

The werecat and the vampire locked gazes, neither saying anything further. After a few moments of this stare-off, I wondered if I could just wander away unnoticed.

Then Kett nodded as if they'd been speaking the whole time. He looked away. "She isn't under my protection."

"Then you have no say," Desmond said.

"No, but the wards on her home speak of great power."

"I have no fear of witches," Desmond snorted.

"You are young," Kett answered without the heat of any accusation.

They both turned to look at me. Okay, I had wandered off a bit, just to see if they'd notice. They did, damn them.

"The witch knows the magic that raised the dead werewolf," Kett said, far too casually for someone delivering a death sentence. Bastard.

I groaned and closed my eyes. Noticed, did he? Damn. I'd hoped to slip away and sort through everything in my head for a day or two. Okay, maybe a week — and my Gran's return.

I opened my eyes and offered what was meant to be a charming smile. It felt shaky across my stiff face.

That freaky green glow rolled over Desmond's eyes as he returned my smile with a nasty one. "Oh, there will be blood tonight," he whispered.

As his magic brushed over me, I shivered as if it had been an actual breeze — though warm, not cold, so that my reaction had nothing to do with temperature.

There always was blood in the deep, dark depths of despair and tragedy, wasn't there?

It was Rusty's practically dormant necromancy I'd sensed in the morgue, before and after the zombie rose. I was actually having a difficult time shaking off the residual of it, still coating my throat and nostrils even heavier than the actual smell of the morgue. I'd cleared that scent out after only a few fresh breaths of alley air.

Rusty's magic didn't feel evil. Just twisted in a way I'd never felt from him before, which gave me pause and stopped me from naming him.

I slumped against the cement wall I'd been skirting in my attempt to exit the alley unnoticed. Kett and Desmond closed the distance between us in a single step each. I turned my face away from Desmond's glowing green eyes and Kett's impassive expectancy.

Kandy had returned from the car, which I guessed was parked nearby. She stood off to one side, flexing and massaging her hand. I realized she was pushing claws through the tips of her human fingers, as if practicing the technique. I wondered if it hurt.

Desmond growled, low and quiet. It was a warning sort of noise like a cat might make. A very large cat.

"What if I'm wrong?" I asked no one in particular.

"You recognized the magic, though?" Kett reconfirmed.

"Yes, but it felt twisted, not evil. Not like the trinkets."

"Have you ever been around the caster when he or she raised the dead?"

I locked eyes with Kett, looking for some understanding from him. I didn't want to get a friend killed. "The caster shouldn't have been capable of such a thing."

"The same caster who's been killing werewolves and siphoning off their power?" Desmond asked, rather rhetorically. Between blood lust and feeding, Kett and Desmond had obviously had time to chat.

"You're saying he's stolen the power?"

Desmond threw his hands up in the air, then spun to walk away down the alley. "You deal with her," he growled at the vampire. "You just tried to rip out her throat, but she obviously trusts you more than me."

"I don't trust either of you!" I yelled after Desmond, but he didn't turn back. Kandy followed him without looking at me. Once again leaving me alone with a vampire ... now in a slowly darkening alley. The sun would be setting soon. The location was new, but the trepidation was old hat.

"We can't seek justice without proof, Jade. Especially because this is an interspecies conflict, which is also one of the reasons Desmond asked me to continue to aid in the investigation after I'd ruled out vampire involvement."

"That's a good thing, is it?"

"Yes," Kett answered with a sigh. He then tousled his blond hair until it was more bed head than slick skier. Magic glinted off his skin in tiny gleams of color now. I wondered if the werewolf blood strengthened him even further because of its magical potency. I wondered if repeated ingestions would actually alter his own magic.

"Why do you act more human after you've fed? I understand the change in skin and eye tone, but why the personality change?"

Kett stilled. "I was unaware I was less ... human ... between feedings. Thank you for sharing your observation, I'll take it into consideration during our further interactions."

I thought maybe I'd hurt his feelings. Feelings I'd been previously unaware he even had. "Maybe I'm just getting to know you better," I said. It was a lame recovery effort, but I so hated having people pissed at me. I'm a fixer.

Kett narrowed his eyes at me. "The magic?"

Right, so he'd noticed the stalling. I closed my eyes again, but it didn't make any difference. I could still feel him staring right through me, his gaze eating into my soul. I could also feel his magic — along with the magic of the shapeshifters waiting around the corner, all of it looming over me — just as well with my eyes closed as open. "You'll wait for actual evidence before the murder and mayhem commences?"

"As I indicated earlier."

I was obligated to answer. I could almost feel the life debt bond forcing the name from my mouth. "Rusty."

"Rusty is a necromancer?"

Um, yeah? Hence the raising of a dead body? I quashed my need to deflect through sarcasm — especially since it was rare for a necromancer to be male — and answered the vampire politely, "His mother is."

"And this Rusty has some sort of latent ability?"

"An affinity. But it's spotty, unfocused, and really nowhere near powerful."

"Powerful enough." Kett touched the side of his smooth, unblemished neck. Reassuring himself he wasn't still missing a chunk of flesh, I guessed. His regeneration was terrifying. I wondered if this would all be old news and everyday to me soon. I shuddered at the thought of such a life, jaded by fantastical magic. That drew Kett's attention. "What are you waiting for, witch?"

"I was hoping for a nap."

"The shifters will drive."

"Are you two telepathically linked or something?"

"Certainly not." Kett seemed a little over-the-top enraged at this suggestion — in his completely offish, icy way. "I'm simply not stupid. They always travel in multiple vehicles. They are pack." *Pack*, I gathered from his tone, was a loathsome thing to be.

"For protection?"

Kett shrugged one shoulder and strode off down the alley. Then he almost immediately stepped back and forced me to follow alongside him. Geez, he didn't even give me a second to straighten off the wall. "For hunting, Jade. They are a pack even though he leads them. He might hunt alone if he wishes, but the rest hunt as a pack. Something you might have remembered in the dance club."

"I'm not the bad guy here."

Kett continued through the mouth of the alley and crossed toward the parking lot. Every time I matched his stride, he sped up a little more, as if it pleased him to drag me just a little bit. It appeared that dominance games weren't just for werewolves. "You play with magic. That makes you irresponsible. You don't know your own strength, and you leave magical objects hanging around for anyone to take or manipulate."

"Trinkets," I spat.

"Not just trinkets," Kett snarled as he whirled on me. We were standing in the middle of two rows of parked cars, with more vehicles stretching in every direction. It was a big hospital. To the passing humans, we probably looked like two very blond lovers having a spat after visiting a loved one.

"That knife severed the zombie's magic like slicing through butter."

"Everyone knows that if you destroy a zombie's brain you kill it —"

"Myth," the vampire spat. "You cut off the magic of the necromancer. And that necklace you wear like it's just a pretty thing you've flung around your neck? It's some sort of shielding device —"

"Maybe I'm naturally resistant —"

"No witch should be able to stand before me. And that bruise on your neck? Not only does it speak of a nasty injury, but it showed up within minutes. Bruises indicate the body's attempt to —"

"That's enough," I screamed. Kett seemed shocked and surprised, as if we'd just been having a chat. "You have all the answers and I have none," I said darkly. "I get it."

"Perhaps you aren't asking the correct questions."

"Perhaps I don't want to know."

His face took on that impassive quality again. I glared at him, my fists clenched and chin jutting.

A too-large-for-the-lot SUV pulled up. Kandy was driving. An identical vehicle idled a few feet behind, Desmond at the wheel. He was smirking. Both SUVs were luxury vehicles of some expensive make. I couldn't be bothered to care.

I yanked open the front passenger door of Kandy's SUV, snarling at Kett as I climbed in. "Get your own ride."

Kandy pulled forward toward the exit as I violently snapped on my seat belt. Kett stared after us. I could see him in my sideview mirror.

"I've never seen a vampire speechless before," Kandy said with an appreciative chuckle.

"You're not in my friendly book either. Where was the car this morning when you made me walk in the rain?"

"Not everything is about you."

"But that was calculated. To wear me down? To confuse me? Make me uncomfortable? Upset me?"

"Yes."

"Don't talk to me."

"Where are we going?"

"To the West End. Over Burrard Bridge, loop right. He lives just off Denman."

Kandy's eyes flashed green and she grinned rather maniacally, as if she was already anticipating the hunt, as Kett had called it.

I looked away and hoped I was doing the right thing. Everything was all twisted in my head. I had a feeling — like the earlier walk in the rain — that all this was calculated to put me off, keeping me moving but confused. To what ultimate end, I had no idea. Maybe they did it on purpose, the vampire and the shifters. Maybe I was part of the hunt as well.

I closed my eyes and tried to nap. Tried to at least clear my head before I accused a friend of murder.

I wondered if I should text Sienna. I wondered if Kandy would stop me if I tried.

I stopped wondering and started focusing on the cool of the window glass as I pressed my temple against it. That soothed me, though only a little.

Chapter Ten

*R*usty lived in a fifteen-or-so storey building on the corner of Bidwell and Burnaby Street. He had a peekaboo view of English Bay, and the annual Festival of Lights firework celebration in the summer was spectacular from his rooftop.

Not that I'd known him long enough to be invited more than once.

It was an older building with no amenities other than a laundry room, but his rent was still reasonable in a city where real estate was out of control.

As the shifters illegally parked in permit-only spaces, I realized that I wasn't entirely aware of what Rusty did for work. He traded stocks or played the market, but I wasn't sure if he had any clients, or if he was working off an inheritance or what. And now I was leading predators to his doorstep ... not that there was any correlation between those two things, just ... I was really unsure and numb. But the taste of his magic in the morgue had been unmistakable. As far as I could tell in my limited experience, such things were as individual as scent. My mother's and grandmother's magic, for instance, tasted different even though they were blood related. They both had that witchy earthy base, and the layer that marked them as blood kin, but the spicing was different. I'd never met Rusty's mother; I wondered how similar her magic tasted to Rusty's.

"What if I'm wrong?" I whispered as I looked up at the building from the sidewalk. "Maybe it's someone blood related —"

"We'll figure that out pretty quickly, won't we?" Kandy gave me a nudge with her shoulder toward the building's front door.

Rusty lived up on the fourth floor, and a quick glance up at his balcony only confirmed that his curtains were drawn. I couldn't remember if he usually opened them during the day.

I found myself staring at the buzzer panel. It wasn't listed by apartment number, but I finally remembered Rusty's last name. I wasn't sure I'd ever seen it written down anywhere before. Rusty didn't answer the buzzer. I waited and tried again.

"Maybe ... I could call," I said, my voice sounded hollow even to my own ears.

Desmond reached past me and snapped the lock on the glass front door with a simple twist of his thumb and forefinger. He tossed the broken dead bolt in a nearby planter and held the door open for me.

I thought about just giving them the apartment number and walking away. I was currently surrounded by four shapeshifters and a vampire. I had no doubt I was a prisoner. I just hadn't tested the strength of my cage yet. Honestly, I was scared to do so.

"What's your name?" I asked the tall blond werewolf. He'd recovered enough from the vampire's bite to follow us from the second SUV. He looked wan, as did Lara, who was huddled in a short-cropped, burgundy leather coat beside him. On a better day, I would have lusted after that coat, and the matching lip gloss she wore. The young werewolf looked at Desmond, who nodded his head almost imperceptibly.

"Jeremy," he answered.

"All right, then. I thought it good to know all the names of the people who are probably going to kill my friend, and then me. Maybe with luck, I'll manage some sort of death curse with my final breath."

Jeremy glanced at Desmond with some questioning concern, but I turned away and walked into the apartment entranceway before the conversation could continue. I didn't want their platitudes or cajoling — or maybe even torture — if I balked further.

The building manager's door stood to the left. Two elevators were directly in front of the entrance doors. I opted for the stairs, not wanting to be crushed into an elevator with this group. I was fairly certain I would hyperventilate, and showing them more weakness wasn't high on my to-do list.

I could practically feel Desmond's breath on my neck as I climbed the four flights of stairs, though given how similar in height we were, that should have been physically impossible. It was Kandy's hand that reached out for the fourth-floor door when I paused at it.

Kandy entered the hall ahead of me, holding me back as if she was protecting me or something. Then she turned and nodded to me. I led them to apartment 403. The varnish had worn away from around the door handle and the mail slot, and the door had a peephole. I really hoped Rusty used it when I knocked. The muddy teal carpet was worn but not shabby underneath my feet. Why was I noticing such stupid things?

Rusty had a one-bedroom corner suite, maybe 550 square feet if I was estimating generously. The shifters and Kett stepped off to the left so Rusty couldn't see them through the peephole. They lined themselves along the short, perpendicular wall that ran between Rusty's door and his south neighbor's. Kandy was right next to the door, her hand hovering over the knob.

I knocked.

No one answered.

"Rusty? Sienna?" I called, though not terribly loudly. I knocked again.

No answer.

"No movement within," Kandy murmured. Desmond nodded and Kandy popped the lock with a single twist of her hand. The deadbolt wasn't engaged.

The green-haired werewolf slipped by me and entered the apartment. I followed, not waiting for the all-clear even though I knew I was supposed to.

A small, rather messy bathroom stood to my immediate left. The toilet seat was up. A discarded light gray bath towel had fallen between it and the tub.

I turned right, avoiding the bedroom in front of me with its partly closed door, and walked by the tiny galley kitchen into the empty living room. I passed Kandy on her way out of the kitchen, though why she'd need to enter what her eyes could clearly see was empty I didn't know. Dirty dishes sat in the sink, with clean ones drying on the counter.

Two wineglasses were on the floor by the futon couch. An old, barely-used TV occupied the corner of the living room. The drapes covering the balcony doors were just as closed inside as they'd looked from the outside.

Kandy was methodically opening the doors and checking the closets that ran parallel to the kitchen entrance. I wandered over to the west window — the one with the peekaboo view — and watched the sun begin to set. The dust on the drapes suggested that Rusty never bothered to close them on this window, probably because the building was angled toward a park so there were no nosy neighbors.

The apartment was empty. I knew that the moment Kandy had opened the door. I couldn't feel any magical signatures beyond those of the shapeshifters and the vampire. They'd probably all known it as well; they were hunters, after all, with heightened senses. I gathered that Kandy's continued search was for clues.

I'd always loved watching the sunset from English Bay. It was as if you were standing directly in front of the sun, with nothing but the ocean between you.

"Witch, you're going to want to see this," Kandy called from the bedroom. I was very certain she had no idea what she was talking about.

I turned from the window, unaware that the vampire had joined me in the living room. Great, he could dampen his magical signature. That wasn't scary at all.

"I didn't know you were here," I said before I could stop myself.

Kett shrugged. He already had his arms crossed as he watched me watch the sunset. "You are preoccupied."

"Witch!" Desmond snapped from the other room. With a sigh, I obeyed the command in his voice.

The bedroom barely fit the double bed and the side table. The stink of old magic hit me as I turned from the short hall.

I stared at the furniture arrangement from the doorway. The bed had been shifted to the middle of the room and placed inside a black-painted pentagram. That paint was going to be a bitch to get off the worn cork floors. The open closet held a set of shelves containing what I guessed were spell ingredients and collectibles, as well as clothing on hangers and an overfull laundry basket. The bird wing from our spell in the bakery basement sat on one of the shelves, among other animal bones and dried furry corpses I didn't look at too closely.

The sheets on the bed were well mussed. Tangled, even. Kandy stood, her arms crossed defensively, as far away from the pentagram and closet as she could be and still be in the room. Desmond didn't seem as wary, though he was careful not to cross through the pentagram as he circled the bed. He looked up to where I'd stopped in the doorway. The vampire was right behind me.

"Sex magic," Desmond said. He wrinkled his nose.

I nodded and felt Kett do the same behind me. Even I could smell the stale sex that lingered in the air, but the bed in the pentagram was a dead giveaway.

"The pentagram isn't active right now," I said. I crossed a couple of steps further into the room to look down at it. No vessels of any kind stood at any of the five points. I glanced around the room, but, besides the closet shelves, there was nothing else to be seen.

"He's using sex to power spells?" Desmond asked.

I shrugged. "Not sure. I usually cast a circle — north, east, west, and south sort of thing — which is how my Gran taught me. And there aren't any collection vessels, empty or otherwise."

"Raising Hudson had to have used up a bunch of juice," Desmond said, but he was speaking to Kett, not me. The vampire nodded. He'd stepped up beside me. Out of the corner of my eye, he was only a couple of inches taller than me in my heeled sandals. He'd seemed much taller when I was facing him.

"How many magical signatures can you pick up?" Kett asked.

I crossed the pentagram and hovered my fingers over one of the pillows. I didn't want to actually touch the sheets. "Just Rusty and Sienna, I think."

"Sienna, your sister?" Kandy asked from her corner.

I nodded.

"You think?" Desmond said with a sneer as he reached over and pressed my hand down onto the bed itself. "Afraid to get dirty, princess?" I noticed how he waited to cross the pentagram until I did. He'd also wrapped his hand in a sheet before he'd touched mine — a quick move before he'd flicked the sheet corner away. Was he afraid of touching me, or simply of contaminating my readings?

I glared at him, my clenched teeth effectively blocking my angry retort. He stepped back without ceding any intimidation ground. I refocused on the bed. "It's old, residue. Just Sienna and Rusty."

"What spell were they doing?" Kett asked. He hadn't moved any closer.

"I don't know."

"Guess," Desmond growled.

I straightened from the bed and stepped out of the pentagram. I noted he had already done the same. I guessed that standing in a pentagram with a witch could be unnerving. Too bad I wasn't that kind of witch.

"I don't know," I repeated. My jaw was starting to ache from suppressed anger. "I don't do this kind of magic."

"But you know about it," Kett said, his tone dropping to soothing levels.

"It wasn't really on my Gran's syllabus."

Desmond glared at me from the other side of the bed. Kandy kept her eyes on the ground. Kett gave me an encouraging smile. Either that or he was thinking about biting me ... again.

I sighed, my eyes glued to the blue cotton bed sheets, and fished into the depths of my brain to try to pull out some sort of information. It wasn't an easy task. I really didn't retain this sort of thing, because it never much interested me. "As far as I know, sex — the energy from sex — can be captured and used to fuel a spell —"

"But there are no vessels," Kett said.

"Right. So I suppose ..." I swallowed, not really wanting to acknowledge the other possibility. "Sex could be used to ... to directly enhance, or conversely, drain, the magic of one of the participants."

"One? Not both?" Kett asked.

"I don't think so. Like I said, I don't know this type of magic. I sense Rusty and Sienna here, but not their purpose or their ... activities."

Kandy snorted.

"Is Rusty's magic the same here as it was in the morgue?" Kett asked.

"No."

"So this ... whatever it was, wasn't used to desecrate Hudson?" Desmond asked. I shuddered at his word choice, trying to shut out the image of Hudson's beautiful body lurching up from the table.

"No," I answered. "It's different, less pungent. Rusty's magic, yes, but not that darker, deeper version of it. This is grass and fresh dirt and dew on a fall morning, and that was ... was ..."

"Death," Kett supplied.

"Maybe. Blood, but not ... fresh ... not coppery, not alive, for sure. It seethed."

"Can you track this ... scent?" Desmond asked.

"It's not like that. It's not just hanging in the air, and I'm not a werewolf."

"It is just hanging in the air," Kett corrected. "If you know where to look."

"I can't track it. Give me a magical object or point me in the direction of a magical object and I can find it. Like I collected the pieces for the trinkets —"

"You're a witch," Desmond interjected. "Use a tracking spell."

"I'm not that kind of witch. I don't do spells. Not on my own anyway. My magic doesn't work like that."

Desmond looked at Kett with a raised eyebrow. Kett tilted his head in some obscure response, then crossed to look at the items on the shelves in the closet.

"What about these? They're magical," the vampire said.

"You can see magic?" I asked, intrigued despite my ire. I stepped up beside him. I couldn't help it. I'd never met anyone who could see magic without being caught in or wielding it — and that was usually just a feeling, I'd been told. A person usually had to be connected to, or spelled by, magic to feel it.

Kett turned his head just enough to look at me. "Not like you can. It was a gift of mine, before."

"Before? Before what?"

"The turning comes with its own set of gifts, but we sometimes retain some from our lives before."

Before he became a vampire, he meant. He'd been turned, not born a vampire. I thought vampires had to be born to be as powerful as Kett. That anyone who'd been badly bitten and managed to live just carried the secondary effects such as light sensitivity or the need for blood and not much of the magic. The magic was what gave Kett his strength, immortality, and other vampire gifts, as he called them.

"What is this? Show and tell?" Desmond snapped.

"Take these items and make one of your trinkets to track Rusty," Kett said, as if just saying such a thing would make it possible.

I stared at him, then laughed. It was a short laugh. "I don't make magical objects. We've been over this before. No one does."

"Someone does, because such things exist."

"Fine. Someone powerful, maybe. You can't just infuse magic into inanimate objects. It's not compatible, and energy can't be created or destroyed —"

"But it can be directed —"

"Magic can tint or tinge the things we hold close to ourselves over a long period of time. Like these wedding rings. Or it can occur naturally, such as in a piece of jade I find in a river. But you can't take that rock and just tell it to find someone. Do you think I'm stupid?"

"No. I think you can do it." Kett spoke as if I were five years old. "I think you made this ..." He reached up to touch my necklace. "And your knife."

"And you make these," Desmond said, gesturing toward a trinket that was hanging off a nail on one of the shelves. Yeah, I'd noticed that. I'd also noticed that there were more empty nails with nothing hanging from them. I'd kind of hoped no one else would notice, though.

"I cobble together items that hold bits of residual magic. I placed some spells on a knife I carved. I don't make these things function as something they aren't, like a tracking device."

Kett didn't speak further. He just looked at me, as if waiting for me to have some sort of epiphany.

Desmond batted at the trinket so it swung off its nail with a series of clicks and chimes. "You owe me, witch."

"I can't do it," I snarled. "No one can."

"What good are you, then?" Desmond spat.

"Well, I have a cell phone, why don't I use it? That would be the sane, modern thing to do." I shoved past Desmond — aware that he was letting me go, or I wouldn't have been able to move him at all — and pretty much ran into the living room. The bedroom was just too filled with magic, both stale and radiating off the shapeshifters. It was claustrophobic.

I dug my cell phone out of my satchel. But instead of calling Sienna, I opened my browser and googled the hotel my Gran was staying at in Tofino. Yes, I was utterly aware I'd been stupid not to do so before. I should have begged her to return a day ago, but I so wanted to handle this on my own. I'd wanted to prove I could do more than just make pretty window decorations and yummy cupcakes. Was I going to spend my entire life hiding behind my Gran's skirts or in her shadow? Probably, yes. But I wasn't going to risk Sienna's safety any further than I already had.

Kandy and Kett joined me in the living room. Desmond stormed out of the apartment — slamming the front door like a child — as if he couldn't stand another moment inside. The other two werewolves, Lara and Jeremy, hadn't entered the apartment at all.

I found the number for the Long Beach Lodge and dialed. The hotel operator answered, but I barely heard her greeting.

"Pearl Godfrey's room, please," I blurted into the phone.

"One minute." The phone clicked and some saccharine music blared in my ear. My thoughts drifted to the mussed bed in the other room ... of how tired but happy Rusty had been the last two times I'd seen him ... of Sienna wearing my trinkets like they'd protect her. In fact, she'd been wearing a lot of my things lately ... had she needed protection? How could I have missed it? I was freaking blind to anything outside my own tunnel vision.

"My sister," I whispered as I met Kett's eyes.

He nodded. I almost believed he, too, was a little worried.

"The coven should have dispersed by now," he said, rather incomprehensibly.

"What? What coven?" I asked, but then the phone clicked.

"That guest has checked out, ma'am," the Hotel Operator said.

"When?" I asked.

"This afternoon, a late checkout, about two hours ago."

"Thank you." I hung up. I hadn't taken my eyes off Kett. "You're suggesting my Gran is in some sort of coven? Rather than surfing?"

"Perhaps she surfs as well," he answered.

"And this coven was meeting in Tofino?"

Kett furrowed his brow and didn't immediately answer.

"How would you know?"

"The first step of any investigation I conduct is to open communication, or check in, if you will, with the proper people when I arrive in any given city or territory large enough to host a magical community."

"And my Gran is on the Vancouver list?"

"Your grandmother is the list. There was a notation about your mother, of course, but I understand she isn't in residence."

"That's why you showed up at the bakery."

"The building is listed among your grandmother's properties."

I suddenly felt a little ill. I was aware I'd been in blind denial with all the things Kett had been suggesting about my powers, my magic, and parentage. But for some reason, this news that my Gran was someone the vampires had on a list, let alone on a list of people they considered important to speak to ... I knew how political the vampires were supposed to be.

"It is odd that someone of your grandmother's prominence chose Vancouver as her territory."

"She met her husband here ..."

"I see. It was also odd that your existence didn't even warrant a footnote. Hence my surprise in meeting you."

"My magic isn't foot-notable, I guess."

"No? I certainly wouldn't agree. I plan on correcting the list as soon as it is appropriate."

That was just peachy. I loved the idea of being on a vampire list. I swallowed the bile that rose unbidden in my throat and powered forward with the information gathering. "Sienna and Rusty also don't appear on any list."

"No. They were of little consequence."

"And Rusty's mother?"

"The necromancer? Why would I ever need to speak to her?"

"She would be on another list?" I asked. And the vampire grinned as if he was proud of my deduction. The vampires must like their lists, and I'd guessed they had one noting who to avoid as well.

"If she was powerful enough."

"Like my Gran."

"Yes. But anyone on the Convocation would be considered among the most powerful."

"The Convocation. Is that different than the coven you mentioned?"

Kett inclined his head.

I hated his serenity as I worked to piece everything together. "A witches' Convocation, as in a governing body?" I added. "Like your vampire Conclave?"

"If you wish."

The idea of a governing body rang a dim bell for me, of course, as in it had been somewhere on Gran's syllabus years ago. Seeing as I had no interest in anything I wasn't good at — such as magic — I never paid very close attention to such things. But my Gran was supposedly some sort of a member of this Convocation? That didn't sound right; the vampire must be confusing his witches.

"What I find more intriguing is why they all seem to be hiding you," Kett said, casually dropping his next mind-boggling bomb.

I thought about sitting down and not getting up for a while as I pieced bits of a lifetime of secrets, and maybe even betrayal, together. But Kandy shifted impatiently in my peripheral vision and called me back to the more immediate concern. Sienna, my sister, who might be drained of magic and helpless somewhere.

I dialed her number.

Muffled music started to play nearby — "Die Young" by Kesha. Sienna's ringtone.

Kandy crossed to the futon and pulled Sienna's cell phone out from underneath it.

Damn it. I held out my hand for the phone, and Kandy gave it to me without question. As I scrolled through Sienna's favorites, Rusty's number appeared just under my own. I dialed it without hope of him answering. He didn't. I hung up without leaving the vicious message on the tip of my tongue.

I put both phones in my satchel and looked at Kett. "It's seven hours from here to Tofino, if the ferry's on time and there are no issues with the roads."

He nodded his head as if I'd just gifted him with some valuable piece of information.

"Sienna might not have seven hours, or even five more if we assume my Gran is already on her way." Kett didn't react to this. I thought furiously about what to do next ... the implications were staggering and piling up ... the sex-mussed bed, the pentagram, Sienna's 'lost' phone ... my trinket hanging off the nail in the closet ...

Then, fishing my phone back out of my satchel, I made a last-ditch effort to avoid involving myself further in this growing nightmare, and I did something I had never done before in a crisis. I called my mother.

She answered on the first ring. I should have called two days ago. She called me "darling" and I could hear the smile in her voice. She always smiled.

I blurted, "You and Gran have been hiding things. Sienna's missing. And a zombie werewolf just almost incapacitated an ancient vampire, who might still be thinking about draining me."

Kett sighed and muttered, "I'm not that old." I turned my back on him. I was pressing the phone too hard against my ear. It hurt, but I didn't stop.

The smile left my mother's voice. After all these years, I'd finally managed to shake her, though her tone betrayed nothing further. "Did you neutralize the zombie?"

"Yes."

"And Sienna is involved?"

"No, her boyfriend."

"I'll be on the next plane."

"Thanks, Mom." I wouldn't — couldn't — cry with relief, but it was a near thing.

"Cast a seek spell for Sienna," she said then.

"By myself?"

"You have to either wait or do this yourself, Jade. I'll explain why, as well as I know it, later. But ... you mentioned a vampire?"

"Yes."

"The damage is already done if there is a vampire in Vancouver. It is difficult, as I am sure you have discovered, to hide certain things from their senses."

"Like I'm not half-witch, half-human."

"Yes, but I can't address the complications of that over the phone. Not now, Jade. Soon."

I let it drop. My sister was in trouble. I had to focus on her. "And Sienna?"

"Perhaps, if the vampire is friendly enough, he can help you close the circle?"

"All right, but I can't cast something so complicated on my own."

"Pearl ... your Gran, she's just protecting you, Jade. She worries that your magic might backfire and hurt you. The most the seek spell will do is just not work. If you close the circle properly. If you don't cross its boundaries once it's active."

"I know that."

"I know you know. I'll be there as soon as I can. And Jade? Don't worry about your Gran. If you're ready to hear it, I'll tell you anything you want to know."

"Okay." More questions flew through my head. I could hear my mother moving around, opening drawers or doors on her end. I opened my mouth and simply asked, "How far away are you?" So I guess I wasn't ready for any of her promised answers.

"At least four hours. If I can get a flight that quickly." That wasn't what I wanted to hear. I squeezed my eyes shut and tried to persuade myself to not be such a baby.

"Jade?"

"Yeah?"

"You're far more capable than you've ever tried to be." Well, if that wasn't the kettle talking smack about the pot, I didn't know what was. "Call me if you need me. I'll keep the phone on before and after my flight."

"Okay. See you soon."

"Love you, darling."

"I know. Bye." I hung up and took a couple of shaky breaths. Then I turned to Kandy and Kett. Kandy was pacing but stopped when I caught her eye. Kett was imitating a statue — a statue that was obviously listening in on my conversation, but still with complete immobility.

"I need to make two stops. I've never cast alone before. I'll need to do it from the basement of the bakery, if I have any chance, because the last spell I did there actually worked ... at least in part. And I'll need my Gran's spellbook."

"And something personal of Rusty's?" Kett asked.

"No." I swallowed my trepidation, and for a moment it got caught in my throat. "I'll cast for Sienna."

"Better connection."

"More chance it'll work."

"Or you could do it the way I suggested."

"I'm not fiddling with trinkets based on your say so, vampire. Gran's spellbook is my best chance. Keep it simple, stupid."

Kett inclined his head, accepting but doubtful of my choice. Hell, I was doubtful. I'd never even attempted to close a circle on my own before, let alone cast a tracking spell. I needed four things of Sienna's ... that might help anchor and direct the magic.

I strode out of the apartment without another word.

Kandy and Kett followed.

Chapter Eleven

A quick stop at Gran's yielded her spellbook — though not the one that Sienna had used for the reveal spell, which only added to my mounting concern — and a baby blanket from Sienna's childhood. I was pretty sure it was the only family thing my sister still owned. It was blue and crocheted — she was supposed to have been a boy — and unraveling at one end. I wondered why Sienna hadn't fixed it, or asked Gran to. I'd found it draped over the rocking chair in one of the guest rooms where Sienna was known to crash between living arrangements, but I didn't find anything else usable for the spell. It was obvious Sienna hadn't slept here in a while.

I tried to not fret about taking the spellbook through the wards. Sienna had removed the other one without difficulty, but I wouldn't have been surprised if Gran had spelled the books to disintegrate if they were removed. Though maybe anyone keyed to the wards would also neutralize any latent spells also keyed to the wards … yes, all this magic theory was confusing as hell.

I'd pretty much ordered the others to wait in the SUVs, not that they could get through my Gran's wards without my invitation anyway. Anyone keyed specifically to the wards here or at my apartment, for instance, could invite people through. I didn't need any extra magic coming into contact with the heavy-duty spells, though. Kandy had already suggested that Desmond might be able to break through some wards.

I wrapped the spellbook in the baby blanket and stepped out into the darkening evening. I tried to think only one step ahead. Any further and I started to panic.

The two dark SUVs filled Gran's driveway like the foreboding harbingers of doom they actually were. The predators they contained still scared me silly stupid ... predators in human skin, waiting, watching me. I stumbled, my feet betraying the trepidation I was trying to hide from my thoughts.

I climbed into the passenger seat beside Kandy. "We can park in the alley of the bakery," I told the green-haired wolf, happy that my voice sounded sure even though I wasn't.

Kandy put the SUV in gear and waited, her eyes on the rearview mirror, for the other vehicle to clear the drive. Pulling onto Point Grey Road was always a patience game, but werewolves didn't play by those rules. I squeezed my eyes shut and clutched the spellbook to my chest as Kandy darted backward into oncoming traffic. I forgot to breathe — though honestly, it wasn't just the crazy driving freaking me out, though that certainly didn't help. No, it was the next few steps — steps I was fairly certain I couldn't pull off — that were causing my stomach to do flips.

All I could do was try.

I let Kett, Desmond, and Kandy through the bakery wards off the alley entrance. I refused to invite the other two werewolves — hell, I'd only learned one of their names half an hour before — and I refused to give anyone access to my apartment above. Letting them into the bakery was bad enough; I wasn't inviting them in where I slept. Desmond nodded the other two werewolves off into the shadows of the alley without questioning my decision, and I guessed that he was just as happy to have them on watch. I still felt like a bit of a bitch, but that was my own ongoing needing-to-please issue.

The thing was, I didn't think I had enough magic on my own to close the circle, let alone work a seek spell. So I had to bring the other three inside.

With a quick visit upstairs, I found a toothbrush, hairbrush, and sweater of Sienna's. I deemed that bounty good enough and headed into the basement. I would have used the cell phone that Sienna was usually never without but I thought it better if I had the potential of trace DNA to anchor the spell. I didn't stop for the nap or the chocolate that I was crazily craving.

Desmond followed me down the stairs so closely that I could once again feel his breath on the back of my neck. It was in no way comforting.

Kandy was practically vibrating in anticipation of "doing magic," and it set my teeth on edge. I tasked her with lighting the candles that Sienna had neglected to clean up after the botched reveal spell. I should have known my sister wouldn't listen. At the time, I'd been surprised that the spell had worked to any degree; I guessed now that Rusty had been building his power even then. The thought of him bringing stolen power into a witches' circle bothered me. I'd been taught that witch magic was earth bound and a sacred trust ... not about blood and deceit.

"Do you cast down here often?" Kett asked.

"No. Once. Last night. I don't usually cast at all, not unless Sienna drags me into it. This set up is hers ... and Rusty's."

"And the magic residual in here is from last night? What sort of spell did you cast?" Kett was staring thoughtfully at the brick wall where the outline for the doorway had appeared. And, yeah, I could still feel the energy coming off that wall as well, as if the door was sleeping now, but ready and willing to wake.

"A reveal spell. It shouldn't interfere with this new cast, though."

"Ah." The vampire let the subject drop. I was happy he did. I didn't need to be worrying about hidden doors. I needed to be solely focused on my sister; otherwise this had no chance of working.

With a broom I'd brought down from the bakery, I swept the circle that was still inscribed in the dirt, then drew a new one with the broom handle, slightly more to the eastern side of the basement. That wouldn't make any difference; a new circle was a new circle, even if I hadn't relocated it. But I always had an affinity for the eastern placement. The others watched me. I realized there wasn't much else for them to do, but I wished they wouldn't stare.

"Is that okay?" Kandy asked as she crossed to light the candles on the north side of the room. "No pentagram? No salt? Don't witches use salt to seal a circle?" Her disappointment was evident.

"Not me," I murmured. I placed the toothbrush at the north inner edge of the circle, the hairbrush at the south, and the sweater at the west. "Don't touch the items or intersect the circle in any way."

The three nodded in unison. It would have been funny, except I couldn't laugh. I could barely feel anything past the achy lump in my chest that I was pretty sure was my fear for Sienna, scrunched into a tight ball in my heart.

I sat in lotus position at the east side of the circle facing west — my usual spot — and unwrapped the spellbook from the baby blanket.

I folded and placed the blanket inside the edge of the circle just on the other side of my feet. I opened the spellbook across my lap to the page I'd previously marked.

"Okay," I said and looked up at the others. "If you'd grab a candle each, the flame is sort of a focal point for your magic ... in theory. And it'll give you something to focus on."

They did as I bid. The remaining candles ringed the room, and I paused to notice there seemed to be more than before. A lot of black candles. Sienna liked the irony of black candles. The color actually didn't make a difference to the magic, though I noted that both the shifters picked white candles and Kett was holding a red one, so ... seeing as how magic was partly about perception and belief, maybe I was wrong. The extra candles made it pretty clear that Sienna had continued casting here, even though I'd asked her not to.

I glanced around the packed dirt floor. The candlelight cast deep shadows, but I was fairly certain I couldn't see any evidence of residual magic or spell items, other than the faint thrumming from the wall behind me. Sienna had probably just been obsessing over opening the door, if it was, in fact, a door. It should piss me off, but it didn't. I just wanted her safe and sound.

I shook my head and focused on the now. "Kett, if you would sit west?"

The vampire floated down into lotus position like he was sitting on a velvet pillow rather than a dirt floor. He didn't question my placement choice; his face was more serene than his usual icy stoicism, though. Placing him west put him in Sienna's spot, because I was guessing he was the strongest magic user of the three. At least, according to him, he had been before his current vampiric incarnation.

I gestured Desmond to my right — north — and Kandy to my left — south.

Kandy's eyes gleamed green in the candlelight. Her fingers were creating dents in the three-inch wide candle she held. Desmond kept his eyes on the middle of the circle, and was more contained than I'd ever seen him. I imagined he was doing it for my benefit. Neither McGrowly nor his half-beast personas would be helpful here, though they were both riddled with explosive, tangible magic. I marveled at his ability to rein himself in.

"Do we join hands?" Kandy asked eagerly.

"No!" I responded sharply, and instantly regretted my tone. "I don't ... I'm not sure I could balance your magic if I was touching you. This is a junior sort of spell, not even the exact wording is important. It shouldn't need that much power. We're simply scrying Sienna."

"Without water? Or a bowl?" Kett asked.

"The circle is the mirror. Sienna's items are the focus. Our magic is the conduit. Or engine, if you prefer."

Kett nodded, and I took that as a signal to begin.

"First we close the circle ... blow a bit of your breath through the flame of your candle. Not enough to blow it out, but toward the circle, like this." I blew a light huff of breath on the pink pillar candle Kandy had lit for me, then placed it on the very edge of the circle, careful to not overlap the line I had drawn in the dirt. I could feel a little bit of my magic hum in the candle. Kett went next, placing his red candle directly opposite mine. The hum in my candle increased, though I doubt anyone could feel it but me. We hadn't closed the circle so carefully when we'd done the reveal spell, and then

I'd crossed it to add my blood to the bowl of water. I wasn't repeating that mistake here.

Kandy and then Desmond added their candles and their magic to the circle. As Desmond placed his candle down, the circle snapped closed. Just like that, I could feel the ring of magic as if it were slightly raised, maybe an inch or so, off the ground. If one of us snuffed out our candle or intersected the circle, it would break just as easily as it had formed, but I was happy nonetheless that we'd managed this set-up.

I referenced the spellbook spread in my lap, but like I'd told the others, this spell was born of intention — not fancy words or special ingredients. I rested my hands on the thick parchment paper, feeling the indentations of the handwritten words. I wondered if Gran had crafted this particular spell, or if it had been her mother, or grandmother. I let myself sink into the stillness, the simplicity of my steady breathing. I listened. I heard the long, deep breaths of Kandy and Desmond. Kett either didn't breathe or was too far away to hear. I opened myself to the magic in the room. The taste of Desmond's, Kandy's, and Kett's magic flooded my mouth. The shifter magic was earthy chocolate, as it had been on the dance floor. I pushed the immediate thought of Hudson from my mind. The vampire's magic was cool — peppermint icing with something else underneath, something spicy, stronger than cinnamon or cloves. I couldn't place it, so I let it go.

"Sienna," I murmured, picturing my sister as I'd last seen her — straight, dark hair falling over her darkly lined brown eyes, mouth turned up in a smirk. I'd half-hoped to find her in my apartment, her cell phone simply forgotten at Rusty's, but my place had felt hours empty ...

"Where are you, Sienna?" I whispered, as I opened my eyes to gaze on the center of the circle.

The magic called forth by us swirled as a light breeze would, over and around the four items placed in the circle. It flitted to the edge in front of Kett, Kandy, Desmond, and me, almost as if trying to return the bit of breath we'd offered it, but it could not cross out of the closed circle.

"We seek Sienna, who we believe to be in some sort of trouble. Sienna, let us see you."

The magic swirled through the items again, but this time it felt odd. It was less focused than before, as if I'd confused it somehow. As if I'd not spoken the truth as I knew it. I must have said something wrong, given it some sort of conflicting direction.

Self-doubt rose in my chest. The magic dimmed further.

"Damn," I muttered. I shut my eyes to try to gather the magic up again.

"Is something wrong?" Kandy asked, but no one answered her.

I tried again. I felt the residual magic unconsciously woven into the handwritten spell beneath my hands, and I thought about how it would be so much easier to simply transfer this bit of magic through the circle, using the baby blanket as a conduit. Then my Gran's words and thoughts could anchor the spell. Magic didn't work like that, though ... at least it shouldn't ... but if I really focused my intention, then maybe ...

I lifted the spellbook to my face by instinct. I said, "Sienna," so that my breath blew across the pages toward the circle.

The magic responded by coalescing into the center of the circle, hovering about two inches above the dirt floor. I saw it as multicolored — shades of green, red, gold, and blue. I wondered if this was an actual manifestation of our magic.

"Sienna ... show me my sister," I asked the magic, which collected into a small sphere at my coaxing. The colors in the sphere whirled and resolved, and I swore, just for a moment, that I saw Sienna's face within the sphere. Kett stiffened across the circle from me, so I was sure he'd seen it as well.

"Please, where is she? Show us a location." The magic whirled and clouded again. I could see the edges of some sort of building. "What is that? A warehouse?" I asked. Then I pushed the magic a bit, pushed my energy and focus toward it. "Please, she's in trouble. We need to help her."

The magic collapsed with an audible pop that felt like a pinch in my mind. I gasped.

"But ... I ... it was working!" I reached out to grab Kandy's and Desmond's bare forearms, to grab their magic, to focus the spell.

It was a bad idea. All my senses were wide open, and there was a reason I was very careful not to touch on the dance floor, or to bring magical people home to my bed for skin-to-skin contact. Magic, almost like electricity, ran through each of my palms and up my arms. The hand touching Kandy felt warm and tingly, but the hand touching Desmond practically seared me.

I stifled a scream and yanked my hands away. The rest of the magic in the room dissipated. Desmond, looking rather amused, inspected the pink burn mark on his forearm.

"I'm sorry. I thought I might be able to bolster the spell. I just ... I suck."

"This isn't your sort of magic," Kett said, his gaze on me steady. "Maybe with other practitioners here, you could anchor the magic and manifest the spell, but you're working against your strengths. You shouldn't be pushing the magic away. That isn't what you do when you make trinkets, is it?"

I didn't want to hear his stupid theories about my magic. I'd trained under my Gran for years. If I was capable of more, certainly she would have known, certainly she would have directed me ... But what about the trinkets? And the knife? Why would the vampire lie? What would he have to gain?

I realized that I'd woven my fingers through the rings of my necklace. No one else had moved. They sat patiently holding their candles and watching me.

I looked down at the ring charms now on my fingers. I looked at the items laid around the circle. I thought about how I made the trinkets, how I let my fingers surf the tiny drops of residual or natural magic in the items I collected. How I brought that magic together, unified it.

I pulled my fingers from the rings. I felt calm, centered. I ran my fingers along the necklace until I hit a large man's gold ring. I'd found it in a pawnshop last year, on its own, not as a pair like I'd found the ones in the antique shops. There was something inherently sad in a man pawning his wedding ring. It raised so many questions, but now the drop of magic within this ring felt right ... somehow.

"Can you break the solder?" I asked Desmond. "Not the chain, just this connection point?"

Desmond leaned into me. I noticed his forearm was now unmarked, the magical burn completely healed. He delicately grasped the ring I held out to him between his thumb and forefinger, and gave it a slight twist. The ring came off in his fingers. He dropped it into my open palm.

"I'll need the hairbrush as well," I murmured, trying to surf the calm from before and to not panic about my necklace being ruined. I could solder the ring back on in minutes, no worries.

Desmond passed me the hairbrush and I pulled off a clump of hair. Sienna's straight, dark hair. I smoothed it and twisted it into a string. Then I sank further down into my soft focus, my meditative state. I shut everything else out — every worry, every fear — as I wound the twisted hair around the ring. I smoothed the residual magic of hair and ring with my own. I could actually see how I did this now ... like my magic was mortar or solder. When I added bits to the trinkets or rings to my necklace, I must have instinctively done the same thing — mortaring the residual magic with my own, and therefore making a new object altogether. I pushed these revelations aside as I focused on knotting the ends of the twisted hair together. There was just enough to manage this. Then I slipped the ring onto my left index finger.

It just fit.

I looked up to find the vampire smirking at me, but I ignored him. I closed the spellbook, unaware that I'd held it open on my lap this entire time. Clutching it to my chest, I stood. Then, awkwardly, I stuffed the sweater and other things in my bag. It wasn't a good idea to leave personal items lying around in a witches' circle.

I crossed to the stairs, looking back to the others, who'd risen but not yet followed. "What are you waiting for?" I asked. "We have a killer to catch, don't we?"

"Oh, now you get cocky, dowser?" Desmond said. "Wait until you find her, then we'll bow to your magic prowess." He snorted, and then twisted his lips into a begrudging smile. Somehow, with this look of approval on his face, he was suddenly damn sexy. No, I chided myself — scary monster men are not sexy. I tore my eyes away from him, running my thumb over the ring and thinking of Sienna instead.

The ring grew warm on my finger, then cooled just as suddenly. It was up for a game of hotter/colder. I'd always been a stellar player.

Chapter Twelve

After all the terrifying buildup of fear and anticipation, it was a painfully short ride.

Hazarding a guess based on the warehouse-looking buildings I'd seen in the circle, I had Kandy turn east on West Fourth Avenue. The ring agreed with this direction, and I didn't feel the need to turn off Fourth until we'd passed Cambie Street about seven minutes later.

Desmond and Kett had climbed into the backseat of Kandy's car. I was surprised McGrowly fit back there, despite the overall size of the SUV. But then, it was a giant SUV. I imagined the others followed in the second vehicle, but I didn't pay much attention. I tried to just focus on the tiny pulse of magic I wore on my finger. It felt fragile, as if the wrong thought or emotion would unbalance it. I kept my mind as clear as possible. It was a struggle. I just tried to imagine myself baking or making a trinket, and the peace those activities usually brought ... except I wasn't actually doing either of those things.

"You think the trinkets, the baking, are simply my way of ... distracting my magic?" I directed the murmured thought to Kett, but didn't bother to turn around.

"Manifestations, maybe," he answered.

"It was my Gran who always directed me toward those sorts of things ... sewing ... knitting ..."

"Ah." The vampire got it without me elaborating. My Gran had been distracting me, focusing me on mundane tasks so that I worked my magic on a tiny scale — so tiny I didn't even know I was doing it. The question now was why?

We passed Quebec Street on our way to Main and the ring suddenly cooled ... though perhaps it had been cooling before but I'd only just felt it. "Stop, stop! We've gone too far."

Kandy turned right at the next street and then right again to head back west for a couple of blocks. I refocused, pushing thoughts of Gran's possible duplicity out of my head and thinking only of finding my sister.

I hoped that the fact the ring worked meant Sienna was still alive.

This area of Vancouver was undergoing a construction boom, and not many warehouse-type buildings existed anymore. They'd all been replaced by glass and steel towers that occupied the bulk of the city's skyline on the other side of the inlet. This tower development, triggered by the 2010 Winter Olympics, had spread across False Creek. It now almost completely filled the north edge of the area between lower Main and Cambie Street.

There had been some holdouts to this development, though, and I was grateful we hadn't needed to go further east or into Richmond. That was assuming the ring was actually leading us somewhere, however, and that I wasn't just making everything up in my magic-addled mind.

"Slow down ... please," I said. The ring was the warmest it had been since I put it on, but began to cool slightly. "Loop back a block, please."

Kandy took a left and then another left, but when she turned left the second time the ring cooled further.

"Stop. We're near, but I think I need to walk." Kandy pulled the SUV to the curb and we piled out.

The street was dark, though a block north, the new towers were ablaze with light. A block uphill and south, the few homes left in the area promised a warm meal and a soft pillow, but we weren't looking for either. I walked west on the south side of the street. The others trailed behind me. Lara and Jeremy had parked right behind Kandy and were following us up the sidewalk.

A low row of warehouses — as best as I could see between the streetlights — occupied both sides of the block. Most of the buildings had signs declaring their occupants — tile, carpet and marble dealers; some sort of woodworkers' co-op; and a small deli/caterer that didn't bother opening evenings.

One two-storey building, its blue paint in need of a refresher coat, ran half the south side of the block but didn't have any immediately obvious business signs. I paused at the edge of the small, two-lane parking lot that fronted the building. There were no lights on, either inside or out. The warehouse had a flat roof and lots of dark windows, some covered.

"For lease," Kett said, pointing to a sign I hadn't seen in the dark. "It was on my list to check, but then I found you at the bakery." The lease was being offered by Godfrey Properties.

"Gran," I whispered. "Gran owns this."

Desmond suddenly reached down into my satchel and pulled out Sienna's sweater. I quashed the impulse to slap his hand, though I doubt I could have reacted quickly enough to hit him.

He held the sweater out to Lara and Jeremy. They, as if on cue, began stripping off their clothes. I looked back at the warehouse, twisting the ring on my finger and hoping no one was working late in any of the nearby buildings.

"It's a big building. Do you have a plan?" I asked.

"We'll split up," Desmond answered. "You and Kett with the ring and me with my wolves." That didn't sound like a great idea to me — or for Rusty and Sienna. However, I was pretty sure any argument would be ignored, if not punished. Yeah, I still didn't trust a single one of the people I was with.

A pulse of magic hit me from the side. The wolves had transformed. Not into the half-beast creature Desmond had become to fight Kett, but into actual, though rather large, wolves ... big, gray, green-eyed wolves. One was slightly smaller than the other — I guessed it was Lara. Jeremy was a little leggy, like he hadn't reached his full size yet. I made sure to not meet their gaze as Desmond held the sweater out for them to smell.

With a yip, the wolves sprang forward into the parking lot, noses to the ground. They sniffed around in a zigzag sort of pattern, dividing the asphalt between them.

We followed, crossing the bit of grass between the sidewalk and the parking lot. Desmond and Kett were practically glued to my sides, Kandy behind us. As we approached the building, I felt a tinge of that sickly magic from the morgue.

"Wait," I called to the wolves ... too late. They caught some scent at the same moment, springing forward toward the east side door only to run smack into an invisible ward. The wolves collapsed like they'd hit a brick wall. One of them didn't get up ... the leggy one, Jeremy. Lara stumbled to her feet and staggered a few steps back.

I sprinted past her, the ring burning on my finger. I held my hand up to the ward, not touching — just trying to sense it. Kandy knelt before Lara as Desmond reached down to haul Jeremy away. At the touch of his alpha's hand, Jeremy twitched, then struggled to his feet. Both wolves seemed dazed. That was some nasty magic.

Kett stood beside me and mimicked my movement, holding his hand palm forward to the magic shield barring us from approaching the building. "Can you break it?" I asked the vampire, hoping that was within his power. I didn't want to wait for Gran, who was the only person I knew who was powerful enough to break wards.

"It's nowhere near as strong as the wards on your apartment," he replied.

"Of course not," I scoffed. "Those are Gran's wards. These are thinner, and different magic. They're rooted away from the building, unlike personal wards, the ones you find on residences like my apartment and Gran's house. This isn't a home. It doesn't have the strength inherent in that concept." I shut up, realizing the vampire looked far too interested in what I was saying ... was I blabbing witch secrets? Was any of this a secret?

That was a concept I hadn't thought of before. The tenor of the *Compendium* had made it pretty clear that the Adept didn't interact often or willingly —

"Similar construction," Kett said, calling my attention back to the wards.

"Are we going to break through or not?" Desmond interrupted, his voice edged with anger — and maybe just a bit of the beast within him.

Kett smiled and gestured toward the building. "Have at them, lord alpha."

Desmond took a couple of steps back and pulled his T-shirt off. He'd changed into a green shirt sometime between the morgue and Rusty's apartment. Apparently, he didn't want to ruin it like he had with the last one. Kandy started to do the same, but I didn't really notice the green-haired werewolf as the sight of Desmond's chest momentarily blinded me. Even in the low light, it was magnificently muscled. Too bad he was such an asshole. Why did assholes have the best chests? Kandy had started to pull off her sports bra as I came to my senses.

"Wait!" I cried. "Are you just going to bulldoze through it?"

"The four of us should be able to crack it. I could probably do so myself," Desmond answered as he undid his belt buckle. My mounting frustration made it easier to tear my eyes away from wanting to see what lay behind his zipper.

"Not without a huge backlash," I said. "And it might kill you."

"It won't give me more than a headache," Desmond snarled back. Kandy averted her eyes from us both, and I had a feeling that I was about to cross some line if I pushed or questioned Desmond further. I yanked my own eyes away from McGrowly's lightly furred pectorals. Yes, he was suddenly close enough that his broad, gorgeous chest was pretty much the only thing I could see. I turned to glare at Kett, who smiled.

"You're baiting them," I said, more stating the obvious than accusing him.

Kett shrugged.

I shifted my focus up to Desmond's chin. The shifter was directing his scowl to the vampire, who didn't have a problem with meeting his gaze. "Plus," I added, "if they break through like that, they alert the caster for sure."

"More ideas and less critique, dowser," Desmond said. He hadn't pulled his shirt back on, and neither had Kandy. The color of her sports bra perfectly matched the werewolf's green hair. She smiled when she caught me noticing.

I turned back to the ward and raised the hand wearing the ring. I pressed this hand against the ward's magic and watched it react — swirling toward the ring, not away from it.

"The ring?" Kett said quietly. By his own admission, he couldn't see magic like me, but he must be able to sense it to some extent.

"Maybe," I answered. "You'd all need to be in contact with me if I'm to pull you through with it."

Kett immediately curled his fingers around my right hand, as if this was some invitation he'd been eagerly awaiting. Desmond stepped up on my left — he'd put his shirt back on, thank God — and placed his hand around my waist. Kandy curled her fingers around my belt at the small of my back, while the two wolves pushed inside Kett's and Desmond's legs to press their shoulders against my thighs.

I shuddered as all their magic welled around me. There was another reason I avoided contact with the Adept — it was too easy to get lost in the wave. Five powerful magical beings were a lot of wave.

I felt my focus splinter, and gasped as the ring burned hotter. I struggled to pull my attention back. Desmond's arm was delightfully warm cupped around my waist ... I hadn't realized the night was quite cool. In contrast, Kett's skin was almost icy against my right hand, his fingers individually defined where they touched my skin. I shuddered again, then rather embarrassingly felt my nipples harden against my tank top — the silk tunic I wore over it would leave nothing to the imagination. I moaned, lightly but still more than audible.

"All right, dowser?" Desmond asked. "We'll move with you."

Move with you. My mind exploded with the possibilities. Oh, sweet Jesus. My unintentional abstinence was really not helping —

"Breathe," Kett suggested. His cool voice actually felt like it was moving over my shoulder, along my collarbone and dipping down —

I clenched my teeth. I could see Kett's and Desmond's profiles in my peripheral vision. Thank God no one was looking at me.

I exhaled all the air in my lungs as I pressed my hand against the ward. The magic of the shield danced against my skin, resisting me. It hurt. That helped. I concentrated on the way the magic reacted to the ring, and specifically to Sienna's hair twined there. I felt the pressure ease, then imagined that ease moving down my hand, my arm, coasting over me and falling over the others. Then I pushed through the wards.

It hurt like hell. The wards seemed to know they should keep us out, but they couldn't quite grasp onto our magic to block us. A pure human wouldn't have even noticed the barrier.

I ground my teeth and tried to ignore the pain. The others got hit worse. Desmond snarled. Kandy stifled a moan. Jeremy, still in wolf form, stumbled and fell away from my leg, panting in pain. Desmond grabbed him by the scruff of his neck, and then we were on the other side of the ward.

I immediately stepped away from the others. They let me go. Desmond knelt on one knee by the hurt wolf.

I resisted pulling my tunic and tank top away from my erect nipples. To calm my racing heart, I kept my back to the rest of the group under the guise of surveying the building.

"The wards were keyed to allow your sister to pass through them," Kett said. He'd stepped next to me and was speaking in a hushed tone, but by the way the shifters stiffened, I had no doubt that they heard him. They didn't look or interrupt us, though.

"I did consider that ... or he's used her magic." My voice broke and I snapped my mouth shut. I shoved my right hand in my jeans pocket, letting the ring on the left guide me toward the door that had drawn the wolves' attention earlier. This attempt to act normal, and my worry for Sienna, helped my pent-up arousal abate further.

The others followed. Kandy stepped in front of me to snap the lock on the outer door before I could stop her. No magic sparked at the werewolf's contact, so the door wasn't spelled. Whoever had set up the outer ward had banked on it being enough of a deterrent. Or maybe they hadn't wanted to waste too much magic on defensive spells when there were werewolves to drain and corpses to raise. What a delightful thought.

The door didn't open easily, but a swift kick from Kandy remedied that. I was seriously happy this wasn't a residential neighborhood. Otherwise, I would have been sure the police were already on their way.

Desmond's hand on my shoulder stopped me from following Kandy into the building. I guessed that I was still precious cargo or helpful prisoner, depending on the perspective. I half turned to Desmond but didn't look directly at him. I wasn't pleased with my reaction to his touch — like he was a warm cashmere blanket and a cup of dark, hot chocolate rolled into one sexy, well-muscled, dangerous package. I could only hope he hadn't felt my mounting excitement as I pulled him through the wards.

And that he didn't feel my pulse jump when he touched my shoulder. Actually, it was odd he was touching me at all, when he'd been careful to minimize contact before.

"You should let me go through ahead in case there are any more wards or spell traps," I said.

Desmond shrugged and shouldered by me in response. Well, that was definitive. The wolves followed at his heels, spreading out to explore the first room at some unseen/unheard order from him.

"Shifters," Kett muttered in my right ear. I jumped at his proximity. His smile with all its white teeth easily cut through the darkness of the night. "Don't like being told what to do. These three are his enforcers, and the alpha hates how the politics of pack structure mean that they go into danger before him. Most alphas don't make it through their first five years of being pack leader. Stubborn."

"Stupid," I countered, and Kett gave me one of his blazingly human smiles. I looked away, not offering one of my automatic response smiles. I was sure the vampire had known exactly how I would react to all their magic so close ... so intimate, and so utterly delicious ...

I shook off the memory and tried to ignore the residual magic still pulsing lightly through my body. I had a feeling it was all going to get worse before it got better. Though before I stepped forward into the warehouse with the vampire at my side, I did wonder if I could drown in magic ... what a blissful way to go ...

The further I moved into and through the warehouse, the less I could see. After I stumbled a second time, a growled order from Desmond brought the two wolves back to press to either side of my legs. Delightful. My very own seeing eye dogs, guaranteed to get you through the darkness — unless they got hungry and stopped for a human snack. I guess the idea of splitting up hadn't lasted very long.

I'm sure that in the daylight or under fluorescents, the building was tidy and fairly empty. Shelves, chairs, and perhaps partition walls were stacked neatly to the sides. At least I was pretty sure that's what the boxy, long shapes were against the walls. I walked with my hands spread in front of me, feeling for magic ahead, the ring consistently hot on my finger.

The wolves pressed against me if I wandered too close to anything. No one else stumbled, of course. Predators, it seemed, had no issues seeing in the dark. *What large eyes you have ... all the better to see you ...* in the dark when you're vulnerable and afraid and oddly turned on ... okay, maybe that was just me.

The ring led me to a set of stairs. Thankfully, a bit of moonlight filtered down from an upper landing window. The stairs were painted wood, likely as old as the building and not blocked by any doors. I was fairly certain that would violate building code these days. Then I wondered why my mind cared about, and supplied, such stupid observations in stressful situations. I was annoying myself.

I stepped up and could only hear my own footfalls and the light click of the wolves' nails on the wood. The other three, somewhere behind me, were deadly quiet. I would have thought the slow pace would chafe them, and that they'd prefer to rip and plunder through the building. Obviously, I was wrong. They were patient hunters, and somehow that bothered me more. It was like thinking of Rusty as a monster, a murderer, when only a couple of hours ago, he'd been a mild-mannered friend. I didn't like how the shapeshifter package didn't accurately advertise the contents.

On the landing, I picked up on a pocket of Rusty's 'unliving' magic that made my empty stomach roll. I moaned with it and felt instantly stupid when the wolves pressed against me to halt my movement. Their heads turned, assessing whatever danger I could see but they couldn't.

"It's all right," I whispered as quietly as I could verbalize. "Just a me thing." I grasped the hilt of my jade knife, still in its invisible sheath on my right hip. The effects of the 'unliving' magic dissipated.

A cool hand slid over mine, and I was pleased I didn't screech at the touch. Kett whispered into my right ear, his breath not as cool as his skin. "Leave it sheathed. Too dangerous in the dark."

I nodded and tried to ignore the hair prickling on the back of my neck. I hadn't realized he was so close. He masked his magic somehow, or my senses were already overloaded. Monsters slid in and out of the dark all around me ... how the hell did I get here again?

I made it up to the second floor, which wasn't as open as the main floor had been. A long hallway ran east to west. Windows on the north side of the building helped with illumination, but everything was still deeply shadowed. A few doors, well spread out from each other, stood open. Farther along the hall, more doors were closed.

I stepped west and the ring instantly cooled. I pivoted to correct my direction. Kandy stepped in front of me, half blocking me from the first closed door we approached. When I held my ring hand up to the door handle, it cooled, so I shook my head at the green-haired werewolf. We continued along the hall.

The silence was tense and strange. Shouldn't we be able to hear the traffic, or even just the noises of the building? Was it ever this quiet so near the city? The wolf on my left — Lara, I thought — pressed her nose to my palm. I dug my fingers into the hair on the back of her neck, aware I was treating a hundred-and-fifteen-or-so-pound wolf like a dog. A wolf that could rip off my arm with a single nod of its head. Ah, well. I was obviously desperate for comfort.

Ahead of me, Kandy slipped in and out of several open rooms, but I hardly spared them a glance as I passed. I also hardly needed the ring to guide me now — because the presence of the 'unliving' magic continued to grow the closer we got to the east side of the building. It was somehow hulking and malicious, though it had no mass.

Finally, we reached the closed door at the end of the hall. The magic was thick there, making it slightly difficult to breathe. Nothing like the morgue, but putrid nonetheless.

As Kandy reached for the doorknob, I loosed my hand from the wolf's ruff to grab her shoulder. She turned back to look at me, the green gleam of her eyes luminescing. She flashed me the whites of her teeth in what could have been a smile, but might also have been a warning.

I held my left hand up to the door, the ring searing my finger so hotly that I was forced to pull it off. It cooled in my palm instantly. I had let go of my knife hilt and was instantly hit by an extra onslaught of 'unliving' magic. I thought I might vomit, but didn't. I sucked on the burned spot on my index finger and tucked the ring in my jeans front pocket.

Blowing on the now wet burn to cool it, I held my right hand up to the door. I couldn't sense anything particularly magical about it, though I shuddered at the magic behind it. I fretted for a moment too long, not sure if I was so overwhelmed by all the surrounding magic that I was missing something on the door itself. Kandy brushed my hand away and kicked it open.

As Kandy and the wolves surged into the room beyond, I was literally pinned in place by the onslaught of 'unliving' magic. I was unable to close my eyes to the terrible sight revealed beyond the door as it seared itself into my brain — as if I'd never again be able to close my eyes to what I saw there. I would never forget the dozens of candles that illuminated the mangled body, its four limbs all that was left to identify it as human on first glance. The body was sprawled in a black-painted pentagram painted dead center in the middle of the room, twice the size of the one at Rusty's apartment. The carpet and plywood had been pulled back and piled in one corner, revealing wood slat flooring underneath. Pools of blood surrounded the body, running over the edges of the pentagram as if it had been lacerated repeatedly and left to bleed out. Whatever spell had been at work here was also dead. The blood that had seeped across the pentagram boundary made that obvious. Not that that helped with my revulsion.

In the other corner, my sister cowered in a protection circle, though I wasn't completely sure in that first glance if she wasn't dead and the circle wasn't actually a prison.

I turned and vomited bile all over the doorframe as Desmond and Kett brushed by me. Only a second or so had passed.

Sienna screamed. I looked up, still fighting my heaving stomach to see her scream again and press herself as far away from the oncoming wolves as the circle would let her. She raised her badly slashed forearms to cover her face. The wolves stopped before they crashed into her circle, then nosed around it.

Kandy was suddenly back at my side and urging me forward to the body in the pentagram, but I really didn't want to see it. I wiped the spittle from my face, a sudden tenderness in my jawline calling my attention to the fact that I had a splitting headache — the instant kind you get from champagne, but far worse than I'd ever felt. Like my brain was bleeding.

Rusty was the bloody body sprawled in the pentagram.

Something had eaten his eyes out, as well as all the soft parts of his belly ... and below —

I moaned and turned away to heave again. Nothing came out this time, but still my stomach tried again and again. A cool hand held my hair away from my fevered, drenched face. It felt good, so I didn't fight the touch.

As I straightened, using various parts of Kett as handholds, I was aware of Desmond and Kandy stepping away from Rusty's body to cross to Sienna's circle.

My body trembled with post-vomiting shakes. Maybe thirty seconds had passed.

"Can you break the circle, dowser?" Desmond asked over his shoulder.

Sienna raised her eyes from her hands and saw me. "Jade! Oh, God, Jade!" she screamed. "Please, please, Jade. Help me."

I rushed toward her. Desmond stepped back, but Kett was there to block my way. "Is it a prison or a protection circle?" the vampire asked.

"What does it matter?" I hissed as I tried to dart around him.

"Did she close it herself or not?"

"Of course I closed it," Sienna shrieked. "That thing ... that thing was eating Rusty!"

Relief flooded through me. I know, weird timing, but if something else, some other creature was involved, then ... "It wasn't Rusty, Sienna? He wasn't killing and —"

"No, it was him, Jade." Sienna sobbed. "I didn't know. He was drunk on the power. He tried to call something into being, but it was trapped in the pentagram with him. It ate him. When Rusty died, it ... it faded away, but first it tried to get me. Jade, please." Sienna's terrified eyes darted around at the werewolves and the vampire. She didn't need me to break the circle; she could do that herself. She was just too scared to do so.

A lot of things didn't make sense, like why Rusty would have been in the pentagram in the first place instead of casting from safety, or how a being trapped there could have forced Sienna to slice her own forearms to create the protection circle. But I knew nothing about the dark side of blood magic, and I just saw my terrified sister and wanted to take her home. I held my hands out to her.

"Safe passage," she said. It was an oddly formal request.

"I'll take you home," I answered.

"No, Jade. It's them I'm worried about." Sienna, not quite so terrified now, was looking beyond my shoulder. And, indeed, all the eyes on Sienna were glowing in a most intimidating way.

"I'm going to take my sister home," I declared.

After a moment, Kett nodded his head. Desmond turned away with a growl.

Sienna sighed and scrubbed her foot across the edge of the circle. She'd sealed it in blood — her own,

I imagined — for it to work. The blood smudged underneath her foot. The magic protecting her fell as she reached forward to grasp my hands.

Her magic felt odd. But then, I wasn't sure I was exactly in tune with it anymore. I felt coated in the 'unliving' magic Rusty had been wielding. I didn't want to think about Sienna cutting herself to inscribe a rudimentary but powerful protection circle. She must have been terrified and out of options. Blood magic was temperamental and addictive. A last resort. I was probably just picking up on the residual of that.

"We'll have questions," Kett said.

Once again, he sounded like he was standing too near me. I turned my head to find he was at least a couple of feet away, so maybe the room just had weird acoustics.

The vampire stared at me for a moment, then turned back to the body in the pentagram. The wolves and Kandy were sweeping the room, presumably for clues.

Sienna hadn't moved out of the circle. "I'm scared, Jade," she whispered.

I almost told her not to bother, that every ear in the room could hear her anyway. Instead, I squeezed her hands. They were cold. I couldn't remember what Desmond had done with her sweater, and I'd wrapped the spellbook in her baby blanket and locked it in my office safe before I'd left the bakery. I had nothing to warm her with.

"It's going to be all right," I said. "Gran is on her way —"

"Tonight?" Sienna interrupted.

"Yeah, so it'll be okay soon. Well, except for ... except for —"

"Rusty." Sienna spat the name like she was more disappointed than upset. I guess if my boyfriend had used me as a power boost, I wouldn't be happy either.

"It'll take us a while to clear up here," Kett called out as he fished what looked to be an iPad mini out of his invisible satchel. As he started shooting pictures of Rusty's body with the device's camera, I tried to not boggle at the idea of a tech-savvy vampire.

"Will they let me pass?" Sienna asked. She looked ready to open a vein to reform the circle.

"Yeah. They said so, didn't they?"

"Jade, I … thank you for finding me."

I smiled and loosened my hands from hers to pull my necklace off. I dropped it over Sienna's head and neck, and she clasped it with surprise. I'd noticed she wasn't wearing any trinkets. "There. That's the best protection I can offer."

I let go of the necklace. Instantly, I felt the sickening magic surrounding me dig a little deeper into my skin.

"Thank you," Sienna said. She cast her eyes oddly to the ground. The gesture was similar to the deference the wolves used with Desmond, but it also looked like she might be hiding her thoughts. I was so overwhelmed and so over reading every little thing.

"I can't stay here any longer," I said, and Sienna dutifully stepped out of the circle. I quickly crossed back to the door with her trailing behind me. I couldn't look at the body, and Sienna couldn't look away.

"I have to get out of here," I said to no one in particular, but it was Kett who responded by pressing a set of car keys into my hand. Sienna had shied away from him when he approached.

"All right to drive?" he asked.

"Once I get away from here."

"I'll call," the vampire said, his eyes and frown now focused on the necklace around Sienna's neck.

"We'll be by later, dowser," Desmond called after me.

But it was Sienna who looked back, not me, as I shouldered my way out the door and away from the terrible magic as quickly as possible. Without the protection of the necklace, I was so nauseated I couldn't think. Funny ... I hadn't even known what I'd made or was making as I collected those rings and their residual magic together. And now I could barely function without them around my neck.

"And who was that?" Sienna asked as we hit the stair landing.

"Who? Kett?" I had a feeling she'd been talking and asking questions all the way down the hall without me hearing her.

"No, all muscle and lots of trouble."

"Desmond, Lord and Alpha of the West Coast North American Pack." I said it without any of the humor the pompous title should inspire.

"Tasty," Sienna said.

I was awed at her ability to prioritize. "Yeah, he'd say the same to you, right after you said 'what big teeth you have.' "

"Oh, he's a wolf."

I shrugged. And breathed in deeply as we exited the warehouse. I noticed the malignant ward seemed to have dissipated as we crossed through the parking lot to the sidewalk. Sienna was still holding me like I might fall, and I shifted my arm behind her until we were both half hugging each other.

"Are you ... are you going to be okay?" I asked, aware my question was premature, but childishly needing some assurance.

"Yeah … they seemed … cool," Sienna answered.

"Who? The wolves and the vampire? Cool is not the word I would use."

"Powerful, then. It's never a bad thing to have powerful friends," Sienna said, her voice verging on wistful.

"They're not my friends."

"They had your back when you came to rescue me."

That wasn't exactly how it went down, but I didn't want to get into explaining the sequence of events to Sienna. I didn't want her feeling like a footnote in all of this.

"No. We have each other's backs."

"Sister-witch power. Just us against the world." Sienna murmured the silly childhood mantra we always evoked whenever teenaged life had gotten one of us down.

"Exactly." I tried to laugh, but it came out forced and a little shrill, so I gave Sienna a reassuring squeeze. Her sharp intake of breath reminded me that all wasn't right with my sister. "Hospital?"

"No," Sienna quickly answered. "These cuts are shallow, and … you know they'd call the police and a shrink probably. Will you just take me home, sister?"

I shifted my arm up around her shoulder and led my sister from the warehouse to the SUV. I'd thought the worst tonight. I'd thought her dead. I wasn't sure what I would have done if that had been her half-eaten in the pentagram, rather than Rusty. I pushed the nasty thought away and took Sienna home.

Chapter Thirteen

I'd never been so relieved to feel the protection wards on my apartment slide over me as I did that night. In fact, I'm not sure I'd ever noticed them as intensely before. My sense of relief was palatable, and coming home tasted a lot like my go-to one-bowl chocolate cupcakes.

The apartment felt foreign, though, like I'd been gone weeks instead of hours. Sienna, still clutching my necklace around her neck, fell onto the couch and instantly burrowed underneath one of Gran's woven blankets. She refused to move further, muttering that she'd shower the blood off later.

No matter how exhausted I was, leaving my sister bloody and bruised on the couch wasn't going to happen. I bathed her arms in diluted tea tree oil and wrapped them in strips torn from an old cotton pillowcase. I had no idea if that was the correct approach, but I had to do something.

Sienna watched me with sleep-hooded eyes but didn't pester me with questions. I, on the other hand, desperately wanted to ask her about Rusty. About his mother and his other friends and how this could have gotten so out of control. When had Sienna known? Not until tonight? How had Rusty hidden everything from her? How and when had Rusty managed to kill Hudson?

Sienna sucked in her breath as I dabbed the tea tree oil-soaked cloth over a particularly deep cut on her left forearm. I quashed all the questions in my head and just focused on caring for my sister. Someone would have answers tomorrow — probably Gran when she swept into town to clean up the mess.

"We've never left such a big pile before," I said. And felt instantly deplorable for referring to the bodies of Hudson and Rusty as a 'pile.'

"What?" Sienna asked.

I shook my head and tucked the blanket up higher underneath her chin.

"Thank you," she murmured as I stood to take the bloody rags and used tea tree oil into the kitchen. I left the light on over the stove so Sienna wouldn't wake and find herself in darkness, but I was pretty sure that wasn't enough to give her sweet dreams.

I was dead on my feet, and didn't manage to do more than brush my teeth and strip down to my panties and tank top before I crawled into bed.

As I drifted to sleep, I was acutely aware that there were many things Sienna and I hadn't talked about. Gran would show tomorrow — I assumed I'd see her bright and early — but I didn't have any of the answers she would be seeking. Perhaps Sienna did. Perhaps 'why' wasn't important at all right now. Perhaps all we could do was figure out 'how' and hope there wouldn't be any sort of further retribution. It wasn't as if I or the shifters or Sienna had killed anyone, but Rusty's mother was a necromancer. Presumably they had rules of conduct as well?

I was starting to think like the vampire, Kett. Gran wasn't going to like him at all. And with that delightful thought in my head, I sank into blissful unawareness ... for a moment, at least.

Though I had fallen asleep with no problem, I almost immediately began dreaming of being surrounded by different levels of blackness. Rationally, I knew my brain was just trying to work through the previous terror of feeling trapped in the warehouse and walking through the dark, with no idea where each step was going to take me. Unfortunately, the rational side of my brain didn't conquer the dream. The inky blackness shifted — now pressing against me, not just surrounding me as before. I was actually having a difficult time breathing, but fighting the dark oppression only made it worse. I began to panic, then to hyperventilate. Right before I thought I might be dying, might be suffocating in the blackness, a shudder ran through the darkness and it released me.

I woke sitting upright in bed with the taste of Rusty's 'unliving' magic in my mouth. I was covered in rapidly cooling sweat, shivering in it. My hand was wrapped around the hilt of my knife. I was holding the blade before me as if warding off an attack. It should have been sheathed in the pile of clothing at the side of the bed. How had I laid hands on it in my sleep?

My heart was racing as if I'd been running or ... fighting. Fighting off the effects of a spell ... I breathed in deeply and slowly exhaled, attempting to gain control of my body and mind. Where had that idea about the spell come from? I'd only been subjected to ill-intended magic a few times in my life — most notably and recently when Kett tried to compel me in the morgue. It hadn't felt like that oppressive darkness.

I toweled off my sweat-soaked limbs and torso with the bed sheet, managing to keep the knife in hand while doing so. And then I did something I'd never attempted to do before, never thought to do before. I reached out with my dowser senses and tasted the magic of the apartment wards. Lavender and berries filled my senses, calming my heart rate further. The wards felt fine, uncompromised. I was sure no malignant spell could have gotten by them.

Had I left a light on in the kitchen? Oh, yes. But was the stove light usually that bright? Maybe Sienna was watching something on the TV. I slipped out of bed, noted the time on the bedside table clock — 2:08 a.m. — and exchanged my sweat-soaked tank top and panties for clean ones and Lululemons.

I stifled my need to simply call out to my sister. I didn't want to wake her if she was sleeping. I padded on bare feet out to the living room.

The couch was empty. Gran's blanket was dumped on the floor. I picked it up and folded it over the back of the armchair as I glanced about for Sienna. The extra light was coming from the craft room on the opposite side of the living room from my bedroom. It, however, looked empty from this angle. I'd noted the bathroom was empty as I passed by it. Sienna wasn't in the kitchen either. Had I left the chain off the front door? Maybe ... I didn't usually come and go that way, but I could have forgotten it, though that was unusual.

The door to the bakery stairs was slightly ajar. But again, that could have easily been me when Sienna and I stumbled home.

Perhaps Sienna was in the bakery seeking cupcakes or chocolate? Except both were easily obtainable in the apartment kitchen.

Instead of heading downstairs, I found myself continuing to the craft room. The desk lamp, its shade made of stained glass, was lit. No werewolves or vampires were perched on the balcony, which was a relief. I leaned over to switch off the lamp, even though I had no idea when I would have turned it on. I usually worked on the trinkets using the overhead light. The lamp was a gift from Sienna, actually, and more of a dust collector than anything useful.

My eyes strayed to the coat rack that held my completed trinkets. I only worked on one at a time, and usually didn't walk away until I felt it was complete. But once complete, I hung the new trinket on one of the arms of the coat rack before taking it to the bakery or giving it away.

The rack was empty. I told myself there should be eight or more trinkets hanging there, but then I just as quickly started to convince myself I was wrong. Yes, I was seriously deluding myself. My brain wanted to click together all the pieces of the puzzle that were the last three days, even as I wanted to acknowledge that there was nothing to piece together any further.

My neck and chest suddenly felt bare, naked without my necklace. I deliberately blanked my clamoring mind and yanked open the desk drawer to pull out three trinkets I'd tucked away a few days ago. Those trinkets had felt unfinished, but I'd had no idea what to add to them at the time. I instinctively knew what they wanted to be now, and as I retreated back into my bedroom, I knotted the ends together until I could wear them around my neck, as Sienna had been ... like Sienna ...

Oh, God. My brain railed at my utterly blind, willful ignorance while my heart lamented the facts I was compelled to acknowledge.

I felt a little more grounded with my knife strapped across my hip. I wiggled my toes into the pink flip-flops I used when I got a pedicure and pulled on a T-shirt over my tank top.

Then I went looking for my sister, though I knew I didn't have to go far. Just two flights of stairs, but somehow, I knew it would be one of the longest walks of my life. I knew ... I had always known what she wanted. What she'd wanted from the moment she set eyes on it. The moment I stupidly agreed to the reveal spell and pricked my own finger. Had she known it was there all along, before she'd suggested the reveal spell? Did she think she'd gathered enough magic to open it now? Open a portal? Because that's what I was pretty sure was in the basement. Knowledge I hadn't been able to accept at the time because I had no idea where it came from.

The stink of the magic hit me in the bakery kitchen, and I suffered a moment of utterly irrational, almost debilitating anger in reaction to my space, my sanctuary being polluted.

I grasped my knife and it calmed me enough to keep moving. I headed for the basement stairs.

The wooden stairs creaked under my weight. I'd never noticed how noisy they were before. Fear that someone could be hiding underneath and grab me through the treads rose to briefly war with the anger still coursing through my synapses. The anger won, and I continued downward into the sea of nauseating magic.

The basement was well lit — perhaps a dozen candles had been added to the ones Kandy lit only a few hours before. Other than that, the storage room looked very different.

I stood on the second stair from the bottom, one hand clutching the trinkets around my neck and one clutching the hilt of the sheathed knife. Now that I knew how to do it, I sought to use the protective magic stored in each as a shield against the swamp of 'unliving' magic that now seemed to live and breathe in the basement. I struggled to find an anchor within the magic of my own creations that would hold against the magic my sister had released. My sister, not Rusty. Or at least it wasn't Rusty this time.

A large pentagram had taken the place of the witches' circle in the middle of the room. Kandy, her eyes wide but unseeing, was spread-eagle within it. Her hands had been staked through their open palms, her legs bound by silver chain. I knew it was silver because I kept a large roll of it in my craft room for making trinkets. Plus, a chain that thin shouldn't be able to hold a werewolf in place. That part of the myth was true, then. Blood — too much to be Kandy's alone, I hoped — soaked the dirt ground beyond, though somehow not intersecting, the edges of the pentagram. In fact, all the dirt in the room seemed oddly dark, and I knew when I took the second of my next two steps that the ground would be wet, soggy with blood under my feet.

Kett, his ice-blue eyes edged with red, turned his head to me as I entered, but his feelings and thoughts stayed hidden behind his typically frozen facade. He was pinned by some invisible force against the south wall. He seemed able to swivel his head with effort, but couldn't move his limbs. He was pale — too pale — but appeared unharmed. Of course, I'd already figured out it was difficult to judge a vampire's health until right before he ripped your head off in a blood frenzy.

Desmond was also pinned in a similar invisible fashion against the north wall, his demeanor the complete opposite of the vampire's inscrutability. By the multiple layers of duct tape over his mouth, I gathered he'd been overly verbal. His eyes were bright green, his fingers edged in two-inch claws. He'd obviously attempted to change — or was still attempting to do so. As I watched, he strained — every muscle on his body tensed — to pull his arms away from the brick wall where they were pinned above his head. He cleared an inch, held his hands there, and then, shaking with the effort, fell back into his invisible binding. His eyes — which had been fixed on my sister where she stood with her back to me, facing the east wall — turned to meet mine. And I then understood the show of strength was for my benefit, but to what end I didn't know.

"Took you long enough," Sienna said, though she didn't turn. "I've been calling for hours." A set of my stainless steel mixing bowls sat at her feet.

"Calling or trying to ... siphon my magic?" I answered. My tone was surprisingly flippant, though I was reeling from the inhuman tableau Sienna had set up.

She laughed and turned to look at me. Her eyes were dark — totally black, as if the pupil had expanded to overtake the whites. I'd never looked into the face of a black witch before ... at least not one unmasked. I tried to not be terrified that this was the face of my sister, my best friend. I tried to just keep that small, screaming voice firmly closeted.

The sickening magic rolled off her, and my stomach lurched in response. How was she so powerful that her binding spell could hold a vampire and a shifter pinned while she initiated a conversation with me?

"I figured out pretty quickly that wasn't going to work with you. I guess you'd have to invite me to your bed, and we both know that would never happen. And, frustratingly, even with possession of the necklace, I can't manage to trigger the outline." She turned back and ran her blood-soaked hand across the brick wall that concealed — or rather, held — the portal. God, she sounded so normal.

"Sienna, have you been bathing in blood?" I heard myself ask, and then wondered why I chose to vocalize that question instead of all the others running around in my head.

"Of course. And drinking it." This drew Sienna to the mixing bowls at her feet. She bent to retrieve one and crossed to Kett. Before I could react, she slashed her fingers across his neck and attempted to catch the resulting gush of blood in the bowl, though some of it sprayed across her face, neck, and chest. Vampire blood all over my necklace and in my freaking mixing bowl! I tamped down on the selfish lurch of my offended brain.

Kett flinched. The wound on his neck healed to a pink line that then quickly faded. My mind reeled as Sienna raised the bowl and drank from it. With her head thrown back, she shook the final drops into her open mouth.

"He heals too fast," Sienna said, her lips in an actual pout. She turned to cross to Desmond. "I like the werewolves better."

"Sienna! No!" I found my voice, though it didn't sound like me — didn't sound like it was coming from my own lungs and throat. I thought I might have been in shock.

Sienna paused and tilted her head at me. "You want some?"

"No!" I cried. "This is insane. What ... how... why ..." I couldn't figure out how to form any sentence. I shut my eyes and tried to focus. Was Kandy still alive? Could I break Sienna's binding spell? Could I get out of here and get Gran? Would Sienna even let me leave? Would she kill them all and flee before I could return with help?

"Jade," Sienna said, her voice soft and cajoling. "You wouldn't believe the power, the feeling."

"Stolen power, fleeting feelings," I said. And with the return of my anger, my voice sounded like my own again.

"No one will ever doubt me. No one will ever tell me what I can or cannot achieve. No one will ever call me a half-blood."

"They'll still call you a half-blood, but with 'crazy' as your given name. Crazy half-blood. Right before they hunt you down and kill you."

Sienna stopped smiling and dropped the mixing bowl. Her attention was diverted from Desmond at least, but she wasn't upset. She was simply flipping subjects.

"That's where you come in, Jade. You're going to open this door. I could feel the power from it when you cracked it before. Think of what it would feel like fully open. This is the root of Pearl's and Scarlett's power. This is what the Godfreys have hidden from us. Sheltering and lying, keeping us in place. This is the fountain of their power."

I made the noise of a buzzer. "Sorry, wrong answer. Try another door."

Sienna glared at me. "I know they're hiding something. I know they're hiding this," she snarled.

"You may be right, but you're wrong about it having anything to do with you."

"It's all about you, isn't it, Jade? That's new. Tell me something that hasn't been beaten into me my entire life. But now, you're not the special one, I am. You better step up if you want to keep up."

"I never did play 'follow the leader' well."

Sienna barked out a laugh. "You don't even know yourself, Jade. You follow Pearl around like a puppy whining for a teat. You don't even know the power that lies dormant in your veins."

"All this blood, Sienna. All the power in it, even if you were to drain me as well. It would never be yours."

"Mine to command, at least. And I think you might be wrong. True, with the others you attracted for me, it was short-lived, but I've learned. I've learned to prolong death, and to take the power within me, to consume it from the blood-filled meat. These two are terribly powerful. A lovely gift from a lovely sister."

I was having a hard time continuing to meet Sienna's eyes, a hard time standing around chatting with her. But Desmond was getting his arms further and further away from the wall, and Kett had just managed to lift one of his legs. Sienna was either distracted or the spell was fading. Either way, keeping her occupied appeared to be a good idea.

"I'm in no way complicit in any of this, Sienna."

"Sure, Jade. It's all just milk and cookies with you. I can pretend for you that you had nothing to do with it. Even though I never would have gotten my hands on someone like that other werewolf — the big, pretty one — without you."

"Hudson," I gritted out.

"He was so perfect for you. So big and strong and comfy. He just walked right into your apartment with that dopey smile on his face. He even brought you chocolate. Three of those twenty-dollar bars you lust after and never buy. Smart werewolf, he already knew that roses wouldn't get him anywhere with you."

I squeezed my eyes shut; she was making me visualize Hudson in my apartment ... in my life. "The damn stools," I muttered. "You knocked over the stool when I was in the shower. And broke my bowl."

"On his head. It took two binding spells to even slow him down. I had to hit him over the head to stop him. Then Rusty was so pissed hauling a werewolf in and out of his trunk."

A keening moan rose in my chest. I had been so fucking stupid, so incredibly fucking blind —

Sienna snapped her fingers. The noise cleared my head and focused me. It was our warning signal. She'd used it the other night in the club. But using it here — in this context — she was reminding me of our childhood pact. That we were cohorts in everything ... stealing cookies, backfired spells, sneaking out to the park to smoke stolen cigarettes and kiss the neighborhood boys. One of us was always the lookout, and one of us the perpetrator. And now, she wanted me with her in murder and blood magic and death. I opened my eyes.

Sienna curled her lips in a smug smile, but her blacked-out eyes didn't change. "Good girl, Jade. Now, come here, hold my hand, and trigger the reveal spell again."

"And why would I do that?"

"Because we're sisters. Because they came for us, they came to stop us. I knew they would. I knew they would blame us."

"You, Sienna. They blame you."

"They didn't call, did they? They didn't knock or even send an email. They just broke in in the middle of the night, but I was here to protect you, to protect us. And now you will do your part."

I shook my head. Sienna's logic was dizzying. Had Kett and Desmond come for us? Come for me? Was I somehow complicit in all of this? Gran always said that not making a choice was a choice in itself. That choosing to turn the other cheek or look the other way wasn't always the best choice either. Had I always known

Sienna was pushing into magic she shouldn't be touching? Magic Gran always warned was addictive? Was I an enabler? Even beyond the trinkets, were Hudson's and Rusty's deaths on my shoulders?

"You love me, sister," Sienna said, interrupting the avalanche going on in my head. "I want this. This is permanent power. You know I need ... need something to be mine."

"This isn't any way to get it."

"I can feel it, like you always said you could feel magic. It burns, scorches me from the inside out. It wants. It needs me. It will fill me up, make me shiny and new."

"That's not ... that's not how it feels to me. That's not how it tastes."

"You are already culpable, Jade," Sienna snapped. "You can't run away and hide behind Pearl's skirts. You think these two believe you're innocent? They came looking for you," my sister repeated. "To tidy up their investigation."

"They came looking for you." I sounded more certain this time.

"Me? Nothing points in my direction. But the trinkets and your magic point directly at you. When I kill them and leave the bodies in your basement, that will tighten the noose nicely."

"No one could ever believe I would be capable of any of this. You reek of it, the stink of the magic seeps from your pores. You've been hiding behind my trinkets and borrowed clothing, but you've gone too far, Sienna. You'll never get the stink out."

"And Jade can't stomach the magic," Kett said, his voice a whispered knife through the tension building between my sister and me.

"We'll see about that," Sienna snarled. She snatched up the stainless steel bowl from the ground and darted over to Desmond.

"No!" I shouted, as I took my first step into the blood-soaked dirt. I stumbled, lost my flip-flop, and ended up taking my second step barefooted. The instant my foot touched the blood, the 'unliving' magic seized me.

Sienna slashed her fingers in some sort of cutting spell across Desmond's neck. Blood sprayed everywhere. She laughed as it splattered across her face and chest but she managed to catch some of it in the bowl.

I struggled to free my foot but ended up toppling forward onto all fours. The magic was leeching up from the ground, imprisoning me as it had done in my dream. My limbs felt sluggish. My heart raced. I twisted and turned but couldn't get away.

Sienna danced away from Desmond, the bowl of his blood held in the palms of both hands. The wound at his neck sealed and he began to fight against the binding spell once again.

Sienna turned to me. My feet, one hand, and one knee were still pinned to the ground. Sienna reached down with one hand and yanked my head back by the hair. "Let's test your theory, vampire," Sienna said, and tipped the bowl toward my face.

Then I saw it. The shifter and vampire blood that had splattered across Sienna's chest was smoking where it touched the necklace.

I stopped struggling. This off-balanced Sienna, who'd been fighting to hold me still. The bowl tipped and she released me to grab it.

Then I laughed.

Sienna's mouth dropped open in a stupefied expression. Her blood-spattered black-lipstick-and-black-eyed look was difficult to pull off when looking fucking stupid. I laughed harder.

"What?" Sienna snapped.

"Look at the necklace, Sienna."

She did.

I freed my hand from the dirt. Seeing my necklace burning off the foreign, unpalatable magic in the blood, I understood how I had sweated out of the dream spell. And why I always threw up when I came into contact with black magic. My magic naturally rejected it. The sweating and vomiting were my body's instinctual means of expelling the dark magic. Now that I knew that, I could use my magic like a shield to create a barrier between me and the 'unliving' magic Sienna was wielding. The black magic might be able to affect me, even incapacitate me briefly, but it had no way to permanently hold me. As a dowser, I was naturally drawn to magic, but now I understood I could also manipulate it.

I punched Sienna in the gut.

She collapsed forward. The bowl went flying.

Then a bunch of things happened all at once.

Desmond ripped himself from the hold of the binding spell and flung himself at Kandy, who moaned as he ripped the stakes from her hands and pulled her from the pentagram.

Sienna flung herself sideways at me and took me down to the floor. We tussled. She was way stronger than she should have been. But then, oddly, so was I. I wasn't totally sure anymore that I could thank the yoga classes for that.

As Desmond pulled Kandy from the pentagram, a flash of dark magic swamped the room. He'd compromised the integrity of whatever spell Sienna had set up. This wave of darkness hit my brain and immediately scrambled it. I collapsed to the blood-soaked ground, aware that Sienna was also screaming and clutching her head.

I blacked out for a bit.

When I came to, I noted that Sienna was passed out beside me. Desmond and Kandy were down and out, off to one side of the stairs. Kett was sitting cross-legged in the pentagram.

As my vision cleared, I watched the vampire puncture the skin of his wrist with his teeth. Before the wound could seal, he squeezed a few drops of blood onto one of the points of the pentagram.

"Dowser, good," Kett said, though his back was to me. "I thought you'd wake first. I'm keeping the unfulfilled magic at bay with my offering, but we will need your sister to close the spell. Unless you know how to do so?"

I pulled myself to my knees and attempted to straighten up. I was only half successful. "Is everyone dead?"

"They still breathe," Kett answered.

I reached over to Sienna and yanked my necklace off her neck. A childish gesture, but still, it was mine.

With the necklace back in its rightful place, I crawled over to Kett, careful not to intersect the pentagram. Then I remembered what he'd said about Sienna, so I crawled back to drag her with me.

I pulled my sister around until we were sprawled in front of Kett. I noticed — and quickly looked away — that his eyes had dilated fully red.

"No worries, little dowser. I'm not so far gone this time that I will need to instantly feed." Ah, he'd noticed the look.

"She ate Rusty, didn't she?" I asked as I looked down at my sister, crusted in blood and dirt from where I'd dragged her across the ground. Yeah, I was kind of stuck on that point. My hands and knees bore a similar dirt-blood crust, and I was certainly glad I couldn't see my hair.

"I imagine she also would have harvested his heart and liver, if she hadn't realized we were near," Kett answered.

"And drinking your blood ... will she turn?"

"No. It takes more than that ... though ..." — he tilted his head momentarily, as if puzzling through something — "it might have lasting effects."

"Like what?"

"Perhaps it would be better to close the spell, then chat."

"You need her blood?"

"Just a drop."

I grabbed Sienna's hand and hovered it over the edge of the pentagram a few inches away from Kett's feet. I pulled out my knife and pressed the point to Sienna's index finger. A drop of blood welled. I set the knife in my lap and hurriedly squeezed Sienna's finger while I smeared it across the edge of the pentagram.

"Jade!" Kett shouted a warning, though he was only a foot away.

Something nasty stung my waist just below the left side of my rib cage. I dropped Sienna's hand ... actually, I thought it might have twisted out of my grasp.

I looked down. A slash of blood welled through a cut in my T-shirt. I pressed my hand to the wound and looked up in time to see Sienna gain her feet, my knife in her hand. "Sienna?" I whispered.

"Yes, Jade." Sienna's sneer was firmly in place as she then leaned over to stab me in the stomach, about an inch to the right of my navel. "Thanks for those lasting benefits, vampire," she said. She pulled back the knife to stab me again. "Stupid, stupid, Jade. All those years of protection and unbreakable spells, and all you needed was a drop of blood to ensure the knife couldn't be used against you. But poor little Jadey was so scared of the big, bad blood magic."

"Thanks for taking care of that for me, sister," I choked out through the waves of pain from my belly. That gave Sienna pause — just enough for me to grab the knife as she thrust it down and forward. I reached out — as I had when checking the wards upstairs — to find the magic of the knife. Then I sealed it with the magic glistening in my own blood that coated the blade.

Sienna screamed as the magic cemented into the knife and seared into the skin of her hand. She reeled away, attempting to shake the knife free from where it was burned to her.

I somehow stumbled to my feet. My hands were pressed to my stomach as I took a half-hearted step toward the stairs.

Sienna shook off the knife and swung back to me. As I watched helplessly, mired in more pain than I'd ever known, she pirouetted and knocked a back kick into my bleeding gut. Damn those self-defense classes we took together.

Pain exploded from my stomach and radiated through my limbs. I fell backward, unable to bring my arms up or slow my descent. I hit the east wall, smacked my head, and slid down the brick.

Sienna gasped.

I struggled to focus, to right myself. I reached up to find a handhold, only vaguely aware that the outline of the portal had somehow appeared behind me. But my hand, slippery with my own blood, slid across the brick wall and I fell hard onto one knee.

The magic in the room shifted around me in a rush. Pure, white energy flooded my senses. It came without taste ... except maybe freshness. The wall that I was huddled against for support disappeared, and with a flood of golden magic, the portal opened.

A power I'd never felt before filled me, filled every pore of my body with joy ... no ... exhilaration. It was a physical feeling rather than an emotion.

The golden light blurred out everything in my field of vision. It buoyed me to my feet. My arms were lifted to the sides, my head thrown back. Then I was floating in it. I breathed it in, feeling strength flow through my body, my limbs. All the small aches and pains, the wounds of the last couple of days, eased. The deep knife wound on my belly knitted together and healed. The dirt and grime of Sienna's magic was scoured from me, leaving nothing but this golden magic — and me — behind.

I felt invincible. I felt whole. I hadn't realized I'd been missing so much of myself.

Something called from the depths of the magic, but it wasn't a voice, just a possibility. The possibility of moving ever forward, the possibility of knowledge, the possibility of another life waiting just beyond the threshold ...

Darkness moved out of the light and I realized I was facing the room, suspended a few inches above the dirt floor. The magic of the portal glowed behind and flooded past me. The darkness resolved itself into the form of Sienna, who took a few stumbling steps toward me.

Behind Sienna, Kett had flung his arms across his face and twisted away from the golden glow. Desmond was cradling Kandy in his arms, but they both gazed at the portal behind me in awe, not fear. No pain was evident in either of their faces, though they were still battered and bruised. It seemed the portal magic was only healing for me.

Sienna lunged toward me. On some instinct, I grabbed her arm as she tried to pass.

My feet touched down. Sienna yanked against my hold, at first with just a tug and then with a snarling pull. I was immovable. My hold was apparently unbreakable.

"It's not for you, Sienna," I murmured, knowing it to be the truth. "Only death awaits you through there."

Sienna screamed in frustration and tried to twist away.

"No, sister," I said again, utterly patient and understanding — so unlike me. "You must trust me."

"Jade!" Sienna shrieked and clawed her free hand toward me. I felt her magic boil up around her. The golden light of the portal didn't like it. I could feel it pull away, though it still lapped along the left side of my body and face — the side that wasn't touching Sienna.

Sienna raked her clawed fingers toward me. I made no attempt to block her, though she moved as if in slow motion. Her magic hit me from the tips of her fingers — the cutting spell, I thought — and sliced across my jaw, neck, and cheek.

I locked eyes with Sienna. Hers were still entirely filled with black pupil and nothing else. Her expression was frantic, fierce, and utterly hateful. Utterly alien.

The wound on my cheek healed.

Sienna's eyes widened and she stopped straining against me. "Let me go, Jade," she whispered. "You have everything. Let me have this." Her tone recalled late-night conversations under the cover of sleepovers before Sienna's dad had died. Confessions and dreams … none of Sienna's wishes had ever come true. I hadn't completely realized that until this moment.

My grasp loosened and fell to Sienna's hand. She squeezed my fingers.

"Sienna, please ..." I whispered, aware on some terrible level that I had already lost my sister. My best — perhaps my only — friend.

"There is only forward for me, Jade," Sienna said. It was her truth. It always had been, no matter how many walls she hit along the way, no matter that no one loved her as their one and only. No matter that she'd always been lost and floundering, she moved ever forward.

Sienna turned and stepped into the golden magic, our fingers still entwined.

She gasped, like she used to when we were young and experiencing something wonderful.

She turned to look back at me. The golden glow was a halo around her head and torso. Her eyes had cleared. The blood and dirt, the stink of the 'unliving' magic had evaporated.

I stared into my sister's eyes and thought just for a second that I'd been wrong, that everything was going to be okay somehow.

Then Sienna said, "It's so beautiful here," in the softest, sweetest of tones. "Come with me, sister." She tugged my hand. "Come with me, Jade."

I shook my head. I couldn't go with her, and I wasn't ready for the promises the portal had offered. With my feet firmly planted in the earth of my home, I knew this was where I belonged. The magic of the portal held no sway over me.

Sienna laughed, full of joy. The edges of her face blurred. She took another step, pulling her back leg into the golden light.

I clung to her fingers, and she to mine. Then she disintegrated into the magic.

I held onto her as long as I could, longer than I could even see her with my eyes. I held on until there was nothing left to hold.

I exhaled the breath I'd been holding, and felt utterly lost and found at the same time.

The door at the top of the stairs banged open, and a strident voice thundered across the room. "Jade Godfrey, close that portal immediately."

I turned to look up at my Gran where she stood. A tiny woman, she somehow filled the doorway above. Her never-dyed hair was pulled back into a long silver braid. Her magic danced like blue lightning on her fingertips. I'd never seen her do that before. I wondered what spell she was preparing. The urge to instantly obey her — though honestly, I had no idea how to close the portal — came and went. It was as if the golden energy had melted away all the years of my gentle indoctrination along with the 'unliving' magic.

I smiled instead. My best, most winning I'm-not-really-smiling-but-actually-calling-you-on-your-bullshit smile.

Gran frowned. Her eyes swept the room. She looked very displeased with the blood, the black magic, the shifters and a vampire currently occupying my storage room. "I'm the guardian of the portal. Not you. Not yet, perhaps not ever. You will close it." Gran didn't like repeating herself.

Accusations and arguments flitted through my mind. I could press her with the power of this magic behind me — I could press her hard. The golden glow rolled around me in response, supportive if not eager. "Close it yourself," I said, as pleasantly as I could.

Gran's frown turned into a look of concern. She opened her mouth to speak, but then seemed not to know what to say. It was the first time I had ever outright defied her. Yeah, I was a late-bloomer in that area. So what?

Then Scarlett, my mother, shouldered past Gran to make her own assessment of the room. Her strawberry-blond hair hung over delicate shoulders in a perfectly waved waterfall. Her bright blue eyes stood out against her creamy skin, which, as always, she showed as much of as possible without verging on slutty territory. She looked only a few years older than me. I'd always hated that she neither appeared nor acted anything like a mother. She raised a beckoning eyebrow at Kett, though her gaze lingered on Desmond. Then she dazzled us all with a smile, my own paling in comparison.

"Hello, darling," Scarlett said, her voice strong and musical at the same time. "Going to introduce me to your friends?"

"Sure," I responded. "Just as soon as you tell me who the hell my father is."

Scarlett's grin widened. She threw her head back and laughed as if I was utterly delightful and charming. She laughed as if she loved me, as if I could never do or say anything wrong. Charm and charisma were the focal points for my mother's magic and the everyday outlet of that energy, but there wasn't a contrived bone in her body. Charming and truthful was a devastating combination. I'd never seen anyone stand against her when she cared to exert her will. Not even Gran. I had no chance. Plus ... I thought of Sienna, whose touch I could still feel on my fingers, who had no mother rushing to her rescue, no mother willing to step into a room full of monsters in human skin and extend her hand ...

I stepped away from the portal. I stepped away from the soul-filling magic and it closed behind me as if it had never existed. Though I could still feel the buzz of it underneath my skin when I was near.

It was the polite thing to do after all.

I was still going to get some bloody answers, though.

Chapter Fourteen

*E*veryone was okay. Or, at the minimum, they were all functional enough to be bullied out of the basement on their own two feet by Gran. She was going to "raze the remains of the blood magic" — Sienna's 'unliving' magic — "from the face of the earth." I'd never heard her voice laced with so much power or anger before. I didn't stick around to watch.

I thought about going for a walk even though it was still the middle of the night, but then wound up curled up on my couch. Scarlett would come to me — she neither made nor broke promises lightly. I would get my answers and then I would sleep. I just didn't want to wait or demand answers in front of the wounded shape-shifters. Or the far-too-sharp ears of the vampire.

My questions were my own. The answers belonged to me and no one else.

So it turned out there weren't that many answers to be had — at least not from my Gran or Scarlett. Suppos-edly, the identity of my father was actually unknown, other than the fact that he'd been gorgeous, blond, crazy strong, and Australian. I'd never noticed the far-away look my mother got when talking about him. I wondered, for the first time, if she'd loved him. How could you possibly love someone you only knew for one night, during a fertility rite ceremony? Yeah, that was a new tidbit. A circumstance that they — in their collective wisdom — thought it best to keep from me. Mom, while 'backpacking around the world,' had participated in an aboriginal fertility ceremony somewhere in the middle of bloody Queensland. She was sketchy about whether this took place during a full or new moon, and I was pretty sure she'd 'run away' at sixteen rather than 'backpacked.' And, now that I thought about it, she'd been running away ever since. But never back to Australia, not that I knew. I wondered if dear old dad scared her as much as he obviously exhilarated her.

And what the hell did that say about one half of my DNA?

Gran and Scarlett couldn't exactly deny my sudden ability to heal very quickly or imbue things with magic. They'd already figured out that part, and kept it from me for my own protection. *For my own protection* ... that wasn't going to be the last time I heard those words, and they already pissed me off. Magic users who could create magical objects were rare among the Adept — so rare that my freedom could be in jeopardy, according to my Gran.

I had a list of questions rattling around in my pretty little head — questions that might be too big for such a small container. Was there a portal in the basement? Yes. Where did it lead? Gran had no idea, nor had she ever seen it open. The responsibility of hiding it was passed down generation to generation, not that Vancouver was that old in terms of settlement. Was Sienna dead? Again, Gran didn't know, though it seemed likely that only a person in tune with such magic would be able to travel through it. So why the hell was I attuned with it when it seemed no one else was? Again, Gran didn't have an answer for me, though it was pretty obvious it all came around to the question of the other half of my DNA.

When I broached the subject of the life debt with Desmond, which I was pretty sure hadn't been dissolved along with Sienna, my Gran's lips had thinned and I saw the blue of her magic rimming her eyes. Even my mother seemed put out at this information. At this point, it was not-so-subtly suggested that I needed sleep, and I was promptly sent to bed. Seeing as I was utterly exhausted and probably not absorbing the answers to my barrage of questions anyway, I complied.

Desmond was about to be in the line of fire, which pleased me more than it should have. Yes, I should fight my own battles, but it was awfully nice to have a pair of powerful witches at my back. In my mind, the shifter and the vampire had everything coming to them that my Gran and Scarlett could dole out. They'd ripped me from my protective cocoon and showed me a world of magic that scared the shit out of me. The fact that I was still standing had little to do with either of them. The fact that I was walking away was pure choice. The first choice in days that I felt was uninfluenced by forces greater than me.

I felt like I needed to sleep for three days, but settled for the three hours that was all my body seemed to need.

I got up. I baked, though it wasn't my shift — I'd traded with Bryn for Sunday, but at least I knew what day it was — and took a 9:00 A.M. yoga class. Halfway through the class, I realized I wasn't struggling as much as usual, and I tried to just enjoy that feeling. The other option was to acknowledge the weight that the sight of the empty mat beside me seemed to exert on my chest.

Obviously, Hudson had affected me on a level that was at odds with the briefness of our friendship. I wondered if Scarlett felt that way about my father, and I was glad that I hadn't had the chance to be intimate with Hudson.

The ache caused by Sienna's betrayal and apparent death was distinctly different. That felt like a shard of a knife tip broken off and lodged in my heart; the top right section of my heart, to be specific. I'd left my foster sister's mess for my Gran and Scarlett to sort and clean up. That was probably cowardly of me, but I had no idea what else to do. I wished it all felt like a dream, or even a nightmare, but it didn't. The last few days felt very real to me. Terribly real.

I wandered back to the bakery and jogged up the stairs to my apartment, though I usually never entered through the front door. I thought it might be symbolic ... a reclaiming of my life and all that ... But then I decided I was freaking out and reading too much into everything.

A shower soothed me further, and I was feeling somewhat rebooted. Then I took the garbage out. Who knew that such a mundane task would result in the frustratingly unresolved stirring of the beehive of my mind? Not me. Otherwise, I would have let it stink up the place.

A delivery truck was blocking the dumpster behind the bakery. Kandy, of all people, was chatting up the driver.

The green-haired werewolf stepped back when she saw me, offering me a grin. The truck pulled away.

I lifted the lid of the dumpster and chucked the garbage in. It hit the empty bin with a satisfying, ringing thump. It must be garbage day. I was very pleased with this confirmation that I was once again on track with my satisfying, regular routine. I chose to ignore the delivery truck, to ignore the werewolf who was currently closing the gap between us with long strides. I was happy to see her on her feet — just not in my alley.

Kandy sauntered over to me, her grin still firmly in place. She was covered in various-sized bandages on her arms, neck, and chest. She hadn't bothered to cover them with more than a V-neck short-sleeved T-shirt, which bore an obscene cartoon involving an apple and a banana. I didn't try to figure the joke out. Sienna had bled the werewolf so badly that her wounds were taking time to heal. Guilt pooled in my stomach, and I tried to push it away as not my responsibility.

"Morning, neighbor," Kandy said. It was actually just after noon, but I didn't correct her.

"Neighbor?" My voice came out in an unbecoming squeak. Kandy didn't seem to mind. In fact, her grin only widened.

"Sorry, can't talk. Getting an actual fridge delivered, instead of that dinky one you have in the apartment. You know I like my meat cut large and readily available." I didn't know that, actually ... and didn't really want to know that. "Catch you in yoga tomorrow? Sorry I missed today's class."

"Okay ..." Yes, I was a little thrown. Kandy turned back into the bakery via the alley door and I dumbly followed at her heels. She had no issue passing through the wards. But then, I'd given her access only a few hours before.

"Delivery guy wanted to drop it in the alley," Kandy said, chatting over her shoulder as she crossed through the kitchen and into the bakery. "But he can cart it up the front stairs himself."

She walked around the display counter and pushed her way through the line of customers as if she owned the place. The delivery truck had pulled up out front and was now blocking one of the lanes on West Fourth.

Kandy dashed out the front door. The trinkets hanging there tinkled in her wake. I realized I was just standing and staring after her. A few of my customers greeted me and I tried to be polite, but I wasn't sure I'd actually formed words to answer them.

The sun streaming in the French-paned windows glinted off Scarlett's hair, alerting me to my mother's presence in the seating area. I hustled over to her. She was prettily perched on one of the high stools by the farthest round table, awarding me with a blinding smile as I approached. I managed to not falter under its wattage.

"Kandy just told me 'Hi, neighbor.' " I completely skipped any pleasantries.

"Oh, yes. The werewolves have rented the second upstairs apartment from your Gran."

"What?" I was having a hard time keeping the dismay out of my voice. Actually, I sounded a bit petulant, even to my own ears. Not attractive.

"It was some arrangement that the alpha — lord, is he a fine specimen — came to with your Gran. Something about protecting his investment. You'll have to ask Pearl about it, but it's never a bad thing to have a werewolf at your back."

"All the better to eat you," I muttered.

"Oh, darling. Werewolves aren't man eaters, at least not those of the pack. And it seems you need all the powerful allies you can get now … if you're going to fully exercise your magic." There was some sort of chiding in my mother's wording somewhere, some backhanded chastisement, but I didn't absorb it. Scarlett didn't typically play the role of disappointed disciplinarian, so that part was easy to ignore.

I started to turn away from her extreme sunniness and her way of never really answering questions with any substantial information. I also hadn't missed her calling Desmond 'a fine specimen.' I wondered if Mc-Growly, or 'all muscle and lots of trouble,' as Sienna had referred to him, knew he was now on my mother's radar. She'd chew and swallow him whole, and he wouldn't know what had hit him until she was walking away. The thought pissed me off a bit. Not enough to forgive him for the heavy-handedness, or the botched life bond, or anything at all, really. But still.

"Jade," Kett said as he crossed from the counter through my peripheral vision to place an espresso in front of my mother. "I was thinking we could go treasure hunting next weekend. I believe the coast is known for its native artifacts." He sat on the stool opposite Scarlett.

My mother was having coffee and cupcakes with a vampire. Not that Kett seemed to be eating or drinking any of his portion. Ironically, he'd chosen *Sunshine in a Cup*, a lemon cake topped with lemon butter icing. So he did have some sort of deeply hidden sense of humor. My mother brought out the best in every man she cast her gaze on, even vampires it seemed.

"Treasure hunting?" I lamely echoed.

"Oh," Scarlett said. "Like a training session. What fun!" She ran her fingers down my bare forearm in a light caress. I could feel her magic, the charisma of it. It made my skin tingle in the wake of her fingers, which was new.

I turned away, completely ignoring my mother and the vampire. I walked back toward the counter, shutting everything out amid the gentle buzz of the customers' quiet chatter. Though I didn't miss Scarlett whispering, "Give her a few hours, her curiosity will win out."

So ... Scarlett and Kett ... sitting in a tree ... I wondered what Gran thought of that. Not that she'd ever had much control over her daughter. Not like me. Not like I okayed every step, every choice I'd made my entire life with my Gran, who had controlled me — lovingly, of course — with secrets and half-truths.

The trinkets chimed over the door to announce another customer. I looked up from my daze to see the cute lawyer guy enter. I flashed him a smile the moment he found me off to the side of the counter. He'd scanned the entire room. He smiled back immediately, that one dimple firmly and sweetly in place.

I crossed behind the counter and began folding a box for a dozen cupcakes.

"What can I get you, lawyer guy from just down the street?" I called to him over my shoulder, blatantly ignoring everyone in line ahead of him. But then, I wasn't actually working a scheduled shift.

His smile widened. "It's Joe," he answered. Ah, Joe. What a perfectly normal, simple name. "How about baker's choice?"

I laughed and walked over to begin placing my favorites in the box. My first choice was always *Lust in a Cup*, a dark chocolate cake with dark chocolate cream cheese icing. Partway through, I handed Joe a chocolate chip cookie, something I'd baked this morning. I enjoyed his appreciative noises as he ate it. I also very much enjoyed the fact he never took his eyes off me.

Joe didn't want me for my magic. He didn't care if I had rare hidden talents. He simply wanted my cupcakes, my body, and maybe a bit of my time.

And that sounded just perfect to me.

Acknowledgments

With thanks to:

My story & line editor
Scott Fitzgerald Gray

My proofreader
Pauline Nolet

My Beta Readers
Leiah Cooper, Clare Hodge, Dana (Bitchie), ETA:soon, Heather,
Ita Margalit, Joanne Schwartz

For their continual encouragement, feedback, & general advice
Gertie from Goodreads, Headshot Heather,
and Shana from A Book Vacation

To My Friends & Family
Thanks for all the years of taste testing

For their Art
Irene Langholm and Elizabeth Mackey

Meghan Ciana Doidge is an award-winning writer based out of Vancouver, British Columbia, Canada. She has a penchant for bloody love stories, superheroes, and the supernatural. She also has a thing for chocolate, potatoes, and sock yarn.

Novels

After The Virus
Spirit Binder
Time Walker
Cupcakes, Trinkets, and Other Deadly Magic (Dowser 1)
Trinkets, Treasures, and Other Bloody Magic (Dowser 2)
Treasures, Demons, and Other Black Magic (Dowser 3)
I See Me (Oracle 1)
Shadows, Maps, and other Ancient Magic (Dowser 4)
Maps, Artifacts, and Other Arcane Magic (Dowser 5)
I See You (Oracle 2)

Novellas/Shorts

Love Lies Bleeding
The Graveyard Kiss

For giveaways, news, and glimpses of upcoming stories, please connect with Meghan on her:

Personal blog, www.madebymeghan.ca
Twitter, @mcdoidge
And/or Facebook, Meghan Ciana Doidge (Writer)

Please also consider leaving an honest review at your point of sale outlet

Time to stock up on chocolate.

You're going to need it.

Dowser Series · Book 1

CUPCAKES, TRINKETS, and other DEADLY MAGIC

MEGHAN CIANA DOIDGE

Dowser Series · Book 2

TRINKETS, TREASURES, and other BLOODY MAGIC

MEGHAN CIANA DOIDGE

Dowser Series · Book 1

TREASURES, DEMONS, and other BLACK MAGIC

MEGHAN CIANA DOIDGE

Catch a glimpse of
the dowser universe
through Rochelle's eyes...

The day I turned nineteen, I expected to gain what little freedom I could within the restrictions of my bank account and the hallucinations that had haunted me for the last six years. I expected to drive away from a life that had been dictated by the tragedy of others and shaped by the care of strangers. I expected to be alone.

Actually, I relished the idea of being alone.

Instead, I found fear I thought I'd overcome. Uncertainty I thought I'd painstakingly planned away. And terror that was more real than anything I'd ever hallucinated before.

I'd seen terrible, fantastical, and utterly impossible things ... but not love. Not until I saw him.

CPSIA information can be obtained
at www.ICGtesting.com
Printed in the USA
LVOW13s1705200117
521668LV00018B/310/P